BOUND BY ICE AND SHADOW

FROSTFIRE

SOPHEA CHAN

BOUND BY FATES AND ARROWS
THE PREQUEL

In the heart of the Summer Court, Fenelre, a fierce fae archer, is prepared for war. With the Frost King's icy forces threatening the realm, she's tasked with training for battle alongside an unlikely ally: Ravros, an Everwolf—an ancient, sentient creature with the power of the wild. Bound by duty, they begin to train in military tactics, but as they spend more time together, their bond deepens beyond camaraderie. A forbidden love stirs between them, one that could unravel everything they hold dear.

In a world where the rules of court and nature cannot be broken, Fenelre and Ravros must navigate the treacherous waters of loyalty, duty, and desire. As war looms, they are forced to make impossible choices, risking their love and their lives for the chance to be together. But in a realm divided by ancient enmities, can love truly conquer all, or will it be their undoing?

A tale of passion, sacrifice, and defiance, *Bound by Fates and Arrows* is a journey through forbidden love and the unbreakable ties of war.

BOUND
by **FATES** *and*
ARROWS

SOPHEA CHAN

BOUND BY ICE AND SHADOW

Do not enter the house. Do not speak his name. Do not break the spell.

Twenty-eight-year-old Callie Winters is used to being alone. No one knows about the whispers she hears in the wind or the eerie way shadows seem to reach for her. But when she inherits a remote house from her estranged grandmother, Callie discovers that true isolation comes with a price.

In a land where ancient magic lingers in every creaking floorboard, Callie unknowingly awakens Ykazar, the imprisoned Frost King. His voice is silk and ice, his promises as enticing as they are deadly. But a promise is like a noose. The more you struggle, the tighter it becomes.

When rival fae learn of Ykazar's potential freedom, Callie finds herself caught in a dangerous game of power and deceit. The fae have always been creatures of nightmares and bedtime stories... but now Callie is living one, with no way to wake up.

The first mortal to set foot in Ykazar's domain in centuries, Callie becomes bound to the Frost King in ways she never imagined. He will use her to break his curse, no matter the cost to her... or himself. Freedom has a name. It is Callie Winters. Her heart is pure. Her power is untapped. And she's the key to unleashing a force that could reshape both worlds.

Be wary of the bonds you forge, little flame. Even the kindest touch can leave you frostbitten...

PART ONE

CHAPTER I

YKAZAR

My breath billowed out in a cloud of white vapor, crystallizing instantly in the frigid atmosphere. The world around me was a canvas of pristine white, stretching as far as the eye could see. Snow-capped mountains loomed in the distance, their jagged peaks piercing the steel-gray sky.

This was my kingdom. And soon, it would be all that remained.

I, Ykazar, King of Frost and Lord of the Eternal Winter, stood atop a glacier, my icy throne a testament to the power I wielded. The wind whipped around me, carrying with it the howls of wolves and the distant rumble of avalanches.

But I felt no cold.

The chill was a part of me, as natural as breathing. It wrapped around my bones like a second skin, a constant reminder that this was my domain—a place where shadows lingered longer than sunlight, and the air hung heavy with secrets. In this world, the cold whispered my name, inviting me deeper into its embrace. Each breath I took was infused with the crisp bite of frost, a soothing balm that grounded me in the depths of my solitude. Here, in the stillness, I was not just a visitor; I was the master of this realm, where the chill was both my ally and my essence.

My fingers, long and pale as icicles, curled around the hilt of my sword. Frostbite, I called it, for that was what it brought to all who stood against me.

The blade gleamed wickedly in the weak sunlight, catching glimmers of light that danced along its surface similar to fireflies at dusk. Its edge was honed to a cruel precision, sharp enough to slice through bone and soul alike, leaving no trace of mercy in its wake. Each polished curve told a story of battles fought and blood spilled, a testament to its relentless hunger for power. As I held it, I felt the weight of its history, the echoes of countless confrontations reverberating in the air around me. It wasn't just a weapon; it was an extension of my will, a tool of transformation that could sever not only flesh but the very threads of fate.

I closed my eyes, reaching out with my senses. I could feel every snowflake as it fell, every crack forming in the ice beneath my feet. The world pulsed with life, warm and vibrant.

It disgusted me.

For centuries, I had watched as the lesser races multiplied, spreading like a disease across the land. They built their cities, cut down forests, and tamed rivers. They thought themselves masters of nature, but they were nothing more than parasites.

It was time to remind them of their place.

Raising my free hand, palm up, I concentrated. A sphere of swirling ice and snow formed above it, growing larger with each passing second. Within its depths, I could see the world as it should be—a desolate wasteland of ice and snow, where only the strongest survived.

"Soon," I murmured, my voice as cold and unforgiving as the winter itself. "Soon, all will know the embrace of eternal frost."

The sound of horns pierced the air. I opened my eyes, a snarl curling my lips.

They were here.

Far below, at the base of my icy fortress, an army had gathered. Even from this distance, I could make out their banners—reds and golds that burned akin to fire against the white landscape—the forces of summer, rival fae who came to challenge my rule.

I laughed, the sound echoing across the frozen wasteland.

Let them come.

They would learn, as all others had before them, that there was no flame hot enough to melt my resolve.

With a thought, I summoned my generals. They materialized beside me in swirls of snow and ice—the Frost Giants, with their blue-tinged skin and eyes like chips of glacial ice.

The Winter Wolves, their fur white as fresh-fallen snow and teeth sharper than any mortal blade.

And the Ice Wraiths, beings of pure cold that even I sometimes struggled to control.

"My lord," rumbled Joul, the leader of the Frost Giants. His voice was an avalanche, deep and foreboding. "The armies of Summer approach. They bring with them weapons of fire and light."

I sneered. "Let them. Their flames will sputter and die in our winds."

Sadi, alpha of the Winter Wolves, growled low in her throat. "We should crush them now, while they still struggle through the snow."

"Patience," I cautioned, though the idea tempted me. "Let them exhaust themselves reaching us. When they arrive, cold and weary, we will show them the true meaning of winter's wrath."

The Ice Wraith, Ia, spoke next, her voice a whisper of wind through bare branches. "There is something different about this army, my king. A power we have not faced before."

I frowned, turning my gaze back to the approaching forces.

Now that she mentioned it, I could sense it too—a warmth that went beyond mere fire, a light that seemed to push back the very shadows of winter.

For the first time in centuries, I felt a new thrill. After all, I was used to striding through life with unshakeable confidence, like a storm that couldn't be contained. Unease? It was a feeling for the weak, for those who didn't know their power. But here I was, facing a new emotion. Maybe it was a sign that I was still capable of being surprised, still capable of feeling. Or perhaps it was just a reminder that I played in a world where even legends could be challenged. I couldn't help but smirk; if anything, it only made the game more interesting. Let the darkness come—I was ready to dance with it.

I had brought the world to its knees once before, and I would do so again.

"Prepare our defenses," I commanded. "I want blizzards so fierce they'll strip the flesh from their bones. Avalanches to bury their troops. I'll ready the ice dragons—we'll rain frozen death from above."

My generals bowed and vanished, each disappearing into the swirling maelstrom of winter as they set forth on their tasks. I remained atop my glacier outside my castle walls, a sentinel of ice and shadow, watching as my forces mobilized with a precision that was both awe-inspiring and terrifying. The air thickened with snow, swirling in a blinding dance, and visibility dropped to near zero, cloaking the battlefield in an ominous shroud.

Beneath me, the ground trembled, resonating with the impending chaos as massive chunks of ice and snow broke free from the ancient mountains. They cascaded down akin to the wrath of the gods, thundering toward the invading army, a deadly avalanche that promised annihilation. Yet, amidst the howling winds and the fury of nature, the enemy continued to advance, their silhouettes growing clearer, their determination palpable.

I could feel the tension crackling in the air, a prelude to the storm that was about to unleash. Each heartbeat resonated with the impending clash, a symphony of havoc that was both thrilling and daunting. They thought they could breach my defenses, that they could claim dominion over what was mine? I smirked at the thought, for they had no idea what awaited them in the depths of this frozen hell. I was the master of this icy realm, and as the blizzard swirled around me, I prepared to unleash the full upsurge of my army upon them. The battle would be legendary, and I would carve my name into the annals of history once more.

They dare resist? They dare challenge my rule? Did they not understand that this was for their own good?

The world had grown soft, weak—fragile as a snowflake in the sun. I watched as it succumbed to comfort and complacency, drowning in a haze of mediocrity. Only through the crucible of endless winter could it be remade into something stronger, something worthy of my vision. In the biting cold, true strength was forged; it was a relentless teacher, stripping away the weak and revealing the resolute beneath.

The seasons had dulled the spirit of humanity, lulling them into a false sense of security, but I knew better. I alone understood the necessity of this brutal rebirth. The frost would cleanse the earth, eliminating the rot that had seeped into its roots. As the icy winds howled and the snow buried all that was weak, I smiled, knowing I was the harbinger of this transformation.

With every flake that fell, I felt the power coursing through me, a divine right to reshape the world in my image. I was not merely a ruler; I was an architect of a new age, one where only the strongest would thrive, and the weak would be left to wither away. In my heart, I felt a giddy thrill at the thought of the chaos to come—a symphony of destruction that would clear the path for greatness. And in that darkness, I would rise, the unchallenged king of a world reborn.

As the first hints of their advance emerged, a cacophony of shouts and the clash of steel echoed through the air. The invaders, clad in armor that shimmered like the sun, moved through the snow with an arrogance that made my blood boil.

I raised my hand, the frost swirling around my fingers, and the ground beneath us responded. Ice surged upward, creating ramparts and barriers, while the chilling wind howled in a frenzy, ready to unleash its fury.

"Prepare yourselves!" I commanded, my voice rising above the tempest. "Let the bitter winds be our heralds, and the biting cold be our weapon. When they reach us, we will unleash a storm they cannot fathom!"

The Frost Giants hefted their massive axes, their breath misting in the frigid air, while the Winter Wolves crouched low, muscles coiled and ready to pounce. The Ice Wraiths hovered, their forms of swirling smoke, poised to unleash their chilling might at my command.

"Let the frost claim them," I whispered, my heart pounding with anticipation, as the first arrows of fire arched toward us, their flames dancing like fleeting stars in the encroaching gloom.

I raised my hand and unleashed a wave of frost that surged forward in a vengeful tide. The moment the flames met the icy barrier, they hissed and sputtered, extinguished before they could reach us. A cold laugh escaped my lips as I watched their arrogance crumble into fear.

"Now!" I roared, my voice echoing through the howling winds. The Frost Giants surged forward, their massive forms charging through the swirling snow. Joul led the charge, his axe raised high, a living avalanche intent on crushing everything in its path.

The Winter Wolves were a blur of white, darting through the mayhem with primal grace. Sadi howled, a fierce rallying cry that pierced the din of battle. They struck from the flanks, their teeth tearing into the soft flesh of the enemy in spray of crimson across the white blanket before us, a whirlwind of fangs and fur that left devastation in their wake.

The Ice Wraiths followed, gliding above the fray, trailing icy tendrils that froze anything they touched. They unleashed screams that echoed like the voices of lost souls, sowing confusion among the enemy ranks. With every touch, they turned our opponents into statues of ice, their faces locked in eternal terror. The second wave of Frost Giants surged from behind, their immense forms crashing into the enemy ranks and shattering frozen flesh akin to delicate glass.

The invaders fought valiantly, their swords clanging against our defenses, but their flames flickered and waned under the relentless onslaught of winter's ire. I reveled in the sight of their faces, once confident, now painted with disbelief and despair. They had underestimated us, thinking mere fire could conquer the cold.

"Push them back!" I commanded, my voice rising above the chaos. The Frost Giants responded with thunderous roars, swinging their axes with such force, scraping the ice, shaking the ground beneath us. The enemy lines faltered, panic spreading like wildfire as they realized they were not just fighting an army, but a force of nature itself.

I stood at the edge of my icy platform, my presence a chilling specter. With a flick of my wrist, I summoned shards of ice that flew toward the enemy congruent to deadly arrows. They struck with pinpoint accuracy, piercing armor and flesh alike. Each scream that echoed back to me was a melody of triumph, a song of winter's revenge.

But then, amid the calamity, I spotted a figure at the forefront of the invading army—a warrior cloaked in shimmering gold, wielding a sword that blazed. Their aura radiated an unnatural heat, pushing back the cold in waves. My heart sank for a moment; this was the power Ia had sensed, an entity unlike any I had faced.

"Joul!" I shouted, pointing toward the golden figure. "That one is different! We must eliminate them before they rally their forces!"

"On it, my lord!" Joul roared, rallying his fellow giants. Together, they charged, a wall of ice and fury descending upon the warrior.

As they engaged, I felt a surge of heat push against my icy realm. The golden warrior met Joul with a swing of their blazing sword, and the clash sent shockwaves rippling through the air. Flames and frost battled for dominance, a vivid dance of light and dark that threatened to swallow us whole.

"Fight harder!" I bellowed, feeling the adrenaline coursing through me as I advanced forward. "Do not let their fire extinguish our winter!"

Sadi darted through the fray, leading her wolves to flank the golden warrior, while the Ice Wraiths circled above, preparing to strike with their chilling essence. The tension in the air was palpable, a storm ready to break, as the two forces collided.

Just as it seemed we would overwhelm the warrior, a pulse of energy erupted from the golden sword, casting a blinding light that momentarily pushed back my icy grip on the blizzard I created for tactical concealment. I staggered, feeling the heat wash over me.

As the enemy drew closer to the base of my fortress, I clenched my teeth in frustration. Their armor gleamed with an inner fire, and in their hands they carried weapons that radiated heat and light. At their head stood a figure that made my cold blood turn frigid—a woman with hair the color of flames and eyes that burned with the intensity of the sun itself.

"Ykazar!" her voice rang out, clear and strong despite the howling wind. "Your reign of terror ends today! Surrender, and we will show mercy!"

I laughed, the sound sharp and brittle as breaking ice while I swung my sword to the side, decapitated the summer soldier who tried to ambush me. I flicked my blade, spraying blood across the white landscape in morbid artistry.

"Mercy?" I chuckled. "I am winter itself! I am the cold that creeps into your bones, the frost that withers your crops, the ice that claims the lives of the weak and unprepared. There is no mercy in winter. Only death."

With a gesture, I sent a wave of ice spikes hurtling toward her. But before they could reach their target, they melted away to nothing with another pulse of her power, evaporating in a hiss of steam.

When the woman smiled, it was like dawn breaking

after the longest night. A flash of irritation shot through me. "You're right, King Frost. There is no mercy in nature. But there is balance. And you have upset that balance for far too long."

She raised her hand, and a beam of pure sunlight shot toward me, slicing through the storm. I barely managed to erect a wall of ice in time, the frigid barrier rising to meet the radiant onslaught. But even then, I felt the heat sear through my defenses, a reminder of the relentless power she wielded.

Determined not to yield, I called upon all my strength, summoning storms of ice and snow that could have buried entire cities. The air crackled with energy as I unleashed the fury of winter. My armies clashed with theirs, the sounds of battle reverberating across the frozen landscape—a chaotic symphony of steel, roars, and shouts.

Ice dragons soared overhead, their massive wings cutting through the cold air. They swooped down, unleashing torrents of frozen breath that encased enemy soldiers in crystalline prisons, halting their advance. With their hind claws, they shattered the enemies into shards of ice. Yet for every soldier of summer that fell, it seemed two more emerged to take their place, relentless and unyielding.

Their weapons of light and fire cut through my icy constructs with an ease that filled me with irritation, the magic of summer seeping into every crack and crevice of my defenses. It was as if they were fueled by an unquenchable flame, each fallen comrade merely a spark igniting the resolve of those behind them.

I had never expected to meet her, not in a place like this, not in the midst of the ruin and chaos I had so carefully crafted. The rumors of her command resurfaced in my mind —*Laeta*. She had risen through the ranks with a speed that left even the most seasoned fae veterans in awe.

There were whispers—some out of envy, others out of fear—that her ascent had come at the expense of those who underestimated her. But those who truly knew her, the ones who had fought beside her, understood that Laeta had no use for shortcuts. She had earned everything through sheer willpower, and that made her the most dangerous kind of leader.

Commander Laeta.

The very name suited her, though I would come to learn it was not just a title, but a reflection of the fire that burned inside her. A force of nature in physical form, the antithesis to everything I had ever known.

CHAPTER 2

YKAZAR

Her presence alone seemed to disrupt the very air. The battlefield, once dominated by my icy soldiers, had already begun to feel warmer. The frost that clung to the earth like an ancient curse began to tremble underfoot as she advanced, her every step causing the ground beneath her to shudder. It was as if the very seasons bent to her will, the sun choosing to shine more brightly in her wake, the cold retreating in quiet submission. I could sense the power she commanded, not from any magic, but from the raw essence of *life* itself.

The battlefield erupted into upheaval as the ice dragons tore through the air, their massive wings beating like thunder, sending shockwaves that rattled the earth beneath us. They were born of my will, creations of pure frost and storm, summoned from the deepest reaches of winter's wrath. Their scales shimmered equivalent to the coldest diamond, their eyes glowing with a fierce, primal hunger. They were the embodiment of my power—my most terrifying weapons, and my final line of defense against the heat that *Laeta* brought to this forsaken war.

I stood amidst the chaos, watching as my dragons dove into the ranks of her soldiers, their roars shaking the heavens as they unleashed waves of frost breath, freezing anything they touched. The dragons were unstoppable—ancient and powerful, creatures of ice and furor. The soldiers screamed as the frost turned their limbs to ice, encasing them in solid, lifeless prisons.

And yet, through the flurry of snow, I knew *she* was still out there.

Drawn by an unseen force, I cut through the bedlam, detaching limbs from oncoming opponents and painting the snow crimson until I found her effortlessly amidst the fray.

She was tall, her frame muscular yet lithe, and the sword she wielded was a blazing thing, its blade glowing with molten gold. When she swung it, fire would erupt from the steel, sending shards of flame into the air, burning my soldiers down to the bone in moments. I had thought my army of winter might be unstoppable, my forces of frost and snow a perfect counter to anything that dared challenge me. Yet Commander Laeta—her name now felt so small for the chaos she wrought—she was an enigma, a riddle I could not solve.

I watched as she decimated my front lines, a whirlwind of fire and destruction. The way she moved was impossibly fluid, each movement a deadly dance, and the zeal in her eyes was the kind I had not seen in centuries. The sky itself seemed to darken in contrast to her, her fiery path slicing through the clouds like a burning streak of light. She was everywhere, as though the battlefield itself had been shaped to accommodate her might.

And then there was her laugh—the one that rang out akin to the clash of steel on steel, wild and untamed, as if she reveled in the violence she unleashed. It echoed across the fields, a sound that set my teeth on edge. It filled me with a visceral kind of fury, as if her very joy mocked everything I had worked for.

I felt it then—*doubt*. A word I had not felt in centuries. Her laughter, her presence, her power—all of it stirred something in me that I thought had long been buried. I could feel it creeping through my veins, a sudden weight in my chest, a ripple of uncertainty.

For a moment, I hesitated.

That was a mistake.

The ground trembled beneath me, the earth groaning under the weight of her strength. But I would not let this slip away. No. I would remind her. I would remind *everyone* that winter was not to be trifled with. No matter how bright the flame, the storm of frost and snow would always, eventually, return.

With a growl that came from deep within, I advanced further into the pandemonium. I could feel the chill of winter wrapping itself around my limbs, a familiar comfort. The icy winds began to stir around me, swirling in a dance of their own, growing stronger with each step. Snowflakes began to gather, swirling through the air like a thousand jagged daggers, forming into a blizzard that would blind and freeze.

She wanted fire? I would show her something she hadn't

reckoned with: the cold that could strip the very warmth from her heart.

I raised my hand, summoning the storm, and it responded eagerly, as it always had. The wind howled and the snow began to fall, thick and fast, coating the battlefield in a blanket of white. The flames that had been so dominant began to flicker in the growing storm, their brilliance fading against the sheer force of the cold. The world around us began to freeze—slowly at first, but quickly gaining momentum.

I saw her then, standing at the edge of the storm, sword raised high, the heat of her presence barely managing to push against the frost creeping across the ground at her feet. Her fiery glow contrasted with the chilling whiteness of the blizzard, a battle of elements, of power, of worlds colliding.

Her eyes locked with mine across the distance of the battlefield. For a moment, I thought I saw recognition there —something beyond the defiance. But then she smiled, that wild, uncontained grin that set the flames inside her alight again.

"You think *this* will stop me?" Her voice rang clear, a challenge in the howling wind. She thrust her sword toward the sky, and fire erupted from it, as if it were an extension of her very soul. It ignited the air around her in a shockwave of heat, pushing against the growing cold, filling the space with a blinding light.

"You are a fool," I growled, the wind and snow gathering behind me in a solid wall of force. "You cannot fight nature, Commander Laeta. You can burn, you can rage, but in the end, the cold will consume you."

She didn't flinch. "The cold can try," she said, her voice

carrying over the storm, full of fire and defiance. "But I won't stop. Not until I've burned it all away."

And then she charged.

I did not flinch as she closed the distance, though her speed was nothing short of awe-inspiring. She was a blur of fire, her sword blazing with heat so intense it should have melted the very air. Her laughter rang out again, fierce and unstoppable, as she barreled toward me, cutting through the snow and wind as though they were mere obstacles to be overcome. But I was ready.

The Winter Wolves howled with the winds as I raised my hands, my power flaring, the storm exploding around me like a living thing. Ice surged upward, forming jagged pillars that shot out of the ground toward her, each one sharper than the last, designed to cut her down before she could reach me.

She didn't slow. She didn't hesitate.

With a movement too quick to follow, she swept her sword through the air, and a wave of flame cascaded down, burning the ice to vapors in an instant. The ground trembled underfoot as she closed in. I could feel the heat from her flame lapping at my skin, making the chill in my veins seem feeble in comparison. For the first time in my existence, I was faced with something I couldn't quite control. Something I couldn't predict.

She was there, her fiery form leaping toward me, an unstoppable force of nature.

I summoned the storm again, pushing every ounce of my power into it. Snow and wind lashed out, slamming into her with the vehemence of a thousand tempests, seeking to freeze her in place, to smother her flames. The battle between fire and ice had never been so fierce.

And yet, despite the storm, she smiled.

For the briefest moment, I felt a pang of something I could not define. Admiration? Respect? It didn't matter. All I knew was that I could not let this stand.

The fire in her eyes was unbreakable. That was the truth of it, wasn't it? No matter how hard I tried to freeze her, to subdue her with the weight of winter's touch, she would never yield.

And in that moment, I realized something more. She wasn't just a warrior. She wasn't just an obstacle to my rule of winter. She was a challenge. A challenge that could reshape the very way I viewed the world.

But I wouldn't let that happen. No matter how strong she was, no matter how fierce her flames, the cold was *my* domain.

The ground beneath us buckled and cracked as our powers collided again, a cataclysmic clash of elements—fire against frost, warmth against cold, life against death.

I had only one goal.

To put out her fire before it swallowed me completely.

The clash of steel around us rang through the air, a sharp, discordant symphony of fire and ice. My breath came in quick, icy bursts as I locked eyes with her. Her golden blade burned bright, a streak of molten light against the frozen battlefield. I could feel the heat of it from where I stood, a physical presence in the air that made the storm around us seem almost insignificant.

She was fast—faster than I had anticipated—and when she struck, it was as if the sun had descended to Earth, each swing of her sword cutting through the air with blinding speed. I was no stranger to battle, no stranger to blades, but this? This was something else entirely. The raw power in her every movement was as much a primal upheaval as the fire she wielded.

I didn't wait for her to come to me.

With a growl, I dashed forward with Frostbite in hand, the cold surge of winter swirling around my body similar to a cloak.

She met me head-on, her golden sword flashing downward in a downward arc aimed at my chest. I raised my ice blade to intercept, the sharp crack of our blades meeting like a thunderclap. The heat of her sword licked at the edge of mine, sending a searing sting through my arms, but I gritted my teeth and held firm, shoving back with all my strength.

The intensity sent her stumbling back half a step, just enough for me to press the advantage. I surged forward, aiming a vicious kick at her midsection, hoping to knock the wind out of her. But she was too fast. With a twist, she caught my leg, and in a blur of movement, her knee collided with my ribs, sending a shockwave of pain through my side.

I grunted, staggering, but I didn't fall. Her moves duplicated that of fire—unstoppable, a dancing flame leaping from one point to another. As I regained my balance, I swung my blade in a wide arc, aiming for her throat. But she twisted away, her movements almost too quick to follow.

In a flash, she was on me again, her sword a streak of molten gold. She slashed downward, aiming for my shoulder, but I was ready. I sidestepped, feeling the heat of the blade brush against the edge of my cloak as I pivoted, swinging my ice blade horizontally in a brutal arc. The clash of our weapons rang through the storm as her sword barely deflected the blow, but it was enough to leave her open for just a second.

I moved in, slashing upward with a sharp, vicious strike aimed at her face.

But she anticipated me.

She ducked beneath my strike and brought her elbow up, slamming it into my jaw with a sickening crack. Stars exploded in my vision as the pain shot through my skull, but I refused to stumble. I kept my feet, anger fueling me as I fought through the pain.

She grinned as she took a step back, spinning her blade in her hands.

"You're quick, Frost King," she taunted, her voice hot with the thrill of the fight, "but fire never stops burning."

I lunged again, using my momentum to force her back. She parried the blow, but I didn't stop. I moved with the storm now, faster, more unpredictable. Each step I took sent shards of ice flying in every direction, each one aimed at her. I saw her hesitate—just for a moment—before she leaped over a shard of ice that flew past her like a spear.

In the split second she was airborne, I knew what I had to do.

I dropped low, sweeping my leg under hers, catching her by the ankle and pulling her to the ground. Her fiery sword flew from her grip, skidding across the icy floor, leaving a trail of molten residue in its wake.

For a heartbeat, we were both on the ground, the sound of her body hitting the frost-covered earth echoing despite the buzz of the battlefield. She was quick, though. Too quick. She immediately rolled, shifting her weight, aiming to get back to her feet. But before she could fully rise, I was on her, pinning her down with the full weight of my body.

I had no intention of killing her—yet—but I would end this battle on my terms.

I pressed my ice blade against her throat, just hard enough to send a clear message. The chill of the blade, cold enough to freeze the very air around it, pressed against her skin, and I could see the slight shudder in her eyes. But she didn't look afraid. No—she looked *challenged*, as if this moment was exactly where she wanted to be.

Her gaze never left mine as she reached up with both hands, grabbing my wrist and twisting with surprising strength. I was momentarily caught off guard, just enough for her to break free and roll to the side, using the momentum to spring back onto her feet.

I sprang to my feet as well, still holding the ice blade, but now, I was met with her fiery gaze. She was more than a challenge—she was an *equal*, a force that could not be ignored, and that made her dangerous.

"You think you've won?" she taunted, her voice thick with confidence. "You think you can stop me with ice and snow?"

I narrowed my eyes, shifting my stance, the cold storm within me rising to a crescendo. "Fire is fleeting. It burns bright, but it always fades. And when it does, the cold will still be here."

She tilted her head, her grin widening. "We'll see about that."

In a blur of motion, she charged, her feet practically leaving the ground as she lunged at me, her bare hands now reaching for my throat with the ferocity of a wildfire. I barely had time to react, but I caught her wrist, locking it in mid-air. The raw heat of her body pressed against me, the flames of her spirit nearly burning through my clothes as we grappled. I pushed against her with every ounce of strength I had, my ice blade still in my hand, but neither of us was willing to make the first move.

We locked in a brutal standoff, neither of us able to break free. Her breath came out in short, fiery bursts, and I could feel the sweat beginning to collect on my brow despite the cold, her presence almost unbearable. We were polar elements colliding—one of ice and one of flame, neither willing to yield.

With a sudden move, she jerked me closer and leaped, using my momentary distraction to bring her knee up into my abdomen. The brunt of the blow left me gasping for breath, and for a split second, my vision blurred. She didn't hesitate.

She grabbed my arm, pivoting around it with the speed of a serpent, and before I knew it, my own ice blade was at my throat, her arm around mine, twisting it, forcing me to the ground. Her golden blade—a blade that had almost killed me—was now pressed against my chest, the heat of it unbearable, searing through my cloak and burning into my skin.

And yet, even as the heat radiated from her sword, the battle was far from over.

"You'll burn out eventually," I rasped, my voice cold despite the fire. "You can't keep going forever."

Laeta smirked, her blade unwavering. "Neither can you."

At that moment, with the cold blade of my own ice against my skin, I knew the truth.

Inch by inch, her army advanced with the unexpected addition of Everwolves at their backs, a blur of obsidian.

My Frost Giants fell, their icy forms shattered by weapons of molten metal. My Winter Wolves were driven back, their fur singed and smoking from the rival fae of summer, many of them caught in a bloody battle of jaws and snarls with the Everwolves. Even my Ice Wraiths, beings of pure cold, found themselves outmatched by the searing light of the Laeta's power.

"It's over, Ykazar," she said, her voice tinged with something that might have been pity. "Your winter has ended."

"No," I snarled. "I am eternal! I am—"

"You are defeated," she whispered in my ear.

Her hand shot out, faster than I could follow.

Light exploded around me, brighter than a thousand suns. I felt my power draining away, my very essence being stripped from me.

As consciousness faded, I had one last, terrible thought.

This isn't the end. I will return. And when I do, the world will know a winter from which it will never thaw.

Darkness took me then, and with it came the cold embrace of defeat.

I awoke to silence.

CHAPTER 3

YKAZAR

Gone was the howling of the wind, the clash of battle, and the thunderous roar of avalanches. In their place, a profound stillness enveloped me, a heavy silence pressing against my ears like a physical weight, smothering the chaos that had raged just moments before. It felt as if the very essence of winter had drawn back, holding its breath, as if the world were waiting for the darkness to swallow me whole.

I tried to move, birse rising within me, only to discover that I was bound—not by chains or ropes, but by a power far more insidious. Magic, ancient and insurmountable, coiled and serpentined around me, tightening with every desperate attempt to break free. It pulsed with a vibrant energy, familiar yet foreign, resonating with the primal depths of my being but somehow subduing it.

The chill that usually coursed through my veins now felt

sluggish, as if the very cold had been siphoned away, leaving me vulnerable and exposed. How long had I been unconscious? A sense of dread crept in, clawing at my insides as shadows flickered at the edges of my vision, teasing my senses with glimpses of movement that I could not fully comprehend.

The air felt thick, heavy with a darkness that clung to my skin, warping my thoughts and distorting my perception. Phantom echoes of battle cries and snarls faded in and out of my mind. Were they memories or mere visions? Time lost its meaning; seconds stretched into agonizing eternities as I struggled to piece together what was happening. The ground beneath me felt unstable, shifting as if the world itself were caught in a tempest of confusion.

Desperation surged as I realized I was not just physically confined; I was ensnared in a realm that toyed with my mind.

"I will kill you all!" I roared into the void, the echoes of my voice crashing back to me.

Whispers slithered through the silence, fragmented voices rising from the shadows like crawling tendrils.

"We will annihilate them all!"

Each word seemed to crawl under my skin, twisting in my mind, planting parasitic seeds of doubt.

"Your reign has come to its end."

"The King of Frost has fallen."

The air grew thick with their presence, a cold, suffocating breath that gnawed at the edges of my sanity. It was as if the darkness itself was speaking, mocking me, feeding on my fear.

"Our king will never fall!"

Were they the echoes of my fallen soldiers? The voices of those I had lost, now twisted by time and grief? Or was this just another layer of the curse that bound me here, feeding on my isolation?

"He will rise again!"

"He is imprisoned for his ruthless ambitions. And so will you all!"

The thought physically hit me—sharp and crushing. Even in this endless darkness, I realized with horrifying clarity that I couldn't trust my senses. The whispers could be real—or they could be illusions, born from my own tortured mind. In this place, I was no longer sure what was truth and what was torment.

Time dissolved into nothingness, the weight of eternity pressing down on me, its cold grip tightening around my throat in a noose. *This cannot be!* I strained against the bindings, a futile effort that only seemed to amplify the pulse of the magic around me. It resonated like a heartbeat, a cruel reminder that escape was not just unlikely; it was seemingly impossible. My breaths quickened, and the walls of my icy resolve began to crumble under the weight of despair.

As I struggled, a flicker of defiance ignited within me, a faint glimmer in the suffocating blackness. If this magic sought to bind me, then I would not be broken. I began to gather what remained of my will, drawing on the primal essence of winter that still lingered in the depths of my spirit. The chill of revenge flowed through me, mingling with the darkness that sought to overwhelm.

Though shadows loomed closer, taunting me with their sinister embrace, I refused to surrender.

Howls of agony, followed by yelps of pain reverberated

in my thoughts. Were they imprisoned with me? Or was it a trick of the mind?

Time continued to slip through my fingers as my eyes adjusted to the gloom. I was in a cave, deep beneath the earth. The walls glistened with moisture, a mockery of the ice that had once been my domain. The only light came from my prison itself, a soft, pulsing glow that did little to illuminate my surroundings.

"Comfortable?" a voice cut through the growing madness, dripping with false concern.

I turned my head—the only movement allowed to me—and saw her. The Summer Queen stood just beyond the boundary of my prison, her fiery hair now subdued to a warm amber in the dim light.

"What is this place? Where have you brought me?" I demanded, my voice a mere shadow of its former power.

She smiled, but it was not a friendly one. "Your new home, King Frost. A place where you can contemplate the balance of nature without disrupting it."

I snarled, straining against my invisible bonds. "You can't hold me forever. I am a force of nature itself!"

"Perhaps," she conceded. "But we can hold you long enough. Long enough for the world to heal from the wounds you've inflicted. Long enough for people to forget your name and your terror."

She stepped closer, her gaze piercing into mine as sharp as the crown that now sat atop of her fiery mane, exposing her delicately tipped ears. A cruel smirk played on her lips. "You'll learn the true meaning of survival here, Ykazar. You'll endure in this cave, with nothing but your own thoughts for company. No power, no subjects, no eternal winter—just you and the darkness."

Her words crashed over me like a tidal wave of glacial water, cold and claustrophobic. Anger flared within me, a bitter frost that spread through my veins, pushing back the creeping chill of despair. This wasn't merely imprisonment; it was a calculated attempt to strip me of everything I was, to influence me into a hollow existence. The realization twisted my gut with a phantom blade.

"How dare you!" I spat, my voice a low growl. "You think this will break me? I am winter incarnate! I will not be reduced to mere shadows and echoes. You will regret underestimating me!"

The walls of the cave seemed to vibrate with my lividity, and for a moment, I envisioned the ice storms I could summon, the blizzards that could bury entire armies. But that thought was quickly smothered by the weight of my confinement. This was not just an affront to my power; it was a personal betrayal. She sought to bind me, to erase my very essence.

"You think you can trap me in darkness?" I snarled, my breath coming in sharp huffs. "I will carve my way back, and when I do, your little game will be the first to feel my wrath!"

The shadows loomed around me, and even as they pressed in, I vowed that I would not be merely a victim of her twisted designs. This would not be the end of me; it would be a reckoning. I would rise from this darkness, and she would tremble before the fury of winter unleashed.

I let out a humorless chuckle. "Without winter, without the culling of the weak, the world will—"

"The world will thrive," she interrupted, her tone dismissive and condescending. "It will find its own balance, as it always has. Without your interference."

The weight of her words crashed into me, and a surge of indignation erupted within me, freezing my insides like a burst of ice from a shattered glacier. How dare she speak so casually of balance when she was the one threatening to plunge me into this abyss?

"You think you can just turn your back on me? You think the world can survive without the relentless bite of winter? I am its embodiment! I am the storm that cleanses the weak from the strong!"

She turned to leave, and panic clawed at my insides, a primal, choking terror that twisted my gut. I felt betrayed by my own emotions. Rage followed, sharp and blistering, parallel to ice shattering under the pressure of a sudden storm. The thought of eternal solitude—of being extinguished from existence—was unbearable. It was as though the very act of her departure fractured something deep within me, and I felt the wrathfulness surge, cold and unstoppable, burning through the numbness that had settled over my mind.

"You can't leave me here!" My voice cracked, the anger mingling with desperation. "You have no idea what you're doing! This is my essence, my legacy! You would doom this world to chaos and ruin!"

Her indifference only fueled the fire within me, and I struggled against the magical bindings that held me captive.

"You think you can erase me? You think I'll wither away in this darkness? I am Ykazar, master of winter! The very air trembles at my name, and I will make you regret the day you crossed me!"

The cave walls reverberated with the force of my resentment, echoes ricocheting off the stone like thunder. I could feel the darkness pressing in, threatening to swallow me whole, but I refused to be consumed. I would not allow her to dismiss me as if I were nothing.

"I will rise from this pit," I seethed, my voice low and dangerous, laced with a promise. "And when I do, the world will know true winter once more. I will unleash a blizzard that will bury your precious balance, and I will reclaim my throne. You think you can walk away unscathed? You have only sealed your fate, and when the cold comes for you, you will remember this moment!"

She paused at the entrance of the cave, just for an instant, as if my words had pierced her facade. "Goodbye, Ykazar. May your winter of discontent last an eternity."

As the last flicker of her form vanished, reality slammed into me, its brutal finality shattering the fragile heat within. The entrance to the cave sealed itself with an eerie permanence, rocks grinding together like jagged icebergs colliding, until no trace of escape remained. I was alone, entombed in a tomb of frost, the cold closing in around me, sealing me in a coffin.

The stillness wrapped around me like a suffocating shroud, thick and oppressive. I strained against the bindings that held me, but the ancient magic tightened its grip, feeding off my frustration. I could feel it seeping into my mind, coiling around my thoughts, whispering doubts and fears that had long lain dormant.

The silence began to morph into a cacophony, an insidious chorus of my own thoughts amplified by the void around me.

"This is a trick," I told myself, but the words felt hollow, echoing back with mocking laughter. "I am winter incarnate! I will break free!"

But with each declaration, the certainty that once fueled my resolve eroded away, leaving only the gnawing realization of my isolation.

Days—or was it weeks?—drifted by in this dark prison, time losing all meaning. I could feel the shadows creeping in closer, thickening with every breath I took. Memories of past victories began to blur, replaced by a suffocating weight of despair. I had faced countless foes, yet none had prepared me for this mental onslaught.

With a surge of strength, I fought against the restraints only to bite my tongue, relishing in the tangy, warm taste of copper in my mouth to keep me grounded to reality.

The whispers grew louder, taunting me with visions of my own demise, echoing my failures back to me.

The walls pulsed in response, echoing my thoughts back with cruel precision. I sank to the ground, my hands clawing into the cold earth until each nail cracked and peeled away from my flesh, blood making my fingers slip against the grooves I had created. With a snarl, I punched the stone, the crack of my knuckles echoing around me. "No, I am Ykazar! I cannot be forgotten. I will not be erased!"

But doubt gnawed at the edges of my mind, each moment stretching into an eternity as I rocked in place, smearing my bloody fingers across my temples. I began to speak to myself, the echoes of my own voice my only company.

The shadows danced around me, mocking my spiraling thoughts. I could almost feel them reaching out, pulling at my sanity, whispering secrets in a language I could almost grasp. Fragments of memory flickered in my mind—frozen landscapes, fallen foes, and the icy grip of power I once wielded—but they felt distant, half-remembered dreams.

I shouted into the void, my voice cracking, desperation clawing at my throat like serrated blades. But the silence swallowed my words, leaving only the echoes of my own doubts reverberating back.

"No!" I roared, my voice rising to a frantic pitch. "I will not accept this! I will not fade into nothingness! I am the cold that scours the weak from the land!"

As madness began to creep in, I could feel the icy grip of fear wrapping around my heart. The darkness grew denser, pressing in on me, constricting my thoughts until they became a tangled mess of rage and despair.

With a desperate laugh that bordered on hysteria, I shouted, "You think you can take me? You think this darkness can hold me? I am the storm that chills the marrow in your bones!"

I cackled at the imagery and thoughts of what I planned to do to my enemies. The taste of blood in my mouth was only a prelude to what I had in store for them.

But deep down, I felt the truth gnawing at me. The shadows were growing thicker, wrapping around my thoughts.

With each passing moment, I felt my grip on reality slipping, the shadows weaving tighter around me. I could almost hear their whispers now, urging me to surrender, to embrace the darkness as it consumed me. My heart raced, panic clawing at my insides. The scent of old blood clung to the air, enveloping me from all sides, as if it were conspiring against me, a silent witness to my torment.

I was losing myself, and I could feel the last remnants of my sanity fraying at the edges.

As the shadows closed in, I sank back to the ground, cradling my head in my hands, teetering on the brink of oblivion. In this suffocating silence, I realized that I might not just be a prisoner of stone and magic; I might also be a prisoner of my own mind, lost in a darkness that promised to devour me whole.

I clung to my hatred, my desire for vengeance, using it as a shield against the encroaching insanity.

But as time passed—how much, I couldn't say—even those thoughts began to fade. I felt myself slipping away, piece by piece, memory by memory.

In my darkest moments, when the silence threatened to drown me entirely, I clung to one thought.

Someone would come.

Someone would find me.

And when they did, I would be ready.

This is not the end of my story.

It is merely the beginning of a new, colder chapter.

PART TWO

CHAPTER 4

CALLIE WINTERS

It started like any other Monday, a day marked by the weight of the world pressing down on my shoulders like a particularly heavy toddler. The morning light filtered through my grimy apartment window, illuminating the dust motes swirling in the air—yes, the same dust motes that had been swirling for months, mocking my inability to clean. I stared at the pile of bills on the coffee table, each envelope a reminder of my many failures. Seriously, if bills could talk, they'd probably laugh at me.

My job as a barista barely covered rent, and my social life was a barren wasteland punctuated only by marathon viewings of reality TV and the occasional text from friends I hadn't seen in months.

"What are you doing tonight?" one of them would ask.

"Binge-watching 'The Great British Bake Off' and pretending I know how to make a soufflé," I'd reply, avoiding eye contact with my microwave, which had become my closest friend.

As I shuffled through my morning routine, a sense of heaviness settled in my chest, as if I'd just eaten a burrito the size of my head. The city outside buzzed with life—horns honking, people shouting, dogs barking—yet I felt as though I was moving through a haze, trapped in a life I hadn't chosen but had somehow accepted like a pair of ill-fitting jeans.

I absentmindedly poured myself a cup of coffee, taking a moment to appreciate the irony of needing caffeine to get through my caffeine-fueled job. I plopped onto my threadbare couch, scrolling through social media with a mix of envy and resignation. Everyone seemed so happy, so fulfilled—smiling at brunches I'd never be invited to, sipping cocktails at rooftop bars I'd only seen on social media picture feeds. Meanwhile, I was drowning in a sea of mediocre choices, all while wearing pajamas that had definitely seen better days.

Just as I was about to give in to the siren call of self-pity and slide back under the covers, I shook myself awake. "Get it together, Callie," I muttered, forcing myself to get up.

I threw on some clothes that were at least clean-ish, half-heartedly brushing my teeth while attempting to tame my hair into something resembling human. Spoiler alert: it didn't work. I dashed out of my apartment, nearly tripping over the stack of shoes I hadn't bothered to organize since last spring.

The subway was a whole other level of chaos. I squeezed into the car like a sardine, inhaling a mix of body odor, cheap cologne, and the lingering scent of last night's takeout. I felt as if I was in a claustrophobic horror movie, praying I wouldn't have to make eye contact with the guy eating a breakfast burrito as if it were the last meal on Earth.

Finally, I stumbled into the coffee shop, my sanctuary— or so I liked to think.

My boss, Frank, greeted me with a raised eyebrow. "You're late, Callie. Did you lose track of time again?"

"No, I just enjoy making a grand entrance," I shot back, grabbing an apron and tying it around my waist. "I thought I'd keep everyone on their toes."

Frank rolled his eyes but couldn't hide a smirk. "Just get to work. We're swamped today."

As the caffeine-hungry crowd began to pour in, I jumped into the fray, trying to remember the difference between a caramel macchiato and a caramel latte while juggling orders.

"What can I get for you?" I asked a frazzled-looking woman.

"Um, a pumpkin spice latte?" she stammered.

"Sure, and would you like that with a side of existential dread?" I quipped, flashing her a smile. She blinked at me as if I was an alien.

"Just the latte, please," she said, backing away slowly.

I laughed to myself, shaking my head. At least my humor hadn't died along with my social life.

The morning rush was a blur of grinding beans, steaming milk, and trying to decipher the cryptic notes left by coworkers. "Add extra unicorn magic" seemed to be a popular request today. By the time I took a breath, my apron was splattered with coffee stains that resembled modern art.

At one point, I accidentally handed a double shot of espresso to a kid who looked barely ten. The mother looked horrified.

"He's already bouncing off the walls!" she shrieked, pointing at her son, who was indeed vibrating like he'd just consumed a whole candy store.

"Sorry! My bad!" I said, my cheeks burning with embarrassment. "Next time, I'll include a complimentary nap for him!"

As the hours dragged on, I felt my sanity teetering on the edge. The clock seemed to mock me, moving slower than molasses in winter. I narrowly avoided a spill with a cup of hot coffee—thank goodness for my ninja-like reflexes—only to bump into a customer carrying a massive pastry box. The box tipped, sending croissants flying through the air akin to buttery missiles.

"Whoops!" I exclaimed, dodging a rogue pastry as I tried to help clean up the disaster. I could only imagine the Yelp reviews: "Great coffee, excellent pastry projectile range!"

Finally, after what felt like an eternity, the rush subsided, and I leaned against the counter, wiping my brow with a sigh of relief.

Frank, with his silver-streaked hair slicked back and a walrus mustache that seemed to have a life of its own, threw me a grateful nod. His thick, calloused hands were adorned with a few rings that glinted in the light—old-school Italian flair that hinted at a colorful past.

"Not bad, Callie. You didn't set the place on fire this time."

"Yet," I replied, smirking. "But I'm still considering a dramatic exit involving flaming coffee cups."

"Please don't. The last time you attempted a dramatic exit, you spilled half a gallon of soy milk on my new rug. I nearly had a meltdown," he said, crossing his arms with a mock-serious expression that reminded me of a mob boss assessing his crew.

"Hey, I thought I was giving it a new 'flavored' look," I shot back, grinning. "You know, avant-garde? It's all the rage."

"Avant-garde or not, I'm seriously considering firing you," he said, shaking his head, though the corner of his mouth twitched. "But every time I think about it, you manage to charm the customers—or scare them off. I haven't quite decided which yet."

"Can't argue with the numbers, Frank! My 'unique' customer service style keeps them coming back for more, right?" I leaned in, lowering my voice conspiratorially. "Plus, who else would bring that level of chaos and charm?"

He chuckled, his deep voice rumbling similar to an old engine. "That's what I'm afraid of. I might have to hire a whole new level of disaster to match you. And who would provide the entertainment?"

"Exactly! I'm practically a one-woman show," I said, puffing out my chest. "Next week, I'll start charging admission. You'll thank me later."

"Just try to keep the tickets under twenty bucks," he replied with a grin, his eyes sparkling with mischief. "That's all I can afford for your circus."

With his leather jacket slightly worn and his presence radiating a fatherly warmth, Frank had become more than just my boss. He was the protector of this little caffeine haven, a man who could have easily been an enforcer in another life but had traded the adrenaline for espresso shots and dad jokes.

"Ah, small victories," I replied with a wink, taking a sip of my own cold coffee. "You know, they say the smell of popcorn brings in a lot of customers. Think about it, Frank."

He raised an eyebrow, his walrus mustache twitching with suspicion. "Popcorn? In a coffee shop? I can see the headline now: 'Local Barista Turns Café into a Circus.'"

"Hey, it worked for the carnival last summer! And besides, who wouldn't want a caramel corn latte?" I shot back, trying to suppress a grin. I really didn't work at a circus, but I did attend one. That had to count, right?

"Let's stick to coffee, shall we? I don't need you attracting the local clowns," he replied, shaking his head. "Speaking of, how's your love life? Any more exciting developments? Or is it still just you and your streaming movie account?"

Rude. Did he have to make it sound so blasé?

I sighed, pulling a face as I ground the beans for the next batch. "Same old story. Just me, my coffee, and an occasional text from the ex. You know, the one who cheated on me with the crazy cat lady?"

Frank's eyes widened, a mixture of disbelief and amusement. "How could I forget? I swear, if that guy had any sense, he'd be begging you to take him back."

"Trust me, he's not that bright. I caught him in our living room, cuddling with her as if she was a precious heirloom," I recounted. "I mean, who knew a cat lady could steal a guy so quickly? They say love is blind, but clearly, he had some sort of feline vision."

Inside, though, I felt a familiar pang—a sharp reminder

of the betrayal that still stung. It was almost laughable how easily I could turn my heartbreak into a punchline, as if by wrapping my pain in humor, I could somehow keep it at bay. The truth was, every time I made a joke about it, I was just trying to distance myself from the hurt, building up my walls more and more. It worked temporarily, but deep down, the wounds still throbbed.

I mean, he told me he was a dog guy!

Frank chuckled, leaning against the counter. "Maybe he thought he was getting two-for-one cuddles? Who wouldn't want to come home to a woman and a dozen cats?"

"Right? That's the dream, Frank. A life of cat hair and broken promises. Pass!" I said, shaking my head with a mock grimace.

"Stop it, ya big loaf. Stop trying to butter me up because I've seen that 'Now Hiring' sign outside our window," I teased, leaning against the counter with a smirk.

Just then, the bell above the door jingled furiously as the familiar chaos of our morning routine was interrupted. In barreled Linda, a regular whose frazzled appearance was becoming part of her signature style—hair in disarray like she'd just survived a wind tunnel, and her blouse half-tucked as if it had staged a mutiny.

"Callie! I need a large mocha, extra shot, and a miracle, stat!" she exclaimed, rushing up to the counter, her voice a blend of urgency and caffeine-fueled desperation.

"On it, Linda!" I replied, my fingers already dancing over the espresso machine. "Late again, I see?"

She shot me a look that was both sheepish and frantic. "You know me. I thought I had time to finish my presentation, but then my cat decided today was the day to stage a revolt. I swear, Whiskers has it out for me!"

Frank chuckled from behind the register. "Seems as if the cat lady epidemic is spreading. You should watch your back, Callie."

"Oh, please," I said with a roll of my eyes, pouring steaming milk into the waiting cup. "As if I'd ever trade my life of coffee for one filled with litter boxes and feline drama."

Linda laughed as I slid her drink across the counter. "You'd be surprised what you'd do when you're drowning in paperwork and your boss is breathing down your neck. Coffee keeps me sane. Well, as sane as I can manage with Whiskers plotting my downfall."

"Is this the same cat who gave you that lovely scratch on your arm last week?" I asked, raising an eyebrow.

"Yep, that's my little furball of trouble," she replied, taking a sip of her drink and letting out a blissful sigh. "Mmm, this is perfect. You're a lifesaver, Callie!"

"Just doing my job—saving the day one cup at a time," I said, trying to ignore the pang of longing that stirred within me as I watched her hustle off. Her life seemed so... put together, even amidst the chaos of late mornings and rebellious pets.

"See?" Frank said, waving a hand dismissively. "You're a coffee magician. You could have that life too, if you'd just stop with the self-pity. Look at you—bringing joy to the frazzled masses."

"Joy, sure," I said, leaning back against the counter. "But you're forgetting the joy of those who don't have to fight their cats for an hour before they leave the house. Just saying."

As the door swung shut behind Linda, I couldn't help but feel a mix of admiration and envy. She had her disarray, but at least she was actively living it—unlike me, who was stuck in a loop of late-night TV and self-deprecating humor.

"See? That's why you can't quit," Frank said, snapping me back to reality. "You're not just making coffee; you're the pulse of this place. The life raft for those adrift in the sea of suburbia."

"Life raft or life jacket?" I countered, smirking. "Because sometimes it feels as if I'm the one barely staying afloat while everyone else has their ducks in a row."

Frank grinned, leaning back against the counter, arms crossed. "Just keep your eyes on the prize, Callie. And maybe consider a new coffee blend inspired by your experiences— 'Caffeine for Catastrophes' or something."

"Ha! I can see the marketing now: 'For when your life's a mess but at least your mocha isn't!'" I laughed, but inside, I couldn't shake the feeling that while I was juggling espresso shots, my own life was slipping through my fingers.

As the morning rush began to pick up again, I threw myself into the work, crafting lattes and serving pastries with a flair that would've made any barista proud. Frank watched with a bemused expression, half-shaking his head, half-smiling as I fumbled through the orders.

"You know," he said, wiping down the counter, "if I didn't know better, I'd say you were trying to impress someone."

"Just trying to keep the customers alive, Frank," I shot

back, pouring a perfectly foamed heart into a cappuccino. "Don't want any more heart attacks on my watch."

He laughed, a hearty sound that resonated through the café. "Just remember, Callie, as long as you keep them laughing, you'll keep them coming back."

"Easy for you to say, old man. You've been charming the pants off them since before I was born," I teased, grabbing a few napkins and flinging them his way.

"Ha! Don't forget it," he said, puffing out his chest like a proud peacock. "Now, how about a little less banter and a little more coffee magic? I'm not running a therapy session here!"

"Fine, fine! Just let me pour my soul into these cups," I replied dramatically.

As the hours passed, I lost myself in the rhythm of the café, the bustling atmosphere slowly driving away the remnants of my suburban past. Each drink I made felt like a small rebellion against the life I once knew—one filled with predictable days and unfulfilled dreams. Here, I was carving out my own identity, one espresso shot at a time. And maybe, just maybe, it was a step toward something better.

As the day dragged on and the sun dipped below the horizon, I closed up the shop, exhausted but grateful to have survived another day.

Sitting in the subway on the way home, I sat across from a single mother. It made me think about my own.

My mom, Marissa, raised me on her own after my dad disappeared when I was a toddler. She never talked about him afterward, and I never asked. It was just the two of us, and I was fine with that. She worked long hours at a diner, always putting on a brave face, always telling me, "We'll get through this." She was my rock—strong, independent, and never one to show weakness. I learned to be the same, to handle things on my own.

But when I turned eighteen, everything changed. One morning, without warning, she packed a bag, wrote a note that simply said, "I'm going to find myself," and left. I didn't understand it at first. She'd never given herself a break before, so maybe this was just something she needed. But days turned into weeks, and then months. She stopped calling, stopped writing, and I was left with nothing but silence. I reached out, but I never heard back.

At first, I was angry. How could she just leave without any explanation? But as time passed, the anger faded, replaced by a gnawing worry. Where was she? Why hadn't she come back? I tried to keep going, like she'd taught me, but I never stopped wondering. And now, with everything that's happened in my life, I can't help but think: *is this what she meant when she said she was looking for herself?* Because right now, I'm starting to think I need to find myself too.

"Tomorrow," I promised myself, stepping through my apartment door, "I'll figure out how to adult."

But first, I'd settle into the familiar embrace of my couch and a little more reality TV. Because let's be honest: if my life was a sitcom, it deserved a laugh track.

CHAPTER 5

CALLIE

The letter arrived on a Tuesday, wedged between a pizza flyer and a bill I couldn't afford to pay. I almost tossed it with the junk mail, but the official-looking seal caught my eye. Curiosity won out over my desire to crawl back into bed and pretend the world didn't exist.

"Ms. Callie Winters," I read aloud, affecting a posh accent that would have made my high school drama teacher cringe. "We regret to inform you of the passing of your grandmother, Rose Winters."

I guffawed.

Regret?

Please.

The only thing I regretted was wasting my breath reading this garbage. Rose Winters was about as much my grandmother as I was the Queen of England. Sure, we shared some DNA, but that was where the similarities ended. She was cold, distant, and had made it crystal clear that I wasn't welcome in her life.

I was tempted to chuck the letter in the trash, but something made me keep reading. Maybe it was the faint hope that she'd had a change of heart on her deathbed.

Or maybe I was just a glutton for punishment.

"As per the instructions in her will, you have inherited her property located at 2113 Lilac Lane, nestled in the heart of the Odum Forest."

I blinked. Read it again. Nope, still said the same thing.

"Holy crap on a cracker," I muttered, sinking onto my threadbare couch. "The old bat left me her house?"

Memories flickered through my mind—faded snapshots of a summer long ago. A little girl with pigtails and scraped knees, chasing fireflies in a wild meadow. The smell of pine and woodsmoke. And a home, looming dark and mysterious at the edge of the forest.

I shook my head, banishing the images. That was a lifetime ago, before... well, before everything went to hell in a handbasket.

As I stared at the letter, something clicked.

"2113 Lilac Lane," I read aloud, then snorted. "Of course. Grandma Rose living on Lilac Lane. How very on-brand."

I'd never noticed it as a kid, but now the floral connection was glaringly obvious. Trust my grandmother to coordinate her name with her address. I wondered idly if she'd changed her name to match the street, or if she'd somehow managed to name the street herself. Neither would have surprised me.

The rest of the letter was a blur of legal jargon, but the gist was clear. I, Callie Winters, professional screw-up and barely functional adult, was now the proud owner of a house in the middle of nowhere.

"Well, isn't that just the bee's knees," I said to my empty apartment.

The walls, stained with years of cigarette smoke from previous tenants, offered no response. Even they seemed unimpressed by my sudden change in fortune.

I glanced around at my current living situation—a studio apartment so small you could touch both walls with your arms outstretched. The sink was piled high with dishes I'd been meaning to wash for days, and the air conditioner wheezed like an asthmatic dog. Outside, the constant hum of traffic and occasional shout from the street below served as a constant reminder that I was just one small cog in the great, uncaring machine of the city.

"You know what?" I said, standing up with sudden determination. "Screw it. I'm going to that house."

It wasn't as if I had much holding me here anyway. And Frank had a few interviews just the other day. My job as a barista barely covered rent, and my social life consisted of binge-watching streaming movies and occasionally remembering to water my cactus, which miraculously, was still alive despite my best efforts to neglect it to death.

I spent the next hour in a whirlwind of activity from giving Frank my immediate notice to throwing clothes into a duffel bag and trying to remember where I'd stashed my hiking boots. By the time I was done, my apartment resembled a tornado hitting a thrift store, but I was packed and ready to go.

As I was about to leave, I caught sight of myself in the cracked mirror above my dresser. My dark hair was a mess, sticking up in all directions, and there were dark circles under my eyes that no amount of concealer could hide. I looked exactly like what I was—a 28-year-old woman who had no idea what she was doing with her life.

"Well, Callie," I told my reflection, "you're about to add 'forest hermit' to your illustrious resume. Try not to get eaten by bears, okay?"

With that sterling pep talk, I grabbed my bags, gave a half-hearted salute to my cactus, and headed out the door.

The drive to Odum Forest was long and winding, taking me further from the city than I'd been in years. As skyscrapers gave way to rolling hills and eventually thick forest, I felt a knot in my chest start to loosen. It was like I could breathe properly for the first time in forever.

Of course, that's when my beat-up clunker decided it had had enough of this adventure. The engine made a sound similar to a dying whale, coughed twice, and then went silent. I coasted to a stop on the side of the road, surrounded by trees so tall they seemed to touch the sky.

"No, no, no," I muttered, turning the key in the ignition. The car responded with a sad little click. "Come on, you piece of junk! We're almost there!"

But no amount of pleading or creative swearing could bring my faithful steed back to life. I slumped back in my seat, blowing a strand of hair out of my face.

"Well, this is just peachy," I said to the indifferent forest. "Guess I'm hoofing it from here."

According to my phone's GPS—which was miraculously still working despite the distinct lack of cell service—the property was only about a mile away.

I could do a mile.

Probably.

Maybe.

I shouldered my duffel bag, locked the car—more out of habit than any real concern for thieves, unless the squirrels around here were particularly ambitious—and set off down the road.

The forest was beautiful, in a slightly creepy, fairytale-gone-wrong sort of way. Sunlight filtered through the leaves, creating patterns on the forest floor but it didn't take away the slight chill in the breeze. Birds chirped overhead, and somewhere in the distance, I heard the sound of running water.

"This isn't so bad," I said, trying to convince myself. "It's like a nature hike. With luggage. And possible serial killers lurking behind every tree."

I'd only gone about a quarter mile when I heard it—a low, rumbling growl that didn't sound like any bird I knew. I froze, my heart pounding so hard I was sure whatever it was could hear it.

Slowly, I turned around. There, not twenty feet away, was the biggest black bear I'd ever seen. Granted, I'd only ever seen bears in zoos before, safely behind thick glass. This one was decidedly not behind glass, and it was looking at me as if I might make a nice appetizer.

"Nice bear," I said, my voice an octave higher than usual. "Good bear. You don't want to eat me. I'm all gristle and bad life choices. Probably give you indigestion."

The bear took a step forward, and I'm not ashamed to admit that I may have peed a little.

That's when I remembered the granola bars in my bag. Without taking my eyes off the bear, I slowly reached into the side pocket and pulled one out. With a movement that I hoped looked more graceful than I felt, I tossed the bar toward the bear.

It landed a few feet in front of the massive animal. The bear sniffed the air, then ambled over to investigate. While it was distracted, I began to back away, moving as quietly as I could manage.

Which, given my usual grace and coordination, was about as quiet as a drunk elephant in a china shop.

I'd made it about ten feet when my foot came down on a twig. The snap seemed to echo through the forest like a gunshot. The bear's head whipped up, bits of granola clinging to its muzzle.

Our eyes met, and for a moment, time seemed to stand still.

Then the bear huffed, gave me what I swear was a dismissive look, and turned back to its snack.

I didn't wait to see if it would change its mind.

I turned and ran, my duffel bag bouncing against my back, branches whipping at my face as I crashed through the underbrush. I ran until my lungs burned and my legs felt like jelly, only slowing when I was sure I couldn't hear anything pursuing me.

Gasping for breath, I leaned against a tree, trying to get my bearings. That's when I saw it.

A break in the trees ahead, and beyond that, the dark shape of a building.

"Oh, thank you," I wheezed, staggering toward the clearing.

The house loomed before me, a two-story structure of weathered wood and old architecture. It was larger than I remembered, with a wide porch wrapping around the front and sides. Thick vines climbed up one wall, and the windows stared out at the forest with dark, unseeing eyes.

As I approached, a gust of wind rustled through the trees. For a moment, I could have sworn I heard a whisper on the breeze. A voice so faint I might have imagined it, saying, "Welcome home, Callie."

I shivered, pulling my jacket tighter around me.

"Great," I muttered. "Not even here five minutes and I'm already hearing things. This bodes well."

The porch steps creaked ominously as I climbed them, each one seeming to groan, "Turn back, turn back."

But I'd come too far to chicken out now.

Besides, after my close encounter with nature back there, even a haunted house seemed preferable to a cold night in the woods.

The key was right where the lawyer's letter said it would be, hidden in a fake rock next to the front door. As I fitted it into the lock, I half-expected alarms to go off or for some ghostly voice to boom, "BEGONE, INTRUDER!"

But the only sound was the soft click of the lock turning.

I pushed the door open, wincing at the loud creak of hinges that probably hadn't been oiled since the 1970s.

"Hello?" I called, feeling ridiculous. "Any ax murderers or vengeful spirits want to get the jump-scares out of the way now? No? Okay, then."

The interior of the house was like stepping back in time. Heavy wooden furniture, slightly dusty but otherwise well-preserved, filled the main room. A stone fireplace dominated one wall, and above it hung a painting of a stern-looking woman who could only be my grandmother. Her eyes seemed to follow me as I moved into the room, disapproving even from beyond the grave.

"Nice to see you too, Grandma," I muttered. "Love what you've done with the place. Very 'Gothic horror meets pioneer chic.'"

I dropped my bag on a nearby armchair, sending up a small cloud of dust. The place smelled musty, of old books and mothballs, with an underlying scent I couldn't quite place. It was familiar somehow, tickling at the edges of my memory.

As I explored the first floor, I found a kitchen with appliances straight out of the 1950s, a small study lined with bookshelves, and a bathroom that looked as if it had last been updated when indoor plumbing was considered a newfangled luxury.

"Well, Callie," I said to myself, "looks like you've gone from big city barista to backwoods pioneer woman. Hope you remember how to start a fire without burning the place down."

I was about to head upstairs to check out the bedrooms when something caught my eye. On a small table by the front door sat an envelope, yellowed with age.

My name was written on it in elegant, spidery handwriting.

My heart hammered in my chest.

With shaking hands, I picked it up. The paper felt fragile, my imagination telling me it might crumble to dust at any moment. I carefully opened it and pulled out a single sheet of paper.

"My dearest Callie," it began, and I felt a lump form in

my throat. "If you're reading this, then I am gone, and you have finally come home to Odum Forest."

I sank onto the nearest chair, my legs suddenly too weak to hold me up.

"I know we have been estranged for many years, and for that, I am truly sorry. There are things about our family, about this place, that I should have told you long ago. But I was afraid. Afraid of the responsibility, afraid of the power, and most of all, afraid of losing you as I lost your mother."

My hands were shaking so badly I could barely read the words.

What was she talking about? What power? And what did she mean about my mother?

"The house you now own is more than just a building, Callie. It is a confluence, a place where the veil between worlds grows thin. Our family has been its guardians for generations, keeping watch over the boundary and maintaining the balance between realms."

I laughed, a high, slightly hysterical sound.

"Okay, Grandma," I said aloud. "I think someone slipped something into your wine. Guardians? Realms? What is this, some kind of fantasy novel?"

But as much as I wanted to dismiss it as the ramblings of a senile old woman, something deep inside me resonated with her words. It was like a chord had been struck, vibrating through my very being.

"You have gifts, my dear," the letter continued. "Gifts that have been dormant, waiting to be awakened. In time, you will learn to use them, to see beyond the veil and walk between worlds. But be warned. There is a great danger.

There are those who would seek to use you, to harness your abilities for their own ends."

Of course there is.

Not only was I apparently some kind of mystical guardian, but I also had a target painted on my back.

"In the study, behind the painting of the white stag, you will find a hidden safe. The combination is your birthday. Inside is everything you need to begin your training—journals, spell books, and artifacts passed down through our family for generations."

I scoffed. "Spell books? Really? What's next, a wand and a pointy hat?"

But even as I scoffed the biggest scoff one could scoff, I felt a tingle of excitement.

A part of me—the part that had always felt out of place —had always known there was something more to the world than what I could see. I was practically vibrating.

"I know this is a lot to take in, my dear. You must have so many questions, so much anger and confusion. I only hope that in time, you can forgive me for keeping this from you for so long. Know that everything I did, I did out of love. For you, for our family, and for the world we are sworn to protect."

The letter ended with a final plea: "Be careful, Callie. Trust your instincts, and above all, remember—names have power. The one you must never speak aloud is written on the last page of my oldest journal. Read it silently, commit it to memory, but let it never pass your lips. Our safety depends on this silence. I love you, my dear granddaughter. May your voice be wise and your steps sure. All my love, Grandma Rose."

I sat there for a long time, the letter clutched in my hands, my mind reeling. Part of me wanted to laugh it off, to chalk it up to the delusions of an old woman and go back to my normal life. But deep down, I knew that wasn't an option anymore.

Because as crazy as it all sounded, it felt right. Like I'd finally found the missing piece to a puzzle I didn't even know I was trying to solve.

With a deep breath, I stood up and made my way to the study. The painting of the white stag seemed to glow in the fading light, its eyes following me as I approached. My hands shook as I lifted it off the wall, revealing the safe behind it.

I punched in my birthday, half-expecting nothing to happen. But with a soft click, the safe swung open. Inside was a collection of leather-bound journals, ancient-looking books with titles in languages I didn't recognize, and a small wooden box inlaid with strange symbols.

As I reached for the box, a chill ran across my skin. The air in the room seemed to thicken, and for a moment, I could have sworn I saw shapes moving in the shadows.

"Well, Callie," I said, my voice barely above a whisper, "looks like you're not in Kansas anymore."

I picked up the box, feeling its weight in my hands. Whatever was inside seemed to pulse with an energy I couldn't explain. As I stood there, surrounded by the legacy of a family I barely knew, in a house that apparently stood at the crossroads of worlds, I realized that my life was never going to be the same.

Part of me was terrified.

But another part felt truly alive.

"Alright, Grandma," I said, looking up at her painting. "You want me to be a magical guardian? Fine. But I'm doing this my way. And if any creepy crawlies from beyond the veil try to mess with me, they're going to learn that this Winters girl is no pushover."

As if in response, a gust of wind blew through the house, ruffling my hair and sending papers flying. And in that wind, I could have sworn I heard laughter—warm, approving, and undeniably familiar.

"Okay," I whispered, and opened the box.

CHAPTER 6

CALLIE

My grandmother's old Gothic house came with more than just spiderwebs. How long was this place left unattended? After a brief look into the box which held a strange crystal trinket I was now wearing around my neck for safekeeping and perusing through some of my grandmother's journal with no real direction of where to start my new guardian journey, I momentarily gave up. It was worse than preparing for college finals. I decided the monotony of cleaning would probably help clear my mind before I attempted the journals again, as well as to take my mind off... the name I discovered.

Ykazar.

It had a nice ring to it, I had to admit.

Stop it, Callie. Stop thinking about it.

Right, right.

I shook my head, feeling grateful for the more modern

washer and dryer humming quietly in the background as they cleaned a load of blankets and sheets in preparation for a good night's sleep.

I stood with a bucket of soapy water and gloves in front of the grand entrance that loomed before me. The dark wood paneling and intricate moldings cast eerie shadows in the dim light. I had been cleaning what I could all day, making sure the place was spotless enough for me to walk around barefoot. I mean, if this place is going to be my home now, I might as well make it feel homey. I had nowhere else to go back to. I was sure my former landlord immediately filled the vacancy I left behind.

Plus, with nothing else on my plate since quitting my job, I found myself at a loss. The urgency of my grandmother's note still hung heavy in my mind, but I was, in many ways, struggling to wrap my head around it, to truly believe what I'd read after the initial excitement died down. Maybe it was denial, or just the need for distraction rooted in reality.

With sweat beading on my brow, I set to work, using the small ladder I'd unearthed in the back of the house. The rag I'd been using came back nearly black, and I almost gagged as I rinsed it out in the soapy water, bracing myself for another round of scrubbing. Soon enough the doorway was gleaming and I stood back with my hands on my hips and my chest full of pride.

The house was filled with a history I didn't quite understand, and as I closed the heavy front door behind me, I could almost hear the whispers of memories echoing through the hallways. How was a physical location the veil between worlds anyhow? What did this veil look like? Was there a portal through one of the closet doors or something?

Too many movies, Callie. Wouldn't you think someone would easily stumble through it if that was the case? I'm sure my grand-mother had visitors while she was alive.

Right.

The air in some of the rooms I have yet to venture in were thick with dust, and the scent of aged wood mixed with something musty, something that reminded me of forgotten stories. I stood in the foyer, taking a deep breath and steeling myself against the weight of it all. This was a lot for one person to maintain. It was no wonder it ended up this way. Why in the world would my grandmother choose to live alone?

The more I explored, the more the walls seemed to close in. I fought the urge to call up Frank and turn back to the familiarity of city life and constant sirens. Instead, I grabbed a dust rag, determined to clean up the remnants of time and make this place feel less like a mausoleum.

As I moved through the house, I stumbled upon the parlor, where heavy velvet drapes hung similar to funeral shrouds over the tall windows. I pushed them aside, and a cascade of dust motes danced in the sunlight, momentarily breaking the oppressive gloom. The furniture, some draped in white sheets, seemed to stand guard over the memories of a life lived here. I pulled the sheets off one of the chairs, revealing a plush seat with faded floral patterns. It was beautiful, in a haunting way. Women back in the city would fight for this kind of vintage.

I ventured deeper into the house, my footsteps muffled by the worn, faded carpet that stretched beneath me. It was thick and luxurious once, but now it was stained and smelled of mildew. I made a mental note to call the local hardware shop for a carpet shampooer to rent; I could hardly live in this house with that musty odor lingering everywhere.

The thought of tackling that carpet filled me with dread. Just what I needed—more manual labor to remind me that I wasn't exactly cut out for this whole "adulting" thing. My arms were already starting to ache from the scrubbing I'd done, and I couldn't help but wonder if I should've just embraced my fate as a lifelong couch potato instead. Who knew cleaning could be such an extreme sport?

After rummaging through a kitchen drawer surprisingly filled with old takeout menus and expired coupons, I found the phone book—an artifact from another era. My reception was spotty but I dialed the number for the hardware store, my heart racing at the thought of conversing with a stranger in an unfamiliar town. What if I accidentally ordered a thousand pounds of gravel instead of a carpet shampooer?

Don't be dramatic, Callie. Just do what you need to do and call it a day. It rang a few times before a male voice answered on the other line with a scripted greeting. "Hi, I need to rent a carpet shampooer. Do you have any available?"

"Absolutely! We've got one right here in stock."

Relief washed over me. Let's hope he doesn't hang up on me with the next part. "Great! And, um, do you deliver?"

I waited with bated breath. He probably thought I dialed the wrong number and was really looking for the closest Chinese food joint. I was a hot mess most days, but the slow pace of this town might be just what I need to calm my scattered thoughts.

"We sure do! Just let me check our delivery schedule. Where do you need it sent?"

Say what? I couldn't believe my luck.

"To my grandmother's house—er, I mean, my house, I guess. It's kind of a—how should I put this?—a Gothic mansion-esque building with a bit of a creepy vibe."

The guy on the other line luckily had a good sense of humor, putting me more at ease. "Oh, I love those! Are we talking 'Addams Family' creepy or more 'haunted house at Halloween' creepy?"

"More 'Addams Family'—you know, if Uncle Fester decided to throw a rave in the living room."

I gave him my credit card number, knowing it was almost maxed out and praying it would still go through. When it did, I did a little happy dance. I hadn't had a moment to contact them to change my address and maybe that would play to my advantage for a while.

"Got it. We can deliver it today, but I should warn you: our delivery guy might just refuse to go in if he feels the vibes are too spooky."

I couldn't give him any guarantees but I didn't tell him that.

"Perfect! Just tell him to bring a ghostbuster along. I'll make sure to leave the lights on."

The guy let out a hearty laugh before wishing me a good rest of my day and ending the call.

With renewed energy, I wandered into the living room next, where the air felt thicker, almost stifling. A large, ornate mirror hung on one wall, its surface clouded with age. I hesitated, peering into its depths, half-expecting to see my grandmother's reflection staring back at me. Instead,

I saw only myself, a stranger in this unfamiliar place, surrounded by memories that felt as far away as the last flicker of summer.

Looking around, I found the closest outlet, dusted it off, and plugged in my phone. The reassuring beep of connected charging was a small victory against the oppressive ambiance. It felt good to know that some things still worked, that there was a sliver of modernity amid the decay. Yet, as I glanced around, I couldn't shake the feeling that I was utterly unprepared for the reality of this house—and for the fact that I still didn't have a car.

I was trapped in this Gothic fortress, cut off from the outside world, and it struck me how surreal this entire situation was. Here I was, living in a house that seemed to breathe with the weight of history, but I felt like a ghost myself—lost and wandering through a life I didn't choose. I ran my fingers along the edge of a dusty side table, trying to gather my thoughts.

I'd traded in my bustling city life for a scene straight out of a horror movie—one where the only soundtrack was the eerie creaking of ancient wood. Back in the city, my biggest dilemma was choosing between overpriced avocado toast and a smoothie bowl. Now, I had to contend with the fact that I might need to summon the courage to confront a dusty side table that had clearly seen better days.

I knew I couldn't keep at these menial tasks forever, avoiding responsibilities. There were too many decisions to make, too many things to tackle, and the overwhelming silence pressed in on me. Seriously, I could hear my own thoughts, and they weren't exactly comforting.

"Why did you leave your vibrant coffee shop and yoga

studio for this? The only thing stretching here is the cobwebs!" I imagined my friends back in the city shaking their heads, sipping their lattes as they laughed at my current predicament. Especially over the fact that I didn't have a yoga studio.

"Welcome to the wild, wild west of homeownership!" they'd say, probably posting it all on social media for everyone to enjoy.

In the end, I knew I had to confront this house, not just with a mop and a bucket, but with a sense of purpose. My estranged grandmother had lived here, had loved this place, and it was time for me to do the same, to carve out a space for myself amidst the shadows she left behind despite our lack of relationship.

Just as I steeled myself to face the depths of this house, a startling knock echoed through the silence, jolting me from my thoughts. My heart raced, and I hesitated for a moment, wondering if it was just the house settling or if I'd unwittingly unleashed a ghostly visitor.

Dropping the dirty rag in the bucket, I wiped my hands down the front of my pants as I made my way toward the door. Taking a deep breath, I opened it to find a guy in a hardware store shirt, his hand gripping a carpet shampooer like a weapon. He looked slightly bemused, as if he were bracing himself for something unsettling.

"Hey there! I'm here to deliver your—whoa!" He stepped back, glancing at the house behind me with wide eyes. "This place is... something."

"Yeah, it's got character," I replied, trying to sound nonchalant as I gestured for him to come in, taking a quick glance at the embroidered name on his shirt but not fully catching it. "Or, you know, a lot of dust and questionable life choices."

Similar to the one I was making right now—trusting this guy just because he wore the uniform. Did I have a choice? The shampooer looked legit and so did his vehicle with the Odum Hardware logo on the side.

He chuckled nervously, stepping inside. "You're not wrong. My parents used to tell eerie tales about this house. They said it was haunted by the spirit of a really cranky cat."

"A cranky cat? That's the best they could come up with?" I raised an eyebrow, unable to hide my amusement once my wariness abated a little.

I hadn't seen a single cat since I arrived. Come to think of it, that was odd in itself, wasn't it? Didn't stray cats seek these kinds of places to have kittens or something?

"Hey, it was the '90s! They were less about actual ghosts and more about neighborhood legends. Besides, this place has a vibe." He set the shampooer down with a thud and glanced around. "You sure you want to tackle this carpet? It looks like it might bite back."

He wasn't wrong.

"Bite back? Great, now I have to worry about rogue carpets," I said, rolling my eyes. "But yes, I'm determined to give it a fighting chance."

Plus, I didn't have enough funds to order an entire new area rug of this grand size. This could even be an antique.

There was an awkward, heavy silence in the conversation, and I shifted my weight, leaning back on my heel.

"Alright then! Let me show you what you've got." He started demonstrating the shampooer, a complicated array of buttons and levers. "So, you fill this tank with water and detergent. Then you just push it like you're trying to escape a bad date."

I laughed. "Quite a technique. I'll remember that for future reference."

"Just be careful. If you hear any strange noises while you're cleaning, don't panic. It's probably just the house groaning. Or the cranky cat, you know, making a cameo."

Everyone's a comedian.

"Wonderful. I'll just add 'cat exorcist' to my résumé," I joked. "But seriously, is this place that spooky?"

What was I overlooking, aside from the details on my grandmother's note? Who else knew about my family's bloodline? It had been kept a family secret, I assumed. So what exactly was this guy babbling on about? Urban legends?

"Honestly? It's more the stories that get you. I grew up hearing about this house's dark history—for instance, there was supposedly a secret passageway in the basement that led to the old train station or something."

"Secret passageways? Great. Just what I need: more places for ghosts to hide," I mumbled.

"Right? Just don't go looking for them. I hear they prefer their privacy." He winked, and I knew he was full of it.

As he continued to explain the shampooer's quirks, I found myself feeling a little less overwhelmed by the daunting task ahead. When he wrapped up his instructions, I realized I had a few more questions swirling in my mind.

"So, uh, where's the closest place I can get a car?" I asked, trying to sound casual. Not that I could currently afford one, but, you know, information is power and I was going to need to pick up another job sooner or later.

He raised an eyebrow. "Well, you could try the local dealership some miles down the road toward the next city. They've got a few used cars that won't break the bank—if you don't mind a bit of character, of course."

"Character, huh? Is that code for 'this thing might not start every morning'?" Lord knew I didn't need another one of those.

"Exactly! You're catching on quickly." He grinned playfully. "But hey, sometimes a little unpredictability adds excitement to life, right?"

I stopped for a moment, wondering if his words were a mere coincidence. It had to be.

"Sure, like when your car decides to stall in the middle of nowhere and you suddenly feel you're in a horror movie." My eyes widened briefly. Maybe I shouldn't have shared that much about my situation. *Smart, Callie. Real smart.* It was too late now.

"Ah, classic!" He nodded. "But seriously, if you're looking for something reliable, you might want to check out the local classifieds. Lots of folks are selling their cars these days."

A phone book and now the classifieds. Did I walk into a time warp?

"Good to know," I said, jotting down a mental note. "Speaking of which, do you know if there are any local job openings?"

As if realizing I was here to stay, his smile broadened significantly. I wasn't sure how I felt about that. "Sure do! I think the grocery store needs help in the produce section. And there's a cute little coffee shop in town that's always looking for baristas."

I perked up. Bingo. That would be an easy transition. I wonder if there was a bus stop nearby.

"Ah, I might check that out. Any other places I should know about?"

He thought for a moment. "There's also a vintage bookstore that occasionally hires. If you enjoy books and have a penchant for the odd and unusual, it might be a perfect fit."

I tilted my head. I was probably just reading into things. The guy seemed innocently friendly.

"A vintage bookstore? Just what I need—a job that turns into a black hole of time and reading." The moment the words left my mouth, I was hit with the reminder of the task still waiting to be completed—sorting through my grandmother's old texts and journals and figuring out this guardian of the realms thing.

"Exactly! Just don't forget to clock in before you dive into the world of dusty novels and magical tales."

"Right... Because nothing screams 'responsible adult' like forgetting to show up for your shift because you got trapped in the fiction section," I quickly turned the conversation.

He laughed, and I found my own lips twitching. "Hey, if you do end up in that bookstore, you can always tell the customers it's a time-traveling experience."

Perfect. I'll be the quirky employee who sells books and tells ghost stories.

After he finished showing me the shampooer, I reminded myself to explore what else the town had to offer. He mentioned a local library and my wallet thanked him.

"Alright. I'm going to need you to sign right here for me." He handed me a sheet of paper and I did as he asked.

He lingered on my signature for a few seconds before giving me a quick smile and goodbye. Locking the door behind him, I returned to my cleaning, my thoughts still drifting to the name in my grandmother's journal...

Stop thinking about it, Callie. Concentrate.

After what felt like an Olympic-level workout with the carpet shampooer, I finally finished. My arms were on fire, my back ached in ways I didn't know were possible, and I was pretty sure I was one shampooing session away from a dramatic collapse.

I wiped the sweat off my brow and groaned, "If this is what it means to be a homeowner, I might as well start practicing my Oscar speech for 'Best Dramatic Performance by a Sweaty Adult.'"

I needed air—real, fresh air. I staggered outside, hoping that a quick breath would revive my spirit. The moment I stepped onto the porch, I felt the cool breeze kiss my skin, and I sighed with relief. Winter was coming and the temperatures were starting to drop each day.

As I ambled around the yard, I spotted something peeking out from behind a cluster of trees. Curiosity piqued, I made my way over, and there it was: a vintage bicycle, half-hidden and clearly in need of some love. The rusty frame and dented rear wheel suggested it hadn't been ridden in years, but I could already picture myself zipping around town with the wind in my hair and a slight air of retro chic.

I couldn't help but laugh. *Forget a car. Who needs one when I can channel my inner hipster with this beauty?* I imagined rolling up to the local coffee shop, throwing one leg over the bike, and declaring, "Yes, I know it's a vintage bicycle! It's called style, darling!"

I inspected the bike closer, brushing off leaves and cobwebs. "It might not win any races, but it's definitely got character," I mused aloud. "Everything else around here does. At least it's way more eco-friendly than a gas-guzzler." *Plus, I can pretend I'm in a movie where the main character finds themselves through quirky adventures.*

With a newfound sense of purpose, I grinned.

Taking a deep breath, I gave the bike a little push, but it didn't budge.

"Okay, maybe we'll need to negotiate a bit. Don't think you can just sit there while I do all the work."

I'd have to spend some more time exploring the back-yard to see if I could find a spare tire to replace the dented one, and maybe a pump to go with it.

As I stood there, contemplating my new (or old) mode of transport, I couldn't shake the feeling that this house—and everything that came with it—might just lead to the most unexpected adventures.

CHAPTER 7

YKAZAR

I woke slowly, reluctantly, as if the very act of consciousness was tethered to the restraints that held me. For how long had I been imprisoned? I couldn't say. Time had lost all meaning in the depths where I was bound, where days and centuries bled together into an endless blur. It hadn't mattered, not until now. Something stirred—something subtle, but unmistakable. A tug. A faint pressure at the edges of my consciousness, as though the chains that had held me for so long were beginning to crack.

My name, the very recognition of my existence, had crossed someone's mind. No, not just anyone—a particular bloodline, one whose very memory still ignited hostility within me.

The barrier was thinning. I could feel it, a tremor in the air—soft at first, like the flutter of a moth's wings, barely a whisper against the walls of my prison. But then it grew—

stronger, sharper, more insistent. The veil between worlds quivered, thrumming with an energy I hadn't felt in eons, responding to the thoughts that had summoned it.

A wicked thrill surged through me, wild and frantic. I could feel it, the edges of my mind cracking. The madness of it was overwhelming. With fragility, I held onto a shred of reason while everything I knew—everything I was—began to slip away into nothingness.

I stirred. My mind swam through the murk of dreams and darkness, reluctant to leave the stretch of that endless void. But the pull was undeniable. The veil. The mortal *thought*. I could hear it, faint and distant—*calling*.

My fingers twitched first, struggling to reassemble my form, my essence. Slowly, too slowly, I began to emerge from the depths, my senses stretching out, probing the strange space that was not quite dream and not quite reality. The pressure of existence began to solidify around me, though the clarity came in jagged bursts—fragments of sensation like shards of glass.

There. A scent. The faintest hint of fire and ash that quickly morphed into a subtle warmth. Then the sound of wind, the rush of air. *Ah.* The world... the world had changed. I could feel it in my very marrow, a sharp, foreign ache. It was different from when I had last walked it—long, long ago. But the feeling of the veil thinning was still the same, the same as when I had first been bound in my imprisonment.

But it seemed the world beyond the veil had not forgotten me entirely.

The sensation was maddening in its clarity, a forgotten melody resurfacing in the back of my mind. I was filled with an uncharacteristic hunger. A hunger for destruction and vengeance.

It took effort—exhausting, soul-draining effort—to push my senses further into the waking world. I exhaled. My breath, so long forgotten, a whisper of ice on my lips. The air, so fresh and wild, was foreign. I flexed my fingers and felt the pull of the mortal world stronger now, almost as if I was being led by a silver thread—thin enough to be indecipherable but sturdy enough to allow me through the veil.

With a chuckle and guttural snarl, I clawed at my consciousness.

Bound by the malevolent void of my curse, the walls of my tomb closed in around me, suffocating and oppressive, threatening to drive even the strongest to insanity. The intricate spells wove with the essence of my defeat. I once more strained against the shackles that kept me in position, my muscles screaming in protest as tendons ripped and snapped from bone, as flesh tore open from visceral force. Each tug sent shocks of agony through my limbs and torso, yet that pain became my only control.

As I battled the bindings, I mentally focused on my purpose—the drive that kept me afloat in a sea of madness. Searching for weaknesses, I pulled against the ancient ethereal threads that tethered me to my prison with what strength I had left. Each torn muscle fueled my resolve as I finally felt my shoulder sockets pop out from place, landing me face first a distance that should not have been possible.

I lay there, cackling through the pain—a pathetic shadow of who I once was, as the binds began to retreat, realizing they could no longer hold me. There it was again, my name a whisper of thought across an unfamiliar mind, one that shared a sliver of a tie to my dominion.

My muscles slowly reknit themselves, a cruel reminder of my eternal punishment and the cyclical hell I was trapped in over the centuries. Yet, amidst the misery and torment of time, my resolve had only hardened, transforming my rage into an unyielding determination that fueled my every waking thought.

The crack in the final binding came, surprisingly, like a lover's breath. I sensed a shift in the balance of power, the shackles fraying under my relentless focus... and an unexpected interference. I channeled the strength of my lineage, recalling the one who had wronged me—the one who crafted the very spell that held me captive. With a surge of energy, I pressed harder, my body straining to break free. When the final binding tore, I collapsed once more, gasping for breath, feeling both liberated and burdened by the weight of my past.

My essence strained against the cold slumber that tried to regain its hold on me. I could feel the edge of it, could almost taste the world beyond my prison. The physicality of it was alien to me after eons spent without form—without need for anything but the slow, eternal pull of dreams and nightmares.

As I lay there, gritting through the pain of my tendons pulling my shoulder back into place, a moment of clarity sliced through me.

There was something different about this shift. Yes, I could still feel the blood of the one who wronged me pulsing in their veins, but there was something more... something tainted.

A hint of winter.

In the haze of this awakening, a memory surfaced—a haunting one. A battle. *The final battle.*

I could see it clearly now, as if the fog of ages had been lifted, the scent of blood and steel rising in my nostrils. The battlefield stretched before me, a sea of carnage, the ground soaked in the blood of my fallen warriors. My army was shattered, crumbling, scattered like leaves in the wind. And there she was, standing among the chaos: *Commander Laeta.*

She had been my equal, my opposite. Her blade was lightning, quick and merciless. I had felt her strikes as though they were etched into my very soul. But it was more than just the fight. It was the loss—the failure—that gnawed at my bones, torturous creatures that clawed their way into my marrow. Her eyes locked with mine, filled with a quiet fury, a calm certainty that I would fall. *And I did.*

I could still hear her voice, soft but carrying above the clamor of the dying, *"This ends now, Ykazar. This was always meant to end."*

The thought of her words—her certainty—lingered in my mind akin to poison, still tainting the air as I pulled myself free of the memories. I had been too arrogant, too sure that I could never be defeated. And Laeta had been my reckoning.

A shudder ripped through me, followed by a cackling laugh, guttural and raw. The fragments of my mind twisted together—truth and lies, memories and delusions—until I couldn't tell where one ended and the other began. Everything felt jagged, broken, and I reveled in the chaos of it.

The air around me crackled, thick with a raw, electric charge as my form further solidified. The veil was weakening, tearing at the seams. It seemed the tendrils of the Winter Court had left a trace into the mortal realm during my long imprisonment. And now, that trace had returned to its master, cracking open a door that should have remained sealed forever.

"Oh, how destiny toys with us," I laughed, a bitter edge to the sound. It seemed Commander Laeta had failed to wipe out every last trace of loyalty to me.

I turned over, rolling my reattached shoulder with a wide, sharp grin, then pushed myself to my feet.

The world had waited far too long for the return of its rightful king. But now, they would remember my name—not in whispers, but in the frantic screams of those who begged for mercy.

CHAPTER 8

CALLIE

I squinted against the light streaming in through the ancient windows of my grandmother's Gothic home, which was rapidly morphing into a labor of love—or perhaps a labor of lunacy.

The morning had started out with ambition. I'd managed to call a company to come get my dead clunker vehicle and sell it for scrap metal, rounding up about three hundred and fifty dollars in cash. I was going to need it to gather supplies for my new, terrifyingly empty pantry. I couldn't keep ordering takeout and expect to hang on to the little money I had left.

Heck, I even tried to summon food with what seemed like a simple spell, but nothing happened besides a sting to my ego. I had no idea where I went wrong. I sounded out the words and there weren't any instructions that required extra items. Whatever gifts Grandma Rose was talking about in her letter apparently needed to be tapped another way.

Well, at least the house wasn't flooded with toads or anything.

If I was going to survive in this house, I'd need food, and apparently, I couldn't rely on my supposed abilities and bloodline for dinner.

With my list of essentials scribbled on the back of an old takeout menu—because why wouldn't I use a relic from my takeout-heavy city life?—I took one last look around the dark, creaking foyer, filled with an overwhelming sense of impending adventure, or maybe dread.

"All right, Callie, let's do this. Off to the closest town for supplies."

I stepped outside, feeling the cool breeze ruffle my hair as I made my way down the long, gravel driveway on foot. I was no stranger to public transportation but despite pacing up and down the paved road for a few yards, there was no bus stop in sight, much to my frustration. The bicycle was still in no condition to be ridden and I was stuck with little to no options.

I stared down the empty road once more, a sinking feeling telling me I'd have to ignore my instincts and do what they always did in the movies. I was going to have to hitch a ride with the first passing car. I didn't know how far the next town was and might get lost footing it. Plus, I was still aching from all the cleaning I did.

And if the next town was far, I might not have the energy to walk all the way back.

How do you get yourself into this, Callie?

I cataloged what I had on me in case I required an impromptu self-defense weapon: Shoe Straps, belt, keys that could double as blades between my fingers.

With a deep breath, I waited. The first car passed by without a second glance. I waited thirty more minutes before I saw another one. After a few awkward waves, I caught the attention of someone driving an old pickup truck. He looked a bit confused but more than willing to help a damsel in distress.

I shoved one hand in my pocket, my fingers curling around the cool metal of my keys. The driver slowly pulled to a stop and opened the passenger door from the inside with a metal creak.

Taking a peek, I surveyed the layout of the interior and front bench seats.

Come on, Callie. Who knows when the next ride will come by?

"This is a little too much like a horror movie," I joked to the driver, who raised an eyebrow but chuckled nonetheless. Hey, I figured reverse psychology might make him slip up if he *was* a killer. Then I'd stab him in the eye and leap out of the truck. And if he was, I could pop his eyes with my keys and jump out of this thing. "Just don't drop me off at any creepy abandoned houses, okay?" I tacked on, trying to sound naive.

I was pretty sure my grandmother's house was the creepiest one around these parts so, joke's on him, I was already familiar with the layout and where the kitchen knives were.

"Only if you promise not to scream," he replied, a grin

spreading across his face before he slapped his knee and let out a chortle. "You young folks watch way too many scary movies. Where ya headed?"

My heart stopped for a second before I nervously laughed. With one last pep talk, I made my way toward the open door and climbed into the cab. I still couldn't shake the feeling of vulnerability. "The closest town. Thanks."

"Well, it's a good thing I was already headed that way then."

The ride to town was filled with small talk about the weather and the rising cost of seasonal fruits. I found the tension in my shoulders abating, even if I was acutely aware of the ridiculousness of my situation.

What kind of adult hitches rides instead of having a reliable mode of transport these days these days? But there I was, a wanderer in a Gothic home, trading in my former life for this peculiar new one.

Arriving in town, I thanked my driver—whose name was Jules—profusely before stepping out and waving goodbye.

"You be careful out there, miss. Never know what kind of wack-a-doodles are out looking to pick up a young woman like yourself."

Right...

"I'll grab a cab for my ride back!" I called out and he tipped his head before pulling away.

The town consisted of a small cluster of similar-looking buildings surrounded by a newly slurried road. As I walked, I felt the sun on my back and realized that, despite everything, I was getting out into the world again, starting over as a newcomer.

How many times does a woman have to begin anew before she grows accustomed to this feeling? I'd moved so many times within the city, from one apartment to another whenever the rent shot up, I should have been used to this by now. But this wasn't just another apartment, and this certainly wasn't the city.

Food, Callie. Right.

Continuing along the sidewalk, I quickly spotted a grocery store. Inside, the bell above the door jingled, welcoming me into a world of fluorescent lighting and the distinct smell of canned goods. It was a far cry from the trendy coffee shops back in the city, where I could get a latte that cost more than my first car.

"Ah, the sweet aroma of my new reality," I said to no one in particular, earning a quizzical look from a nearby elderly man who was staring at the cereal aisle with a mix of confusion and regret.

I grabbed a shopping basket that seemed about as old as the store itself and started my quest. Canned beans, pasta, some questionable-looking produce—my culinary repertoire was growing more dire with each item I added.

I really should buy more basic ingredients so I could make things from scratch and stretch the little funds I had. Nodding at the idea, I began putting some of the cans back and pulled up the internet browser on my phone, looking at potential recipes.

As I perused the aisles, I couldn't help but chuckle at the choices. "Do I go for the generic brand mac and cheese or the one that promises 'extra cheesy goodness'?" I mused, only half-serious. "Decisions, decisions. Who knew grocery shopping could be so thrilling?"

Just then, I heard a familiar voice. "Hey, Callie, right?"

I turned to see the guy who delivered my carpet shampooer the other day. He stood by the frozen foods section, holding a box of something that looked disturbingly like pizza rolls.

"I didn't expect to run into anyone I knew here," I replied. Granted he was the only one I truly met besides Jules.

What was his name again? I tried to recall what was embroidered on his work shirt, but the memory wouldn't come. Was it Bob? Jim? Or maybe something completely out there like "Gus the Great"? Honestly, at this point,

"Yeah, well, the frozen aisle is where dreams go to die," he said with a smirk. "I'm just trying to make sure my dinner doesn't involve any actual cooking tonight. How's life in the haunted house treating you?"

"Oh, you know, just me and a questionable carpet," I replied. "But it's slowly coming together. I even found some wheels. Who needs a car when you can channel your inner hipster?"

Tim raised an eyebrow—at least that was what I was calling him. I think his embroidered name on his work shirt had a T somewhere. "As long as you don't show up in skinny jeans and ironic glasses, I think you'll be fine. Just make sure you don't end up stranded on the side of the road, screaming for help because your bike has 'character.'"

There was that strange coincidence again. Or maybe I had a readable face. He'd probably get a good laugh out of my story about hitchhiking with what seemed like a serial killer, only to find out he was just a nice old guy.

"Trust me, if that happens, I'll just wave a white flag

made of grocery bags," I said, gesturing to my sparse basket. "Now I'm just here trying to stock my kitchen with items that might help me survive without resorting to takeout."

I felt a twinge of apprehension about sharing too much. I didn't *really* know this guy—he could easily be a stalker in a plaid shirt, faded jeans, and a friendly smile. Yeah, we had a civil conversation when he delivered the vacuum, but I still didn't *know* him.

How did he know my name, anyway? I didn't remember mentioning it the last time.

"Ah, the journey to becoming a responsible homeowner," he said with mock seriousness. I looked at him then, took him in for the first time. He appeared to be in his mid-thirties, his dark features softened by a faint shadow along his jawline. "You're doing great. Just don't forget the secret ingredient: pizza rolls."

He shook the box, and I was momentarily distracted, contemplating whether I could whip up some DIY snacks with flour and all the other kitchen wizardry I vaguely remembered from watching cooking shows. Everyone knew boxed food was overpriced, and I was on a tight budget until I figured out how to scrape together more money.

"Duly noted," I laughed awkwardly, grabbing a box of the bizarrely enticing snack as if I were going to purchase it.

He chuckled, then glanced over my shoulder, scanning the items in front of me. "You know, if you need a hand moving furniture or tackling more of that house, just give me a shout. I'm basically a one-man moving company as a side gig."

I felt my internal red flags start to wave like a frantic flagger at a busy intersection. Sure, his offer sounded helpful, but it also reeked of suspiciously *overly* friendly vibes. Why was this guy so eager to lend a hand and get back inside my house? I imagined him showing up at my door, box cutter in one hand, ready to reorganize my life—or worse, trap me in a "get to know each other" session that felt more congruent to an interrogation.

"Um, that's nice of you," I said, forcing a smile that felt a little too tight. "But I've got it covered. I mean, how hard can it be to move a few chairs?"

I laughed awkwardly, hoping it would be enough to close the door to this conversation.

"Come on, I'm telling you, I have a knack for it," he insisted, leaning closer as if sharing a secret. "People always underestimate how much work goes into moving furniture. It's like a workout and a puzzle all in one."

I nodded slowly, imagining him watching me struggle with my grandmother's ancient armchair, laughing as I broke a sweat while he lounged nearby, sipping lemonade with a knife in his hand.

"Yeah, I'll keep that in mind," I said, glancing around, searching for an escape route.

"Great! Just think of me as your furniture-moving super-hero," he said with a grin.

I still didn't know his name.

"Right, well, superheroes need to maintain their secret identities," I replied, inching backward. "You know, for the sake of mystery and all."

He chuckled, clearly not picking up on my attempt to distance myself. "I get it. It's always good to have some boundaries. But really, don't hesitate to ask."

I was acutely aware of how awkward the conversation had become.

"I need to get going anyway, you know how it is—errands, life stuff. Very busy." I gestured vaguely as if I had an entire schedule packed with urgent appointments that demanded my immediate attention.

"Sure, sure. No problem," he replied, still looking far too relaxed for my liking. "Just remember, I'm around if you need me. Maybe for a tour of the town?"

The guy doesn't give up.

"Sure, sure," I parroted, practically sprinting away while he waved, the lingering feeling of unease shadowing me.

With a cart full of basic ingredients that would make a baking contestant proud, I finally made my way to the checkout counter, feeling surprisingly accomplished. The cashier, an older woman with thick glasses, rang up my items.

"You're new around here, aren't you?" she asked, eyeing my cart filled with the essentials of a struggling adult.

"Guilty as charged," I admitted, noting that *she* didn't look particularly threatening.

She chuckled, her smile warm. "Just give it time. This town grows on you, like pesky mildew in your basement. Just don't forget to smile at the locals—they're friendlier than they look."

My mind shot back to Tim. Maybe I was overanalyzing it all. After all, they say not every town runs similar to a big city.

"Noted," I said, handing over cash while glancing at the door. The sun was setting, casting a golden hue over everything. I wanted to get back home before nightfall because, let's be honest, everyone knows that after dark is when things get weird.

With my bags in hand, I waved goodbye to the cashier and headed back outside. I pulled out my phone, resolved to call a cab for my ride back to the house. I dialed the local cab number and, after a few rings, managed to secure a ride for a decent price.

As I stood outside, waiting, I took a moment to appreciate the small-town charm around me. The evening air was cool, and I realized that, despite everything, I had to embrace this new reality.

The cab pulled up, and as I climbed in, a friendly older gentleman helped me load my groceries into the trunk. His warm smile and twinkling eyes made me feel a bit more at ease. He reminded me a lot of Jules.

Arriving back at the house, I stepped out of the cab and thanked the driver with my bags of supplies in hand. I surveyed my surroundings in case anything was amiss. The house loomed before me, no longer quite so intimidating. Maybe this journey was less about conquering the ghosts of my past and more about embracing the unexpected adventures that lay ahead.

After all, what could possibly go wrong? I could trip over a cobweb in my "Gothic fortress" or discover a secret passageway that led to a basement filled with taxidermy cats—perfect for my new life as a quirky local legend.

Who was I kidding? I could also end up in a sitcom-worthy scenario where I accidentally host a dinner party for the neighborhood's most eccentric characters, all while trying to decipher my grandmother's cryptic recipes for spaghetti.

Great, just what I needed—culinary confusion mixed with social awkwardness.

I shook my head, trying to shake off my wandering thoughts, and pulled out my phone. I started searching for information on the local coffee shop, eventually finding their job application.

CHAPTER 9

CALLIE

I'd never worked a job quite like this before. In the city, everything was fast—every day was a blur of deadlines, constant motion, and that unrelenting hum of people hustling from one thing to the next. The barista gig I'd landed in this small town was... well, different. It felt as if I was moving through molasses.

I walked into *Brew & Beans* for my first shift with a knot in my stomach. The place was small, the kind of café that felt more equivalent to a living room than a business. The air smelled of roasted coffee beans, cinnamon rolls, and something else—maybe time, I thought. The wooden floors creaked beneath my boots as I took in the scene. *Did everything creak around here?*

There were a few regulars chatting by the windows, the sound of the espresso machine bubbling softly in the background, and the low murmur of a playlist that wasn't quite pop but wasn't quite indie, either. It was the kind of music that didn't demand attention but somehow still managed to settle you into the space.

"Hey, you must be Callie," a voice called out from behind the counter.

I turned to see Andrea, the manager, wiping her hands on a dish towel. She was a few years older than me, with messy blonde hair and an easy smile that reassured me I wasn't about to screw this up. It was a different person who hired me, so this was my first time meeting her.

"Yeah, that's me," I said, giving a small wave. "First day."

She nodded, her eyes scanning me for a second before giving me an approving look. "Don't worry. You'll get the hang of it. Let's go over a few things before you start, okay?"

Her choice of words caught me off guard, especially since I'd mentioned on my resume that I'd worked as a barista for years. Still, I didn't want to come off as cocky, or the typical city slicker. So, I just nodded and kept it to myself.

She showed me the ropes—how to operate the espresso machine, the grinder, how to steam milk just right so it wasn't too foamy or not foamy enough. The technical stuff came easy, but it was the rhythm of it all that tripped me up. In the city, I'd worked at fast-paced cafés where I was constantly juggling orders, frantically trying to keep up with the crowd. Here, it felt equal to a whole other world.

I kept checking the clock, waiting for the rush of customers to come flooding in. But they never did. At first, it was just Andrea and me, with a couple of people trickling in here and there. After a few sips of coffee and a bit of small talk, they were gone. Half the customers simply ordered black coffee. The shift dragged on, and I was starting to wonder if I'd done something wrong. Was there a secret lunch rush I hadn't been briefed on?

I tried to stay busy, cleaning the counters, wiping down tables, restocking napkins and sugar packets. But the more I looked around, the more it dawned on me: it was almost too quiet here.

In the city, my nerves would've been buzzing by now, with the constant movement of bodies around me and orders piling up. My pulse would've been racing as I scrambled to fill drinks, yell out names, and dodge in and out of the tiny gaps between people. But here? I was in some sort of strange time loop where nothing ever moved fast enough.

By the time the first "real" rush came—around 10 a.m.—I was caught completely off guard. Three people came in at once, and I nearly dropped the milk jug in my panic. I tried to make the drinks as quickly as I could, fumbling over the order of the espresso shots and forgetting to ask if they wanted extra foam. The woman at the counter gave me a polite smile as if she could sense I was still figuring it all out.

"Take your time," she said, her voice soothing. "We're not in any hurry."

I blinked. Not in a hurry? *Not in a hurry?* My mind scrambled to understand what she meant. In the city, *everyone* was in a hurry. People tapped their feet impatiently when their lattes weren't ready in two minutes. People shouted across the counter if you got their order wrong. Here, the woman seemed perfectly fine waiting for a drink she could have gotten at any other café, but she wasn't rushing me. Was she even watching me?

I tried to calm my thoughts and finish her order, but I

couldn't shake the weird sense of slowness that had settled in my chest. In the city, that moment of quiet would've been a luxury, a chance to breathe. But here, it was just... odd. No one was yelling. No one was even in a hurry to drink their coffee.

The small crowd shuffled out just as casually as they'd come in, and I stood behind the counter, wondering if I'd missed something.

By the time Andrea came back from the back room, I'd lived through an entire shift in slow motion. She smiled when she saw me standing there, clearly still trying to make sense of the whole thing.

"You good?" she asked.

I hesitated, trying to figure out how to explain what I was feeling. "I don't know... It's just so different from the city. Everyone there is so fast, always moving, you know? I'm used to *constant* action."

Andrea laughed softly. "Yeah, well, we don't do 'constant action' around here. People want their coffee, sure. But they're not in a race. It's more about taking time—time to talk to the person next to you, time to enjoy the drink, time to breathe."

Her words hit me in an unexpected way. *Time to breathe.* I hadn't realized how much I'd forgotten about that until she said it out loud. I'd been so used to the relentless buzz of the city, to the pressure of having to go, go, go, that I'd forgotten what it was like to slow down, to *be* present.

I glanced around at the empty tables, the quiet hum of the espresso machine, and the warmth of the sunlight filtering through the windows. Maybe this place, this pace, wasn't so bad after all. Maybe I could learn to breathe here, too.

But first, I needed to figure out how to stop feeling I was moving at the speed of light while everyone else was happily strolling along at a leisurely pace.

The last person who came in before my shift ended was... Tim. He ordered a black coffee, no sugar, and flashed me a grin that was a little too knowing.

"So you chose the coffee shop. How's the new gig treating you?" he asked, leaning on the counter with an easy smile, his eyes lingering on me in a way that felt just a touch too curious. "Must be a change from whatever you were doing back in the city, huh?"

I froze for a split second. *The city.* How did he know? I hadn't said a word about it to him, and yet he seemed to know *exactly* where I was from.

I forced myself to shrug it off, trying to play it cool. "Yeah, it's... slower here," I said, my voice a little more clipped than I intended.

He leaned in just a fraction closer, eyes twinkling with some hidden knowledge. "I figured. You've got that... vibe. You know, the kind of confidence you only get from certain experiences. You used to be a barista, didn't you?"

The blood drained from my face. I could feel my pulse quicken. *How did he know that?*

Sure, I had some experience in coffee shops, but I didn't wear a physical sign that said *former professional barista.*

I blinked, trying to mask my surprise with a casual smile. "Yeah, a while ago," I said, keeping my tone neutral, though my brain was scrambling to catch up.

He smiled knowingly, as if he'd just solved a puzzle. "I

could tell. You've got the right touch. The way you handled that steam wand earlier? Definitely a barista's hand." He winked, almost too smoothly, as if he were complimenting me—but there was something in his eyes that felt off.

I fought the urge to narrow my gaze. Was he just *that* observant, or had he been paying attention in ways that made me uncomfortable?

"Thanks," I said, forcing the words out. My mind was reeling now. *How long had he been watching me?* The way he'd phrased it—like he already knew my past—didn't sit right.

He took his coffee, his grin widening. "No problem. You'll fit in here just fine, you know. Small town, slower pace, but it grows on you. You'll see." His tone had an edge to it now, something just a little too familiar.

I nodded, but my thoughts were miles away. Tim gave me one last lingering look before he stepped toward the door, the bell overhead chiming softly as he left. I stood there for a long moment, staring at the empty doorway, unease in my chest.

By the time my shift ended, I was exhausted. And it didn't make any sense. The day had been slow—too slow, in fact—but somehow, despite having been on my feet for hours, my brain worked overtime to process everything that had happened, or rather, hadn't. The quiet had seeped into my bones and left me drained in a way I couldn't explain.

The walk along the town square wasn't much of a walk. But the cool evening air was a welcome relief, the kind of crisp chill that reminded you the world wasn't as still as it felt sometimes. I kicked a pebble down the sidewalk, trying to shake off the strange feeling of the day.

During the long stretches of downtime, my mind kept

drifting back to something I'd read in one of my grandmother's journals—the mention of other realms, different races, and strange courts. I wasn't exactly a high-fantasy reader, so most of the terms were unfamiliar—but there were a few that stuck with me, like *the fae.*

It was a word I'd heard before, in passing, but seeing it written in her handwriting made it feel... different. And the more I thought about it, the harder it was to shake the feeling that there was something more to it, something I was missing. How did my family—humans—come to become the guardians of whatever this was? Were we chosen or part of something grander?

I called up the cab company and one was quick to take me home. When I finally stepped through the door of the house, it was the silence that hit me first.

Maybe I should get a pet.

I wondered if Grandma Rose had one to keep her company.

Grandma Rose.

Why had she disinherited my mother after she got pregnant? That question still gnawed at me, even after all these years. I assumed all grandmothers anticipated the day they had grandchildren.

It didn't make sense. It was as if, once Mom was pregnant with me, something in Grandma shifted. Was it my sperm donor? Or the fact that it was a whirlwind romance that fizzled faster than flat soda? He was also the reason why my last name was now Winters instead of Summer.

I never fully understood it and as a kid, I never asked for the details. All I knew growing up was that Mom was never going to inherit anything—not a penny, not a piece of jewelry all because of the man she chose to consort with. It was that very fact that made me resent Grandmother Rose in many ways. How could she blame someone for who they fell in love with? Life was never predictable.

"Yet here we are, in this house with her little apology letter," I mumbled.

Despite the resentment, I slowly began to forgive her—mostly for giving me the house. Maybe, deep down, she'd truly regretted her choices in hindsight. It was hard to say. What I did know was that my mother would never find out. She was still out there somewhere, off on her endless quest to "find herself," completely oblivious to Grandma Rose's end-of-life choices and confessions.

Or maybe my mother was out there looking for my father. That thought lingered in the back of my mind too. From what I could remember of her, he'd always been her one true love—at least in her eyes—despite the fact that he didn't seem to feel the same way. He couldn't have. He left us.

I dragged a hand down my face as if I could wipe away the memories along with the exhaustion that clung to me.

Making my way through the empty rooms, I headed to my bedroom upstairs, shedding my clothes and boots along the way. I didn't bother with the lights. The moonlight filtered through the curtains, casting soft shadows across the walls. I was too tired to care about much else, just needing to get into bed and close my eyes.

After changing into my pajamas, I stood for a moment at the edge of my bed, looking at the small space around me. It was cozy with a chair and a small desk in the corner with one of Grandma Rose's journals sitting on top.

I took a deep breath and stretched my arms toward the ceiling, wondering if the slow pace of this town would be the thing that finally drove me mad.

"Nah. It didn't drive Grandma Rose mad," I mumbled, reassuring myself everything would work out the way it should.

I climbed into bed, pulling the clean covers up to my chin. I closed my eyes, trying to relax, but my mind wouldn't stop spinning. The day had left me with more questions than answers, and I could feel them statically buzzing around in my head, whispers I couldn't quite make out. I wasn't sure if I was tired enough to sleep, but eventually, my mind quieted enough for me to drift off.

I knew I was dreaming because it felt as if I was watching a scene unfold through someone else's eyes. The landscape stretched out before me, blanketed in white, the stark contrast of bloodstains staining the snow. The body I inhabited felt different—*alive* in a way I wasn't. She was giddy, exhilarated by power, her grip tight on the blade as she swung it down with brutal precision, striking a creature I didn't recognize.

There was a strange thrill in the movement, a sharp sense of control that pulsed through her veins, but it wasn't mine. I was just a witness to the violence, detached, yet somehow feeling it all the same.

The scene shifted, and suddenly I was thrust into a deadly dance of clashing blades. My opponent sent sharp ice shards flying toward me, but the body I inhabited felt no fear—only a rush of adrenaline, a thrill that surged through her as she fought back, grappling with him in the snow.

Then, without warning, his full weight crashed down on

top of me. My heart leaped into my throat as he pinned me —*us*—to the ground, the cold bite of a blade against our throat.

But as he held me there, pressing the weapon further into our flesh, I felt something strange stir inside this body —something I didn't understand. It wasn't just the rush of battle anymore. There was an undeniable pull toward him, an attraction that grew stronger with every struggle, every twist of his body against mine. The more he fought back, the more it intensified, an electric current sparking between us.

I felt confused, unsettled. This wasn't me—*I* wasn't supposed to feel this way. But the body I inhabited... it *wanted* him. Wanted him to fight harder, push deeper, feel the tension stretch between us. It made no sense, but I couldn't ignore it.

Why was this body so drawn to him? Why did every movement, every shift in our positions, feel like a dangerous, intoxicating dance? I tried to pull away from the feeling, but it had a life of its own, and I was trapped in it.

The scene shifted once more, and suddenly I was standing at the entrance of a dark cavern, my head heavy with a crown. The air was thick with the echoes of distant screams, their haunting reverberations bouncing off the jagged stone walls.

I jolted awake, my body instinctively rolling to my side. My hand reached for the pendant around my neck as if drawn by some unseen force. The warmth that radiated from it seeped through my fingers, soothing me, and before I knew it, the remnants of the dream slipped away, fading back into the shadows of my mind as sleep claimed me once more.

CHAPTER 10

CALLIE

I'd been in Odom for a week and a half, and I was already starting to lose it every time I was home. The constant creaking of the old wooden structure, the whisper of wind through the trees, and the occasional, unidentifiable noises from the forest were slowly driving me insane.

"Get a grip, Callie," I muttered to myself as I paced the living room for the umpteenth time. "You're just not used to the quiet. This is good for you."

I'd spent most of my time off work exploring the house and its surroundings, trying to make sense of Grandmother Rose's strange collection of books and journals she'd left behind. But every time I tried to delve in, my head would start to spin with information I didn't know what to do with.

But the one page that stayed with me was the mention of an illegitimate child, one whose existence seemed to trace back to the Summer Queen—one of the seasonal courts. A chill ran down my spine as the hairs on the back of my arms stood on end. First, the name I wasn't supposed to speak and now weird court family drama. But what did that have to do with our family? I slammed the book shut, telling myself I needed a break from all this ancient lore and guardian stuff.

I'd occasionally stare out the window, half convinced I'd seen something moving in the shadows between the trees.

On a positive note, I discovered a stash of cash that would tide me over for a good city month in the small wooden box inlaid with strange symbols in her bookshelf, hidden between a couple of old texts. And with my first paycheck coming up in a few days, I should be able to get by comfortably with the rhythm of my work schedule. Thank goodness for small blessings.

As night fell, I decided I needed a distraction.

"Time to channel my inner Pioneer Woman," I announced to the empty room. "I'm going to bake bread. How hard can it be?"

Turns out, pretty hard when you're working with an oven that was probably new when Roosevelt was president. The first Franklin Roosevelt.

An hour later, the house was filled with the smell of what I charitably called "rustic" food. In other words, slightly burnt and oddly shaped. As I pulled the loaf from the oven, a gust of wind blew through the kitchen, slapping the curtains against the walls, extinguishing the candles I'd lit to supplement the house's dim electric lighting.

"Oh, come on," I grumbled, putting down the bread and

fumbling for the matches. "If this is your idea of a haunting, Grandma Rose, it's pretty weak sauce."

That's when I felt it—a chill that went beyond the natural coolness of the evening, seeping into my bones and making my breath catch in my throat. The hair on the back of my neck stood up, and I had the distinct, unsettling feeling that I was no longer alone.

I turned slowly, my eyes straining in the darkness. The shadows in the corners of the room seemed deeper, more substantial somehow. They writhed and twisted, taking on shapes that my mind refused to process.

"Hello?" I called out, hating how small and scared my voice sounded. "Is someone there?"

Silence answered me, but it was a loaded silence, pregnant. I could almost hear it breathing.

Suddenly, the temperature in the room plummeted.

My breath came out in visible puffs, and frost began to form on the windows, intricate patterns spidering across the glass like icy fingers.

"Okay, this isn't funny anymore," I said, backing away from the encroaching cold.

My back hit the kitchen counter, and I yelped as something clattered to the floor. Looking down, I saw the knife I'd laid out to cut the bread lying at my feet, its blade gleaming in the moonlight streaming through the window.

As I bent to pick it up, a voice spoke.

If you could call it a voice.

It was more the sound of ice cracking on a frozen lake, or the whisper of snow falling in the deepest part of winter.

"Callie Winters," it said, my name drawn out into a sibilant hiss that made my skin crawl. "At last, you've come."

I straightened up so fast I nearly gave myself whiplash, the knife clutched in my white-knuckled grip.

"Who's there?" I demanded, trying to sound brave. "Show yourself!"

Stupid, Callie! You know that's how every horror movie starts!

A chuckle echoed through the room, cold and devoid of humor. "As you wish."

In the dim light of the moon, the shadows in the far corner began to twist and swirl, merging into a grotesque, vaguely humanoid shape. As it grew, the darkness pulsed with a sinister life of its own, dark tendrils extending similar to gnarled fingers clawing at the air. A chill seeped into the room, filling it with an oppressive dread. The silence was thick, broken only by the soft creaking of the floorboards beneath an unseen weight. With each heartbeat, the figure loomed larger, its featureless face an unsettling void that seemed to hunger for the light, drawing it in like a black hole. The air grew heavy with an unsettling stillness, void of warmth or vitality, as if the very essence of life had been drained from the space.

It was tall, impossibly so, its head nearly brushing the ceiling. As it stepped forward, details began to emerge—skin as pale as freshly fallen snow, long hair the color of a moonless night, and eyes...

Oh, those eyes.

They were the blue of glacial ice, ancient and pitiless, containing depths that threatened to pull me in and never let go.

I brandished the knife in front of me, though I knew it was about as useful as a toothpick against whatever this thing was. It glinted against the very modern-looking septum piercing.

"Stay back!" I warned, my voice shaking. "I'm armed and... and I make a mean burnt bread!"

The figure tilted its head, regarding me with something that might have been amusement.

"Brave little mortal," it said, its voice sending shivers through me. "Do you truly think you can harm me with that pathetic toy?"

Before I could blink, it was in front of me, moving with a speed that defied physics. A hand as cold as the grave closed around my wrist, and the knife clattered to the floor, narrowly missing my foot.

"Who... what are you?" I gasped, trying to pull away but finding myself frozen in place, despite it phasing in and out of corporeal form.

Those icy eyes bored into mine, and I felt as if I was falling into an endless winter.

"I am the King of the Eternal Winter," it—he—said. "I am the cold that seeps into your bones, the ice that claims the unwary. I am Yk-"

Suddenly, he stopped, a look of frustration crossing his eerily beautiful fae-like features. He wanted to say more but physically couldn't.

"What?" I asked, curiosity momentarily drowning out the terror that gripped me. The last part of his words was lost to the frantic thrum of my racing heart, the sound deafening in my ears. "Is that like a Rumpelstiltskin thing? If I guess your name, do I win a prize? Maybe my freedom and a year's supply of therapy?"

He snarled. "Do not mock me, mortal. I have slumbered

for centuries, bound by magic and betrayal. But now, you have awakened me."

I blinked, my mind spinning. Was this the one Grandma Rose had warned me about? So he was from the winter court. But I hadn't spoken his name—*I was sure of it.* If this wasn't him, then who was he? "I did what now? Listen, buddy, I think you've got the wrong girl. The only thing I've awakened lately is my neighbor's dog when I burnt my toast the other morning."

His grip on my wrist tightened and I grimaced as the cold seeped into my veins. "Your blood, your lineage... it calls to me. You are the key to my freedom, whether you know it or not."

The guy was intense. And he just admitted exactly who he was.

Memories of my grandmother's letter flashed through my mind. The warnings about power, about danger.

What had I gotten myself into? How could this have happened?

"Look," I said, trying to keep my voice steady, "I think there's been a big misunderstanding. I'm just a barista from the city. The only magic I know is how to make a decent latte art. M-Maybe we could, I don't know, talk about this over a cup of coffee? I make a mean peppermint mocha."

For a moment, confusion replaced the intensity in his gaze. "You jest even now, in the face of your doom?" His eyes ran down toward my collarbone and I wanted to shrink away. "Curious creatures, you mortals."

There was that word again. Mortals. It only solidified the fact that he wasn't from this realm one bit.

I shrugged, or tried to. It's hard to be nonchalant when

you're being held in place by an ancient ice demon or whatever he was.

What can I say? I coped with humor. It was either that or scream until I passed out, and I'd really rather not do that.

He released my wrist suddenly, and I stumbled back, instinctively rubbing feeling back into my arm. This icy king —whatever he truly was—began to pace the kitchen, his movements fluid and gracefully predatory. It spoke of a being who was honed for battle.

I watched with eerie fascination as frost trailed behind him, creeping across the floor akin to a living thing, weaving up the walls in a jagged pattern that mirrored his dark intentions.

I could feel the power wrapping around my ankles, icy fingers clutching at me, pulling me closer to his domain. I skipped away in a panic, watching as it retreated back to its master as if laughing at me. With every moment that passed, I felt the weight of his gaze—a mix of hunger and malice—as he circled, an ominous predator hunting in the shadows of the kitchen, and I was his unwitting prey.

"For centuries, I have waited," he said, his voice filled with a longing that was almost painful to hear. "Trapped between worlds, neither fully here nor there. And now, when freedom is within my grasp, I am bound by the very magic that imprisons me."

I edged toward the door, wondering if I could make it to the old bicycle I found before he turned me into a Callie-sicle. "That sounds rough, buddy. Really. But maybe this is a sign, you know? Maybe you're supposed to stay... trapped. Between worlds. Away from people who might get frostbite just by standing near you."

He whirled on me, and the temperature dropped so low I could feel my eyelashes freezing. *Smart move, Callie. Anger the dangerous being you're supposed to keep tucked away with your non-existent guardian abilities.*

"You will not leave," he growled. "You are mine now, Callie Winters. My key, my salvation."

The vehemence in his voice at the end of his sentence sent a shiver down my spine. *How does everyone keep knowing my name? Has he been watching me too? But how?*

"Yeah, about that," I said, my hand finding the doorknob behind me. "I'm more of a warm-weather girl. Maybe you could find someone else? Someone who appreciates a good deep freeze?"

But as I turned the knob, it wouldn't budge. The door was sealed tight by a thick layer of ice, frozen shut and unyielding.

The Frost King's smile was the most terrifying thing I'd ever seen. "There is no escape, little mortal. You are bound to this place now, as surely as I am. But fear not, for I can be benevolent to those who serve me well."

Grandma Rose's letter flitted through my mind. *But be warned. There is a great danger. There are those who would seek to use you, to harness your abilities for their own ends.*

I swallowed hard, my mind burning through every outcome. "A-And if I refuse to serve?"

His eyes glittered dangerously. "Then you will learn why winter is feared above all seasons. Why those lost in blizzards pray for a quick death rather than face the slow, creeping cold."

Well, that didn't sound good. What a horrible pitch.

I needed to think, to find a way out of this mess. But it

was hard to concentrate with the embodiment of winter staring at me as if I was a particularly interesting ice sculpture. He still felt ghostly, despite the unmistakable pressure of his grip on my skin. He couldn't pose that much danger, could he? His name hadn't been spoken.

Maybe I was still safe, despite his looming threats.

"Okay," I said, holding up my hands in what I hoped was a placating gesture. "Let's say, hypothetically, I was interested in... helping you. What exactly would that entail? Because I've got to tell you, my skill set is pretty limited. Unless you need someone to make you a good cappuccino or explain the plot of every late-night original television series, I'm not sure how useful I'd be."

He regarded me silently, his gaze piercing through the heavy air like a dagger. I fought the urge to squirm under the weight of his intense stare, feeling as though he could see right into the depths of my soul, laying bare every fear and secret I held. The shadows around us seemed to draw closer, thickening in the silence, amplifying the tension that coiled between us.

Finally, he broke the silence, his voice emerging comparable to the first chill of winter—soft yet no less menacing. "Your blood holds power, Callie Winters. Power that has been dormant for generations. I will teach you to awaken it, to harness it. And in doing so, you will break the chains that bind me."

I laughed nervously. *He* wanted to teach *me*? What kind of reverse psychology trick was this? "Right, because that doesn't sound ominous at all. Look, Mr. Frost King, sir, I appreciate the offer, but I'm not cut out for the whole 'awakening ancient powers' thing. I can barely remember to water my cactus."

My heart raced as I said it, hoping to mask my terror with humor, but the words felt clumsy and hollow, echoing in the thick silence. I glanced at him, trying to gauge his reaction, but his expression was inscrutable, the corners of his mouth barely twitching.

Great, he probably thinks the last guardian of this realm is an idiot.

But the tension in the air wrapped around me tighter, and I could almost feel the frost creeping in closer, as if it were laughing at my feeble attempt to break the ice—pun intended.

His expression darkened. "You do not understand the gravity of your situation, mortal. You are mine now, to mold as I see fit. Resist, and I will freeze the very blood in your veins."

Another empty threat. How was he going to accomplish this when he wasn't fully here?

I shifted my weight awkwardly, the chill of the floor seeping through my shoes making me shiver. *Focus, focus!* I needed to stay sharp, to keep my wits about me, but the weight of his gaze made it difficult to think straight.

"Has anyone ever told you that you have some serious control issues? Maybe we should work on that before diving into the whole 'unleashing ancient magic' thing."

Not that I planned to. But maybe I could try to placate his anger a little, just in case he *was* capable of following through on his threats. I still needed time to learn how to tap into my abilities.

He moved toward me, his form seeming to flicker

between solid and shadow. *What's he going to do?* The question swirled in my mind, and the last thing I wanted was to provoke him into action. But here I was, floundering in my own ridiculous attempt at bravado, caught in a moment that felt as frozen as the air around us.

"Enough of your prattling. You will obey me, or—"

Suddenly, he stopped, a look of pain crossing his face that sent another jolt of fear through me. *What's happening now?* His expression twisted as if some invisible force had gripped him, and I felt my heart race as he staggered back, clutching at his chest. The moment felt suspended in time, a surreal tableau of dread and uncertainty.

His breath came in ragged gasps, each inhale consistent with a desperate plea for air, and I instinctively took a step closer, torn between concern and the instinct to flee. I mean, it wouldn't do me any favors in this new town if I had to explain a dead otherworldly being in my house to the authorities. What if I lose my job?

"No," he growled. "Not now. Not when I'm so close."

I watched in fascination and horror as his form began to dissolve, ice crystals swirling in the air where he had stood. His eyes locked with mine, filled with rage and desperation.

"This is not over," he growled, his voice fading like the echo of a winter wind. "I will return, and you will fulfill your destiny. Remember... the cold always returns."

With a final howl that shook the house to its foundations, he vanished. The ice retreated, melting away as if it had never been there. The room gradually warmed, and I felt the tension in my limbs ease, allowing me to move once more.

I sank to the floor, my legs no longer able to support me.

My mind was reeling, trying to process what had just happened. A hysterical laugh bubbled up in my throat.

"What in the—" I said to the empty room, "I've gone from making lattes to dealing with ice demons. Mom said I should look for a career change, but I don't think this is what she had in mind. Grandma Rose, what have you gotten me into?"

I looked around the kitchen, now back to its normal, slightly shabby self. The chaos of my recent encounter felt surreal, a bizarre dream I'd soon wake up from. The only evidence of my supernatural brush with the Frost King was a small puddle of water on the floor where he had stood.

I stared at the puddle, half-expecting it to bubble or emit some kind of otherworldly glow.

"Okay," I muttered, shakily pushing myself to my feet. "Step one. Clean up the water before I slip and give myself a concussion. Step two, figure out how to deal with an ancient winter spirit who thinks I'm his ticket to world domination. Step three... find that therapist after all."

When I grabbed a towel to mop up the water, my eyes fell on the bread I'd baked, still sitting on the counter. It was completely frozen solid.

I sighed. "Even my stress-baking gets ruined by supernatural drama. This is so not what I signed up for when I inherited this place."

As I stood there, staring at my icy culinary failure, I thought about my grandmother's letter, the warnings. The books in the study weren't just family heirlooms, the gossip column, or the ramblings of an eccentric old woman. They were real.

Which meant...

"The journals," I breathed. "The spell books. I need to find more answers."

With a renewed sense of purpose, and only a slight tremor in my hands, I headed for the study. If I was going to face off against the Frost boy, I needed all the help I could get. And if that help came in the form of dusty old books and cryptic family secrets, well, beggars couldn't be choosers.

As I reached for the first journal, something told me this was just the beginning.

"Alright, Grandma Rose," I said, opening the book. "Let's see what other surprises you left for me. And maybe next time, a heads up about the hot but homicidal ice demon being able to pop into my kitchen without calling his name would be nice. Just saying."

CHAPTER 11

CALLIE

After my shift at the coffee shop, I nestled deeper into the couch, the musty scent of aged upholstery mingling with the faint aroma of the herbal tea I had brewed earlier.

The study was a world of its own, filled with the scent of old paper and leather. Bookshelves lined the walls, crammed with volumes that looked like they hadn't been touched in years.

The only other new information I came across was that the Summer Queen had a son who, it seemed, had an affair with a human maidservant—one that resulted in an illegitimate child. The discovery of this child didn't come to light until said child, once grown, had already been appointed as the next guardian of the realms. Was this where our bloodlines began? Was I part of something far bigger than just this realm?

What I really needed to figure out was how the Frost King managed to manifest in my kitchen if he was supposedly locked away for eternity. But nothing I had found so far suggested that such a thing was possible. The further I dove, the further these snippets of stories pulled me away from what I was searching for.

That was when my attention span began to resemble the worn-out furniture around me: saggy and prone to collapse under the weight of expectation.

As I squinted at the pages, words began to blur together. Maybe if I stretched a little, I'd regain some clarity—or at least loosen up my creaky joints. I tossed the book aside and stood up, groaning theatrically as if I were an old man getting up from a chair after Thanksgiving dinner.

Rolling my shoulders, I shook out my arms like I was trying to throw off an invisible burden. The truth was, I'd been sitting too long. But the more I read, the more I was peeling back layers of mystery without finding the actual answers I sought.

My grandmother's letter also mentioned training. What kind of training? Didn't I need an instructor for that? How could a clueless person train themselves? I felt as if I was being set up for failure. I was in over my head. Did I really have what it took to keep an ice demon under wraps? I glanced around the room, the weight of the countless books lining the walls and faded portraits pressing down on me.

The thought of mastering whatever skills she envisioned felt as daunting as scaling a mountain in flip-flops. What if I couldn't even make it past the first hurdle?

"Callie, queen of self-doubt," I muttered to myself. "That should be my official title." I chuckled, but deep down, the anxiety bubbled. Could I become who my grandmother wanted me to be? Or was I destined to be the family's biggest disappointment?

"Alright. Time for a break."

With a sigh, I wandered around the living room, stretching my limbs as I went. The walls were adorned with a mix of faded floral wallpaper and dark wooden panels that seemed to watch me as I passed.

"Okay, Grams," I said, half-joking, "what's the secret here? Do I need to cast a spell on one of your old pictures to make you talk to me?"

I glanced at a nearby portrait of a man whose eyebrows looked like they were in a perpetual state of surprise. Was that a family trait? I suppressed a laugh. Maybe my ancestors had a long-standing tradition of overly dramatic expressions.

Continuing my stroll, I found myself drawn to an ornate cabinet in the corner of the room. I gently tugged open the door and discovered a treasure trove of knickknacks—old trinkets, dusty glass figurines, and, to my delight, a photo album.

"Ooh, what do we have here?" I murmured, pulling it out and brushing off the dust with a flourish as if revealing a magician's assistant.

I settled onto a nearby chair and flipped open the album, the pages crinkling slightly as I did. The first few images were of my grandmother, young and sprightly, her hair a cascade of curls that seemed to defy gravity. I chuckled at the styles from decades past—what was once considered fashionable now looked like a time capsule of bad decisions.

But as I turned the pages, my amusement faded into

curiosity. There were photographs of women who shared not just the same facial features but also an uncanny resemblance to me.

A distant cousin? Nah, that didn't add up. Not with how old the photo looked. Maybe it was a great-great-grandmother or something? I leaned closer, scrutinizing their eyes and cheekbones.

"This is getting creepy," I whispered, half to myself. The resemblance was too striking to ignore.

I flipped through more pages, my heart racing slightly as I noticed that the resemblance skipped a generation here and there. I found myself captivated by a picture of a young woman with a particularly dramatic hairstyle.

"Please tell me this isn't where I get my hair ideas from," I snickered, but the laughter faded as I realized how much she looked similar to me at a certain angle.

As I continued to flip through the album, I felt an odd chill creep down my spine. This wasn't just nostalgia—it was a revelation. It was as if the past was tugging at my sleeve, reminding me of a connection I had yet to fully grasp. What did it mean to look so much like these women? Was I going to find an image of the first maidservant somewhere in this album?

Just then, I stumbled upon a page featuring a family tree sketch, meticulously drawn in faded ink. Leaning in closer, I tried to decipher the names, each one a twist in the branches that connected to stories I'd yet to come across in my grandmother's journals. Most of the names I didn't recognize—distant relatives and long-forgotten ancestors.

My mom, after becoming a single mother, rarely talked about the past, aside from complaining about my grandmother. But there it was—my name, sitting at the bottom of the tree. A lone leaf, offshooting from branches that seemed to stretch far back into time.

"Wow, talk about family ties," I mused, feeling a strange sense of pride mixed with bewilderment. But something about this tree felt off. Where was my father?

Suddenly, a loud creak echoed through the house, jolting me out of my thoughts. My heart raced as I glanced around, half-expecting to see one of my ancestors materializing out of thin air, shaking their heads in disappointment over my poor life choices. "Really, Callie? A career in coffee?"

Getting to my feet with the album in hand, I looked around the corner and saw nothing out of place.

Just my imagination, I told myself, noting there weren't any icicles forming or anything.

I shook off the nerves and went back to the chair, focusing on the photo album again. But my concentration shattered when I came across a drawn image that stopped me cold. It was a striking depiction of a woman clad in otherworldly armor, her expression both fierce and ethereal. Her eyes were fixed on the viewer with an intensity that felt unnervingly alive, as if she were piercing through the paper and into my very soul. There was something about her stance, regal yet ready for battle, that sent a shiver down my spine.

"Okay, this is a bit much," I muttered, flipping the page quickly. But that image lingered in my mind, and my imagination ran wild.

I stood up abruptly, the photo album tumbling out of my lap. "I've had enough excitement for one day," I said aloud, forcing a laugh.

With a resigned sigh, I set the photo album back down in its place, feeling a strange mix of reluctance and curiosity. Were all of those women also tied to duties or spellcasting? The woman in armor resembled a guardian of some sort, standing watch over secrets yet to be unveiled.

As I contemplated her fierce gaze, I couldn't help but feel a pang of inadequacy. Here I was, just a regular woman navigating the hubbub of life—grappling with bills, trying to make sense of my grandmother's cryptic legacy, and figuring out dinner for one. The idea of being a guardian of wielding magic or even facing down a metaphorical dragon —or in my case, an unwelcome ice demon—felt like a joke.

The stark contrast between her heroic presence and my day-to-day struggles made me wonder if I was even remotely capable of living up to whatever legacy my grandmother had intended for me. Did I even belong in this narrative? I was more about surviving the grind than standing tall in armor, and that realization sent a wave of self-doubt crashing over me. Who was I kidding? If my cactus from back at my apartment could talk, it would probably have a lot of sassy commentary.

I decided a snack might help clear my head, so I shuffled into the kitchen. My stomach growled as I searched for something that resembled food. Grabbing a box of crackers, I poured a handful into my palm, then plopped onto the counter, still mentally grappling with what I had just uncovered.

Who was that woman in armor and why did it seem there was a memory niggling in the back of my thoughts? Munching on my crackers, my mind began to wander again. This wasn't just about resemblances; there was something deeper—something I was missing that I couldn't exactly pinpoint.

"Okay, Callie," I said, my voice firm in an attempt to chase away the growing self-doubt, "you've got this. Time to turn those breadcrumbs into a full-course meal."

I brushed a few off the top of my bosom and hopped down from the counter, grabbing another handful of crackers. Returning to the room with the cabinet, I was determined to dig deeper into the family history. Maybe I could piece together what made me different and why the ice demon decided to show up now.

I opened the photo album again, flipping through the pages more deliberately this time. My finger traced the images of my ancestors.

"Here's to uncovering family mysteries," I declared to the empty room, raising an imaginary glass.

Just then, I spotted a name in the family tree that I hadn't noticed before; Laeta. It was circled in red ink, a name that felt significant. My heart raced again as I considered the possibilities. Who was Laeta? And why had she been singled out?

I made a mental note to find out more, but before I could dive back into research, a loud crash echoed from the other room. I froze, crackers almost falling from my hand. What was that?

Setting down the crackers and album, I turned slowly, grabbing a hefty candle holder in my grip as a makeshift weapon. Each cautious step I took echoed in the stillness. But as I rounded the corner, all I found was another puddle of water, glistening innocently on the floor, mocking my quest for enlightenment.

Ykazar.

I shook my head vehemently to dislodge his name from my mind.

How is it possible for him to keep reappearing?

Turning on my heel, I headed back into my grandmother's study, determined to find a spell to keep out any random visitors who thought my house was a welcome mat for uninvited guests.

I wandered over to the largest bookshelf, running my fingers over the spines of dusty tomes. One of them had an intricate symbol on the cover that looked suspiciously like a book that would hold the information I was seeking.

"Let's see what you've got for me," I muttered, pulling it off the shelf. The book thudded onto the desk, sending up a cloud of dust that made me cough. "Ugh, why do I always forget to wear a hazmat suit for this?"

As I flipped through the pages, they were filled with complicated diagrams and notes scrawled in a mix of elegant script and chaotic handwriting. I squinted at the text, trying to decipher the spells. There were recipes for potions, instructions for summoning, and even some cheeky commentary about cats being the best familiars.

After several pages of spell components and incantations that could probably raise the dead, I stumbled upon a section labeled "Protection Spells." My heart raced. This was it!

I leaned in closer, my finger tracing the elegant script. "To guard one's abode from uninvited guests," it began, "light a candle of sage, chant the words of closure, and envision a barrier of light..."

"Vision and candles? Sure, why not throw in some fairy

dust while we're at it?" I couldn't help but roll my eyes. What was a candle of sage and how was that different from the candles I had on hand?

I closed my eyes and tried to picture a curtain of light, then cracked one eye open to glance at the incantation. How was I supposed to do both at once? It didn't seem possible unless I managed to memorize the words.

I tried reciting the words while visualizing the light, then reversed it—imagining the vision first and reciting the words after. Nothing worked. Maybe it wasn't me, I thought, clinging to hope. Maybe it was the candle.

I could find some sage. That was in the produce aisle, right? I'd seen it at the store, sitting next to the organic kale and overpriced avocados—things I no longer needed in my life. I could always melt down one of these candles and mix in the sage. A reasonable solution.

Nodding to myself, I flipped through the pages, hoping to find a spell with simpler ingredients and fewer requirements. "Alright, let's see what else you've got."

I kept reading, stumbling upon a spell that seemed promising, but my excitement quickly faded when I hit a line that made my stomach twist: "Caution: performing this spell incorrectly may lead to unwanted consequences. Such consequences may include, but are not limited to, ghostly manifestations, impolite spirits, or a random influx of overly friendly neighborhood cats."

"Fantastic. Nothing like a few extra ghosts and cats to liven up the joint," I grumbled, rubbing my temples. One unwanted ice demon was more than enough. I didn't want to risk it.

I decided to take a break from spell-hunting, not entirely

trusting myself quite yet and grabbed my mug from the shelf. I filled it with water from the kettle I left in the kitchen, determined to have some semblance of normalcy while I figured this out. Maybe I'd just drink my way through the situation until clarity struck.

As I sipped my lukewarm water, the shadows in the room seemed to stretch and shift, and I couldn't shake the feeling that the very walls were watching me. It was as if my grandmother's presence lingered, silently critiquing my every move.

"Shouldn't you be more graceful about all this?" I imagined her saying with a playful smirk.

"Yeah, Grandma, because that's how you kept a haunted house from being overrun by pesky visitors," I shot back, half-amused and half-nervous. "Just whip up a spell and pray for the best, right? I mean, is that why there are no cats around, did one of *your* spells go awry?"

With a resigned sigh, I returned to the book.

But as I rifled through the pages, a loud creak echoed through the house, freezing me in place. I paused, my heart racing. Was it the house settling again? Or was it an actual presence?

My gut nudged me to check it out—but not without a weapon. I glanced around, scanning for something that could serve as a makeshift defense. My eyes landed on a heavy cast iron skillet sitting on the counter.

"Perfect," I muttered, grabbing it. "Nothing says 'don't mess with me' like a good old-fashioned frying pan." I took a deep breath and forced myself to continue searching, skillet in hand, ready to confront whatever—or whoever— might be lurking in the shadows. After all, if this turned into a horror movie, I was determined to be the one wielding the skillet, not the one screaming in the corner.

With the cast iron skillet gripped tightly in my hands, I edged toward the source of the noise, my heart pounding. Each creak of the old floorboards was as if the house itself was trying to dissuade me from moving forward. But curiosity, coupled with adrenaline, propelled me onward.

As I approached the back of the house, the source of the sound became clearer—a faint, slurping noise.

From the corner of my eye, I caught movement—a flicker of something darting just out of sight. My pulse quickened. *Okay, Callie, you've got this.* I advanced further, the skillet feeling heavy but reassuring in my grip.

Turning the corner, I stumbled into another old storage room. Dusty shelves lined the walls, filled with forgotten trinkets and boxes. The slurping noise intensified, and I froze, my eyes darting around, searching for the source.

Suddenly, a wild animal burst into view—a scruffy raccoon, its eyes bright and mischievous, crouched over a puddle of water on the floor. It was licking the ground enthusiastically, completely unfazed by my presence.

"Fantastic. Nothing like a raccoon to liven up the joint," I grumbled, lowering the pan onto a nearby surface. I rubbed my temples.

I looked up at my ceiling wondering if there was a leak in the roof.

I couldn't help but laugh at the absurdity of the situation. "Seriously? You're just here for a drink?" I shook my head, both amused and slightly annoyed, noticing the window slightly ajar.

I spotted the broom propped against the wall where I

had last left it, a reminder of my abandoned plans to clean this room after starting my job at the coffee shop. I grabbed it, hoping to gently guide the raccoon toward the open window.

"Hey there, buddy," I said softly, trying to sound calm. "Time to go home."

As I waved the broom toward it, the raccoon paused, eyeing me with a mixture of curiosity and defiance. It slowly backed away from the puddle, looking as if it was contemplating its next move. Then, just as I thought I had it, it darted toward the shelves, knocking over a dusty box in its haste.

"Great, just great!" I exclaimed, trying to keep my voice steady as chaos erupted in the small room. I swung the broom again, trying to steer it toward the window. "Out! You've had your fun!"

With a few more frantic moments of dodging and weaving, the raccoon finally made a break for the exit. It dashed past me, skidding slightly on the floor before it disappeared into the night, leaving behind a trail of spilled items and a whole lot of confusion.

I stood there for a moment, panting slightly, still gripping the broom like a weapon. "Well, that was unexpected," I said to the empty room.

Shaking my head, I set the broom down and surveyed the mess. "Now I need to clean up," I muttered, sighing as I grabbed an abandoned rag in the corner to wipe up the puddle.

As I moved, my eyes caught on a strange-looking artifact tucked away on a nearby shelf. It had an otherworldly quality, shimmering subtly in the dim light, but I couldn't quite put my finger on what it was. I lifted the charm from around my neck and examined it, comparing the material. In some ways, they were similar—yet in others, they were completely different. Maybe Grandma Rose had a thing for crystals. I wouldn't be surprised. Crystals and spell books go hand in hand in the movies.

Intrigued yet cautious, I placed it gently back on the table, my fingers lingering for a moment longer than necessary. The moment I turned to head back to the kitchen, a chill ran down my spine as if fingers were physically grazing my skin. It felt as if I was being watched, the hairs on the back of my neck prickling in response. I shook off the feeling, chalking it up to my imagination running wild, but the sensation clung to me as I made my way through the house.

CHAPTER 12

CALLIE

I hadn't planned on going to the grocery store the next day, but sometimes life had a funny way of pushing you in a direction you didn't expect. It was the middle of the afternoon on my day off from work when I found myself staring at my fridge, which was as bare as a desert. My stomach grumbled in protest, and the reality of needing real food hit me.

"Alright, alright," I muttered, grabbing my jacket and heading out the door. "I'll go."

I decided to take another trip to town, bringing up the app for the local taxi. They really should add more public transportation here.

The ride was short and uneventful. As we passed the turnoff to the small town, I thought about the things I needed to buy: the basics. Eggs, bread, soup. I wasn't going to attempt making my own bread again, that was for sure.

Thoughts of Yk—the ice demon—slithered into my mind again, and I quickly shook my head, trying to push them away. I needed to stop thinking about him, especially in case I accidentally spoke his name.

I thought about the raccoon.

Pulling up the internet browser on my phone, I did a quick internet search and found that I might need a few oddball items to keep pesky critters away. Specifically, some sort of concoction of ground garlic and chili powder for raccoon repellent. I had no clue how well it worked, but desperate times called for desperate measures, and if the internet said garlic and chili powder would help, who was I to argue?

The taxi dropped me off at the front of the store and I waved him off, giving him a tip through the app. The bell above the door jingled as I stepped inside. The familiar fluorescent lights greeted me, flickering every now and then.

I wandered through the aisles, filling my basket with the items on my mental list. I threw in some frozen meals for when I couldn't bring myself to cook. Taking a quick detour from the frozen aisle, I made my way to the produce section and grabbed some fresh sage.

The place was quiet, the soft shuffle of my sneakers against the linoleum floor the only sound other than the occasional beep of the register as someone checked out.

I wondered what the population of Odum was.

As I turned the corner toward the checkout lane, I spotted the same woman at the register from my last visit. Pushing my cart closer to the conveyor belt, I noticed her nametag: Mrs. Lancaster.

She stood behind the counter ringing up the customer

ahead of me, pushing her thick glasses up the bridge of her nose now and again. Her gray hair was braided down her back in a long, practical style. She had a presence about her, one that was warm but didn't feel like it came with an agenda.

When she saw me, she greeted me with the same easy smile she had last time.

"Well, if it isn't my favorite new shopper," she said, her voice light with a hint of humor. "Back for more, are we?"

I returned her smile, feeling a little more at ease this time. "Guilty as charged," I said, nodding at the simple contents of my cart. "Guess I'm getting the hang of this whole starting over thing."

She chuckled and raised an eyebrow, scanning the chili powder. "Looks to me you've got the basics down, anyhow. Planning on making a hot pot of chili tonight?"

I raised my hands in mock surrender. "No, but something like that."

She laughed, the sound light and easy, like it was perfectly normal to find comfort in the simplest of meals. "Ah, I remember those days. You'll be in good company around here. People get creative when it comes to feeding themselves on a budget."

I couldn't help but grin. There was something reassuring about her easy confidence in the mundane.

She finished ringing up my items and gave me a thoughtful look as she slid them into bags. "So, how are you settling in? Getting the lay of the land?"

The question caught me a little off guard. I hadn't expected to have this kind of conversation today. But since Mrs. Lancaster threw the bait out, I took it.

"It's been... an adjustment," I admitted, shifting the bags in my hands as I secretly contemplated whether I should start a new life as a professional overthinker. "I'm still figuring things out."

I left out the part about the late-night raccoon visitors or the whole ice demon situation. You know, just the usual weirdness that doesn't exactly come up in casual conversation.

She gave me a knowing look. "Yeah, it's like that here. This town doesn't rush you," She winked.

"Tell me about it, I'm still trying to get used to that at the coffee shop, anticipating imaginary crazy rush hours."

Mrs. Lancaster raised an eyebrow. "Oh? I didn't know Andrea was hiring. Well, this place has a way of growing on you, like mildew," she said with a grin.

That was odd. Tim knew about it. And in a town this small, wouldn't everyone know who was hiring? I pushed the thought aside, dismissing it as I laughed at her metaphor.

"Mildew, huh? I'll try to keep that in mind."

She grinned. "You'll see. People here are friendly, once you get to know them. Just make sure you smile when they wave. They'll think you're strange if you don't."

I nodded, trying to portray that I was absorbing this advice. *Smile and wave.* Simple enough, right? But the more I thought about it, the more I felt I was on some alien planet where the rules of normal human interaction had been rewritten.

In the city, waving at strangers was a fast track to getting the middle finger. Or worse, *nothing*—the cold, dead stare of a person who was probably mentally planning out their escape route from the awkwardness. Eye contact was a gamble, and most of the time, you'd end up regretting it. Smiling at anyone who wasn't a barista, a close friend, or a dog was considered borderline insane.

Aside from the basics of customer service at work, we didn't really engage in that level of friendliness. It was as if I'd stepped into some weird, retro version of humanity where people didn't mind being polite, even to complete strangers.

Maybe this would grow on me—like mildew, as Mrs. Lancaster had put it. But I could already feel myself fighting the instinct to roll my eyes and pretend I didn't see someone waving at me across the street.

I nodded, the smile still lingering on my face.

She handed me my receipt with a flourish and a little nod of approval. "That's the spirit. And don't forget—if you need anything else, we're here. Just don't let the shelves fool you. They've got a lot more than you think."

I took the receipt, about to turn away when she tilted her head and fixed me with a curious look.

"So," Mrs. Lancaster said, her tone casual but with a curious edge, "where'd you end up moving to?"

I froze for a split second. What was up with everyone wanting to know where I lived? It felt a little too... personal, maybe. Or maybe I was just getting paranoid. After all, I had been around my fair share of crazy stalkers in the city who followed single women home. Maybe I was overthinking things. It's just a question, right? People in small towns probably just made small talk like this all the time.

I shifted my weight from one foot to the other, trying to keep my voice casual.

"Oh, you know… I inherited my grandmother's old house," I said, attempting to brush it off. I figured that would be enough to end the conversation, but Mrs. Lancaster didn't seem the type to let things go that easily.

Her eyes narrowed, just for a split second, before a knowing smile curled on her lips. "Grandmother's house, you say?" she repeated, her tone almost too casual. "I take it you're talking about that big, old place up on Lilac Lane?"

I froze.

How did she know? I blinked, the words catching in my throat. "Uh… yeah," I said slowly, trying not to sound too suspicious. "That's the one."

Mrs. Lancaster's smile deepened, her glasses catching the light as she peered at me over the top.

"I know that house," she said, as if she was pulling up some long-lost memory. "Used to be old Rose's place. Your grandmother… she was a *strong* woman, wasn't she? I remember her well. Used to stop in here for her canned peaches every other Tuesday. Always had a story to tell, that one."

I swallowed, a chill creeping up my spine. How much *did* she know? Was this just a harmless old woman remembering a neighbor, or was there something more to it?

"Yeah, she was a bit of a character," I said, still keeping my voice light. Even though I didn't have a relationship with my grandmother, she didn't need to know that. "She had her quirks."

Mrs. Lancaster nodded. "Oh, I think you'll find that house has a way of… making you pick up on things you didn't expect." She tilted her head, her smile turning more mysterious, as if she knew a little too much for comfort.

"Things in that house have a way of sticking with you, in one way or another."

I frowned, unsure if I was supposed to be getting some kind of cryptic warning here or if she was just rambling the way old folks do when they're feeling nostalgic. Or maybe cryptic messages came with age.

"Yeah, well, it's... different than what I'm used to," I said cautiously.

She nodded again, her expression softening. "Houses like that, they have a way of... teaching you what you need to know. If you listen closely enough." Her eyes lingered on me for a moment, as if she was waiting for something, before she gave me a warm smile. "You'll settle in soon enough, I'm sure of it."

I gave a tight-lipped smile in return, trying not to let my unease show. With a quick nod, I gathered up my bags, eager to make my exit before she said anything more.

As I turned toward the door, I couldn't shake the feeling that I had just stepped into something more than meets the eye. Maybe it was the way she'd spoken about the house. Maybe it was the way she seemed to know *exactly* which house I was talking about.

As the door swung shut behind me with a soft jingle, I stepped out into the sunshine, but the unease lingered. The quiet, little town had already given me a taste of its strange charm. Now, it seemed, it was offering me a glimpse of its deeper secrets.

And I wasn't sure if I was ready to uncover them just yet.

It was peaceful outside, the sunlight filtering through the trees lining the street. I didn't have anywhere to be, and I wasn't quite ready to go home yet, so I decided to take a stroll. Maybe it was the conversation with Mrs. Lancaster, or maybe I just needed to stretch my legs, but walking felt better than just heading straight back.

The town was quiet, a few cars parked here and there, a couple of people walking in and out of shops. I assumed most of the residents were at their respective jobs.

I passed the antique store with its dusty windows, the kind of place that made you think of forgotten things—old useless items, tarnished trinkets, or mismatched furniture. The florist's shop was next, overflowing with bright flowers in every shade.

As I walked further down the street, my eyes caught something different—a small shop tucked between a pair of more traditional storefronts. The sign above the door read "Mystic Wicks", in gold lettering that was starting to fade from years of exposure to the sun. There was something oddly inviting about it, a quiet pull, like it was calling me without saying a word.

Curious, I adjusted the bags in my hands and stepped closer, peering inside through the windows. The shelves were full of candles in all shapes and colors, each one appearing more intricate than the last. Some were tall and sleek, others were small and round, and a few had odd shapes—twisted wicks, symbols carved into the wax, delicate patterns on the surface. I wasn't sure what it was about them, but there was something calming in the colors, the textures, and the light reflecting off the glass.

Was I going to risk making my own sage candles? I could blame frost boy for my disastrous bread the other night but I knew better.

I pushed open the door, the bell ringing softly as I

stepped inside. The air was thick with the scent of wax, something earthy, maybe cinnamon and clove. It was warm in here, a cozy little cocoon that smelled of a mixture of comfort and mystery.

A statuesque woman with a light tan stood behind the counter, rearranging a few items on the shelf. She looked up as I entered and gave me a smile, one of those knowing smiles as if she'd seen this a hundred times before.

"First time?" she asked in a calm, welcoming voice.

I might as well get used to this by now. At this point, I probably have a neon sign on my forehead that says "Newbie: Please Ask Me About My Lack of Direction."

I nodded. "Yeah. This is a neat little place."

"It's not one of those places you find by accident," she said with a soft laugh. "But sometimes the right people end up here."

I wasn't sure what that meant, but something about the shop felt right. Like I'd stumbled across a secret—or maybe just a space where I could pause for a moment before my arms fell off from carrying these *ridiculously heavy* bags. Seriously, how did people get groceries without turning into human caricatures of their own bad decisions?

I shifted the bags again, trying to keep them from digging into my wrists consistent with an evil form of punishment. I was going to need a chiropractor by the time I got home.

I started wandering through the aisles, my fingers brushing over the candles as I moved. There were so many of them—tall ones in deep blues and purples, small ones with intricate swirls of color. Some looked as if they belonged in a witch's lair, others like they were made for relaxation.

I picked up one of the deep blue candles, its wax smooth and cool to the touch. It wasn't something I would have normally gone for, but for some reason, something told me it might be what I needed.

The woman behind the counter seemed to sense my hesitation and smiled as if she was sharing some cosmic wisdom. "You don't need to know why. Sometimes, it's just about finding the right thing when you're ready for it."

I glanced up at her, still uncertain what exactly I was ready for. Was I ready to find my inner witch? Sorceress? I still didn't even know what Imy bloodline entailed.

"Right," I muttered, half to myself. "Finding the right thing... when I'm ready for it."

I eyed the rows of candles again, now wondering if I'd somehow stumbled into a magical *and* aromatherapy section. What if scented candles didn't count for spells? Would I need to come back for *specific and unscented* candles? The ones that weren't trying to make my house smell like a spa? What if the spell needed something more... unadulterated? No one ever mentioned the nuances of candle choices in the books I'd skimmed. Did lavender *really* help with focusing during spell casting, or was that just for relaxation?

My thoughts were spiraling. Maybe I needed to ask the lady behind the counter, but I wasn't sure if I was ready for *that* level of inquiry.

I took a deep breath, pretending I knew what I was doing, and grabbed the nearest candle that didn't smell like a fruit salad or a "new car scent" air freshener.

Cinnamon. Solid, reliable, *spell-compatible* cinnamon.

"Yeah," I muttered, more to myself than the clerk. "This'll work."

I also grabbed a good handful of sage candles in case I mess up a few times and I paid for them, giving the woman behind the counter a quick, half-hearted smile.

"Thanks," I said, still feeling that strange tug in the air as if something important had just happened. Or maybe I was just overly dramatic from carrying heavy bags for way too long. Either way, I was ready to escape the shop before I turned into one of those people who took candles *way* too seriously.

I stepped out onto the sidewalk, blinking in the bright daylight, and pulled out my phone to call a cab. As I waited, I found myself glancing up and down the street, hoping for a distraction. The place was quiet, just the usual hum of a small town—peaceful in that way where everything feels a little *too* still. The kind of stillness that makes your skin prickle.

That was when I saw him.

Tim—or whatever his name was.

He was standing on the opposite side of the street, leaning against a tree in the corner. I hadn't noticed him at first—he'd probably been there for a while, just blending into the background. But the second I looked up, our eyes met.

He was smiling at me—slowly, deliberately—as if he'd been waiting for me to notice. And then he waved. Not an exaggerated wave, just a casual, one-finger raise of the hand, as if we were old friends who just happened to run into each other.

I frowned, unsure of how to react.

Despite Mrs. Lancaster's talk about friendliness, I hesitated, unsure if I should wave back or just pretend I hadn't seen him. But before I could make up my mind, his expression changed. The smile melted away, and for a split second, his face went blank—empty, as if a mask had slipped on. Something about it made the hairs on the back of my neck stand up.

Then, as if nothing had happened, he waved again, more enthusiastically this time, as if to reassure me. But this time, I didn't wave back. I didn't even blink.

I quickly turned away, focusing on the screen of my phone, pretending to be absorbed in waiting for my cab. My heart thudded in my chest, faster than before. The chill from earlier was back, settling deep in my bones.

It wasn't until I heard the soft hum of the approaching taxi that I dared to glance back over my shoulder. He was gone.

I quickly slid into the taxi, my breath coming faster now. The door slammed shut behind me, and I was suddenly, intensely aware of my surroundings.

The taxi sped away, but that strange feeling didn't leave me.

It followed me.

CHAPTER 13

CALLIE

I stared at the book in my hand, the soft flicker of candlelight dancing around the edges of the room. The candles I'd bought earlier that day—tall, waxy things in shades of deep blue and silver—were arranged in a perfect ring. Their wicks glowed with a soft, steady flame, casting long shadows across the room. I had memorized the incantation as best I could, the words rolling in my mind like a song, and the vision of light, the protective barrier I needed to create was clear in my thoughts.

This was going to work. It had to. It was in my blood.

I took a deep breath, steadying myself, then focused on the candles. They flickered once, almost as if in acknowledgment. My heart raced. I glanced at the script again, just to be sure as if I was cheating on a test.

"Come on, Callie. You've passed multiple exams in a week before. This is just one spell."

I kept the vision of a bright curtain strong as I began to recite the words.

"By light and flame, let no harm pass," I whispered the last line inwardly, my eyes drifting closed as I visualized a glowing barrier, a shimmering wall of light that would encircle me, protecting me from whatever might be out there. The words came with ease, flowing from my memory. I pictured the light growing around me, growing until it surrounded my whole being, until I could feel the shield of warmth.

Nothing happened.

I furrowed my brow, opening one eye to check the candles. They flickered slightly, but otherwise, they remained unchanged. The air around me felt heavy, but nothing more. No spark of magic. No overwhelming sensation that I was doing something right.

I tried again, this time with more intensity. I recited the words in my mind, focusing on the image of the barrier as if I could make it real with sheer will. I imagined the light pulsating, a force that could push back any danger, any ill will that might come my way.

And then, a small pulse.

It was faint, a tiny jolt of static, but it was there. My fingertips tingled for a brief moment, and the candle flames flickered in unison, bending toward the center of the circle. My heart skipped a beat. Was this it? Was this the magic working?

I held my breath, waiting for something more. But after a few moments of quiet, the tingling faded, and the candles returned to their steady glow. The pulse was gone, and the air was still. There was no shining barrier, no wall of light—just the same room I had been sitting in before.

Frustration bubbled up inside me, settling like a knot in my stomach. *This isn't how it's supposed to go.* I had followed the steps, recited the words exactly as the book said—hell, I practically *memorized* them. And I could have sworn I felt something, even if it was just a faint ripple, a shiver of magic brushing against me. Was I doing something wrong? Was I too impatient? Maybe I hadn't gathered the "right energy," or maybe I just wasn't in tune with my *inner* magic yet.

I blew out a breath, letting my shoulders slump. Well, that was a bust.

Then came the voice.

"You give up so easily."

It was low, rich with amusement and something else—something far too familiar. I froze, my breath catching in my throat. I had only heard it once before and it had been branded into my mind ever since. It dripped with arrogance, condescension, and a chilling weight that settled over me.

The temperature in the room dropped several degrees in an instant, and the faintest shimmer of ice dusted the edges of the candles.

I turned slowly, my heart hammering in my chest, dreading what I'd find. There he was, lounging casually against the doorframe as if he had all the time in the world. The Frost King. His presence was suffocating, his gaze appraising, as if he were evaluating a particularly disappointing piece of art. His lips curled into a small, mocking smile, his eyes glinting with cold amusement as he watched me.

"I have to say," he drawled, pushing off the doorframe

and strolling toward me with that unnerving confidence, "I thought your efforts would be... more impressive." He paused, as if considering something. "Not that I expected much, of course."

This was the complete opposite of the person I'd met the first time.

A chill ran through me, making the hairs on the back of my neck stand up. My pulse quickened. *The spell.* The one I'd tried to cast—it had been for him. The barrier, the protection—it had been to keep him out. To protect myself from him.

And I had failed.

I crossed my arms, forcing a smirk. He still wasn't fully corporeal, so that was something. "Well, if the temperatures would stop shifting, maybe I would be able to concentrate better. Forgive me for not wanting to freeze to death, but here we are once again."

The air around me became frigid, the temperature plummeting even further. I wanted to step back, put some distance between us, but my legs felt made of stone. He was watching me, measuring me, and I couldn't stop the flutter of panic in my chest.

"You've been trying to keep me out," he said, his voice dark with amusement, as though he found the whole thing... *adorable.* "How quaint."

He took another step closer, his gaze never leaving mine, the weight of it pressing down on me like an icy hand. He apparently got over whatever ailed him during his last appearance.

"Tell me, Callie," he said, voice smooth and dangerous, "what made you think that little circle of light would hold me back? I've already made it this far. Your spell is for those who haven't yet crossed the threshold."

Crap.

My throat felt tight, as if the very air had thickened around me. And again, how did he know my name? I hadn't spoken it aloud, hadn't even thought it—at least not consciously. I had barely *acknowledged* it in the moments before he appeared, and yet there it was, slipping from his lips as though it was the most natural thing in the world.

I forced myself to take a breath, but it came out shallow, unsteady. "How—How do you know my name?"

I mean, I didn't exactly have any business cards laying around, so that was a *really* good trick if it wasn't a complete creep factor.

His lips curled into that infuriating, condescending smile. He was enjoying every moment of my discomfort. "Your blood," he said, voice dark and slow, "sings beneath your veins. It calls to me, feeding my thirst for vengeance— for the sins your ancestors committed." He chuckled, as if casually admitting to wanting me dead was just part of some afternoon chit-chat. "But," he continued, gaze narrowing, "there's more to you than I expected, little mortal. Tell me, did you feel it too? The pull... when you stepped into this place?"

"Unlike you, I had an invitation," I shot back, forcing my voice to steady, though it came out with more bite than I intended. "Why are *you* here?"

The way he uttered *mortal* made my skin prickle, like a cold wind sweeping over me, though the air was oddly still. His eyes—dark, almost black—held something ancient and knowing, as if they could see straight through me, past my thoughts, past my defenses. I was being pinned under a magnifying glass, each detail of my fear laid bare and under intense scrutiny.

I couldn't look away. Flashes of my previous dream flit through my mind, images of a long lost memory—one that didn't belong to me. The heat of his body pressed against mine, the way I responded.

What was he doing to me?

My body stiffened, my heart drumming louder in my chest. For a brief moment, I felt small. *Powerless.* The kind of powerless you feel when standing in front of a predator, knowing it's the only thing in the room that matters. His gaze lingered for a long moment, too long, and I felt the weight of it as if he were once again on top of me with a blade to my neck. Every ounce of defiance I'd been clinging to threaten to slip away.

"You're not the first to try," he said softly, almost as if the words weren't meant for me at all, but rather a dark thought he was sharing with the shadows. "For centuries, I was locked away. But I knew this day would come. She thought she succeeded, but none ever truly do."

I backed up a step. And my feeble attempt at spell casting was only making my position as guardian look worse.

I wanted to tell him to get out of my sight, but I knew it would be pointless—his arrogance was practically a phys-ical thing, and it seemed impervious to what I had thrown at it thus far. Though his thoughts seemed calm now, I couldn't shake the feeling that beneath that composed exterior, something had to be unraveling inside him. No mind could survive that kind of isolation for as long as he described, not without cracking. Even criminals in this realm lost their grip on sanity after a fraction of that kind of confinement.

Instead, I forced a laugh, trying to mask my fear with defiance. "Guess I miscalculated," I said, my voice shaking more than I wanted to admit. "But hey, I tried, right?"

His lips twitched, the corners of his smile turning colder, more calculated. "Trying isn't enough, mortal," he said, his voice smooth as ice. "Not when it comes to me." He looked me up and down, as if savoring the way I reacted to him, before his gaze locked onto mine with unnerving intensity. "Because of what your ancestors did, you owe me. And there will be a reckoning. Perhaps you'll manage to delay it... if you survive long enough."

His words were a promise, but they felt like a threat—one I wasn't sure I could outrun.

Come on, Grandma Rose. A little help here!

I stood my ground, arms crossing over my chest as I took a slow, deliberate breath. My pulse was still racing, but I wasn't about to let this fae creature—or whatever he was—see me shake. He wasn't that powerful of a person the first time he showed up. He couldn't possibly have gained much more since.

He was still not quite there, his form flickering, his words more of an echo than a solid threat. If he was going to do something, he'd have done it by now, right?

I raised an eyebrow, cutting through the heavy air with a casualness I didn't quite feel. "Owe you?" I repeated, letting the words hang in the air. "Nice try, but I'm not buying whatever ancient guilt trip you're selling. And what exactly *are* you going to do? Fade in and out of the corners of my house and throw threats at me all day?"

He seemed to pause at that, as though my response caught him off guard. For a moment, there was a flicker of something darker in his eyes—like I'd just knocked a chip off his godly arrogance. That gave me a little satisfaction, but I pushed the feeling aside.

"Don't mistake my patience for weakness, mortal," he warned, his voice now a low rumble, but I could feel the edge of uncertainty creeping in. He was still intangible, his form wavering at the edges akin to a mirage. As much as he wanted to seem menacing, he wasn't truly here. Not yet, anyway.

I tilted my head, studying him. "You know," I said, feigning thoughtful consideration, "you keep talking as if you're a force of nature or some ancient king, but you're still... not really *here*, are you?"

His eyes narrowed. "I'm closer than you think."

"Oh, I'm sure you are," I said, voice dripping with sarcasm. "You've got all this power and yet you still can't get past my kitchen table. And you think I owe you something? Please. Your threats are starting to sound like bad movie lines."

I smirked, watching his frustration build. The longer he lingered in this half-formed state, the more I had the advantage. A part of me—okay, maybe a bigger part than I'd want to admit—wanted to keep pushing his buttons, see what kind of reaction I could provoke. Because, frankly, I wasn't exactly quaking in my boots anymore.

His gaze flickered, a flicker of something dark passing through his eyes. He took a slow, deliberate step forward, but I didn't budge. My feet were planted firmly on the ground. "You still haven't answered my question, by the way," I said, keeping my tone light as if we were having a casual conversation. "How exactly are you here? I mean, it can't just be to give me the world's most melodramatic sob story about your lost vengeance. I get it, being stuck in some dead zone for centuries probably sucks, but newsflash—I'm not your therapist."

I flashed a small, sarcastic smile, crossing my arms, daring him to keep this up.

For a moment, I could see the flicker of choler flash behind his eyes, but he quickly smoothed it over. "You think you're clever," he muttered, almost to himself.

"Clever enough to spot a few holes in your story," I retorted, tapping my chin as if I was deep in thought. "You say I owe you for what my ancestors did. Fine. But you've been stuck behind some veil for centuries, so I'm guessing you've just been waiting for someone to open the door for you, right?" I raised an eyebrow, almost amused. "That's a *really* long game plan. Not exactly my fault you're still stuck on the losing side."

I paused, eyeing him with a little more suspicion. "Wait, do you just pop up for all my ancestors, or am I extra special enough to get the royal treatment?" I tilted my head. "Because if this is your usual schtick, I'm starting to feel a little less unique here."

I could feel the air shift, but I didn't flinch. He was a threat, sure. But I wasn't about to play his game. Not when I had an advantage—no matter how small.

"Your mouth will be the death of you one of these days," he said, his voice dropping to an icy, bone-chilling tone. His form flickered once more, he was losing his grip on the reality he'd shaped around himself.

That was offensive. I happen to know many people who enjoy my sass. I didn't flinch. "Yeah, sure. Whatever," I muttered, keeping my stance steady.

There was a flicker of madness behind his icy blue eyes as it contracted a few times before he spoke again.

"Your blood... it's unlike the others. I can feel it. It *calls* to me in ways I didn't expect."

His words lingered, and for a moment, everything in the room seemed to go still. A strange, cold weight settled in my chest. The air had thickened around me. *Unlike the others? Was this why I couldn't get a handle on this training? What exactly was he inferring?*

My mind raced back to snippets of conversations I'd overheard as a child. My grandmother's arguments with my mother. The fact that I still couldn't figure out why my father wasn't on the family tree. At first, I thought it was because of my Grandmother Rose's disdain for who my mother chose to fall in love with. But how could anyone hate another that strongly simply for falling in love?

I felt a tightness in my throat. *My blood.* What had Mother been hiding? I mean, my mother's maiden name being Summers is just a coincidence, right? And my father's last name...

"I'm not sure what kind of twisted games you're playing," I said, though my voice was shaky now, my thoughts racing. "But I'm done with whatever's happening, ice prince. It's time for you to go."

His lips curled into a smile, but it wasn't one of victory. It was more a promise of something far worse. "Oh, little mortal," he purred, "You have no idea what you've gotten yourself into."

Before I could respond, he was gone. Disappeared into the shadows as easily as he'd appeared.

But his words lingered, curling in my mind like smoke, thick and suffocating. *My blood... unlike the others.* What had my family—my mother—gotten caught up in? Did she know about this? Or had she been just as blind to it all, just as much a pawn in this twisted mess of family drama and guardian nonsense as I was?

Closing the book that was still in my hand, I reached forward to snuff out the candles, each one hissing as I leaned over them.

I sat back onto a nearby chair, letting my hands rest in my lap.

I had felt that small pulse during the spell casting. It had to count for something, right? Maybe it was just the beginning. The first spark of magic was always the hardest to ignite, I told myself.

"Grandma Rose, you should have made this easier on me. I'm just a barista," I mumbled.

I replayed Frosty's words in my head. The spell wouldn't work on someone who had already crossed the threshold. So, did that mean he'd been *invited* in somehow? But by who? I hadn't had any visitors. No one had been through my door except for me—and the carpet shampooer. And honestly, I highly doubted Tim knew anything about ice-boy or whatever twisted history I had with him.

My logical mind insisted that somehow, it had to be my fault. But what *had* I done? I'd followed my grandmother's instructions to the letter, kept his name locked away, buried deep. The more I tried to piece it together, the more my brain throbbed. I was hitting a mental dead-end at full speed.

Did I accidentally summon a roommate when I was just thinking about getting a pet? No, that was *ridiculous*. I snorted, laughing out loud at how absurd the idea was. But honestly, with him lurking around, it wasn't doing wonders for my sanity.

Maybe I needed to try something simpler first—something that didn't require as much concentration. A little grounding, perhaps. Some basic spellwork to build up to something bigger.

With a sigh, I rose to my feet, brushing off the frustration that was beginning to settle in. I had come to fully take on my role as the next guardian of the realms, and part of that was learning magic, learning how to protect myself. But if tonight was any indication, it wasn't going to be as easy as I thought.

I stared at the candles, a flicker of determination rising in my chest. *It's just practice. I'll get it.*

CHAPTER 14

CALLIE

I woke up with a start, heart pounding, drenched in sweat. The remnants of the nightmare still clung to my mind like cobwebs, thick and suffocating. Another one. Another night of him—*the Frost King*—haunting my dreams.

But this time, it wasn't just his icy presence that unsettled me. It was what I'd seen, what I'd felt, buried deep in my bones as if I had been there.

I couldn't shake the image of him in battle. The way he moved, similar to a predator. Efficient. Relentless. Each strike with his sword carved a path through the enemy, blood and ice splattering in his wake. His eyes—cold, merciless, but *sharp*—never wavered. He didn't fight to win. He fought to dominate, to *break* everything that dared to challenge him.

I could see the way his form had flickered through the battlefield, his every motion so precise, so unnatural. The way the wind seemed to bow to his will, ice bending around him, whispering a quiet, bone-chilling respect. There was something disturbingly beautiful about it all—his power, his grace in destruction. He was a force of nature, a storm that couldn't be outrun or defeated.

I shook my head, pushing the thought away. But the phantom echoes of one of my previous dreams lingered beneath my skin. The way she had responded to him. The way she *wanted* him.

Running a hand down my face, I groaned and turned over.

No, stop it. You don't like him. You can't like him. This is just residual stuff from these weird dreams. It's not real.

But the image of his smile—no, not a smile, something darker, more twisted—haunted me. His lips had curled in a predatory grin as he stood over his fallen enemies. And in that moment, *he was everything*. He wasn't just a king. He was a hunter, a creature born to rule, to conquer, to break. Snow and blizzards whipped through the air, tangling his long, dark hair as he surveyed the kingdom he had reduced to its knees.

Why am I thinking this? I cursed myself silently, sitting up in bed and running a shaky hand through my hair. *What is wrong with me?*

I had to remind myself that I didn't know him other than what was warned. The visits I had were all tense and uncomfortable, leaving a lingering bad taste in my mouth. What started as simple, awkward encounters had somehow turned into something I hadn't anticipated. Every interaction with him left me more confused. He was a puzzle I couldn't quite piece together. It wasn't just his presence—

cold, unyielding, like the sharpest winter wind—it was something in the way he *looked* at me, as if he saw through every layer of pretense I'd carefully built.

I didn't know whether to feel anger, fear, or something else entirely.

All I knew was his arrogance, his threats, and what I saw in those dreams. My grandmother's journal never highlighted anything other than his title, the things he did and his position as a threat to the other courts in the realm. He was dangerous. A tyrant, a being of destruction. And I knew he wanted me dead. Or worse. And yet... I couldn't stop thinking about him.

It made no sense. He was a monster. But somehow, I couldn't push him out of my mind. Maybe it was his power that called to something in me. Maybe it was the way he controlled the world around him, like a man with absolute certainty, who knew he could have whatever he wanted—and *would* take it.

I shivered under the blankets, curling back into bed and pulling them up to my chin for comfort.

No. I needed to stop romanticizing him. The dreams were manipulating my mind and body's reactions. He was a nightmare, a reminder of everything my grandmother and ancestors had warned me about, of everything I should be avoiding.

Ugh!

Jumping out of bed, I forced myself to move, shaking the lingering dream from my limbs. My pulse was still too fast, too erratic, as if I had been running for miles. *This is just your mind playing tricks on you,* I told myself, but the whisper of the dream still lingered, darker than the room around me.

I grabbed my phone from the nightstand and glanced at the time. 3:42 AM. Of course. Another sleepless night.

I stumbled into the kitchen, needing something to ground myself. My eyes wandered over to the candles on the counter—the ones I had been trying to use to protect myself. I hadn't even finished that last spell; maybe I was just avoiding it because part of me didn't want to face what was coming. Or worse—*what he was already bringing.*

As I flicked on the kettle and waited for the hiss of boiling water, my mind wandered again, unwillingly, back to him.

He was a king, forged from ice and fury. But what would it be like to be under his rule? With an army at his back, didn't that mean he had commanded loyalty from across the lands? What made them follow him? What was it about him that inspired such unwavering allegiance?

I gritted my teeth, slamming my palm against the counter. *Stop it.* But the thought kept coming back. The more I tried to push it away, the clearer the image became— the Frost King, looming over me, standing tall as if he owned every inch of the world, every fragment of power.

And me? A mortal, a pawn in his game, someone who was meant to be *nothing* to him, yet somehow... I was.

I squeezed my eyes shut, forcing the vision of him back, the sounds of the battlefield still echoing in my mind, the clash of metal, the screams, the cold wind that seemed to rise whenever he moved. But then I remembered his eyes. The way they locked onto me in that instant. His cold gaze, yes, but... calculating. Measuring.

I felt the pull toward him, despite not being of his realm. A strange, magnetic connection that I couldn't explain. His words echoed in my mind—*something pulls us together.* It was unnerving.

He knew me—by name. And that was the part that unsettled me the most.

Could this be what my mother went through? How had she met my father, and why did they end up separating? I was too young to understand back then, but now, with the perspective of adulthood and everything I'd learned from my grandmother's journals, I started to piece things together. Yet, with every connection I made, more questions arose—questions no one seemed willing or able to answer.

"Your blood... it's unlike the others. I can feel it. It calls to me in ways I didn't expect."

I had to pull myself together. I couldn't let myself be dragged into his world. I couldn't. My only responsibility was to keep him locked away—neither here nor there—and prevent him from causing any more chaos.

But the more I fought it, the more his presence haunted me. I couldn't even get a decent night's sleep anymore without him twisting my dreams into something so real, so tangible, that I almost thought I was awake.

Was this his doing? Was it some extension of his powers? I refused to believe it. He still seemed powerless in his current form, nothing more than a lingering shadow of what he once was.

I swallowed hard, pushing the thoughts away. I wasn't going to let him take me over. Not mentally. Not physically. I wasn't some plaything for a king of ice. I had to remember that.

I took the kettle off the stove, poured the boiling water

into a mug, and stared down at it. The steam curled up, swirling like the icy mist from his dreams.

Get a grip, Callie. I muttered to myself, shaking my head. Seriously. What was I doing, freaking out over some ice king wannabe who couldn't even bother to show up in a solid form? If I was going to survive in this weird little town, I needed to stop letting my nerves get the best of me—especially over something that hadn't even made a real physical appearance. *Get it together, girl. You've dealt with far worse than this. Remember that time you tried to brew your own kombucha? This was nothing.*

But somewhere deep down, a part of me couldn't help but wonder... What would it be like to be one of his loyalists, to stand at his side in that frozen kingdom? To let go of all morality and follow a being bent on the destruction of everything? If I hypothetically allowed myself to fall into that cold, dark world with him, would I even make it out— or would I become just another lost soul, consumed by his madness?

I shook my head again, trying to shake off the thoughts. This wasn't me. This wasn't who I was. I wasn't some damsel waiting for some dark king to take me.

And yet... he had already crossed my threshold. And maybe, just maybe, I was already too far gone to avoid him.

I needed a break. Being stuck in my own head was slowly driving me mad, and the idea of another hour spent pacing around that quiet, creaky house was enough to make me lose it. So, I grabbed my jacket, slammed the door behind me, and grabbed a taxi to town. I headed straight toward the only place in town that could offer me any kind of distraction—the bookstore.

Odom's Books had a cozy, lived-in feel that immediately calmed me. It reminded me of my grandmother's study, just more open, less Frost King. The scent of aged paper and dust greeted me as I stepped inside, the musty air familiar and oddly comforting. The place was small, with narrow aisles lined with shelves that threatened to spill over, and the soft creak of floorboards under my feet made me feel as if I was walking through someone's private collection rather than a store.

There was something inherently peaceful about it, like stepping into another world—one where I didn't have to think about ice demons, family secrets, or whatever strange pull had started twisting in my chest ever since I set foot in this town.

I ran my fingers over the spines of the books as I drifted aimlessly, letting the titles guide me. I was searching for something light, something that wouldn't demand too much from me. But even as I tried to lose myself in a random paperback, I couldn't shake the feeling that I wasn't alone.

I turned a corner, and there she was.

Mrs. Lancaster, out of her grocery store uniform, on a day off.

"I didn't know you were off today," I quipped with a small smile.

"Ah, Callie." Mrs. Lancaster's voice was soft, familiar, as if she'd been waiting for this moment longer than I had. "I hope all the ingredients you've been stocking up means cooking has kept you busy. Maybe one of these days I'll come over and make something for you to give you a break."

"Oh, you don't have to do—"

She cut me off with a wave. "I insist. It's the least I can do for Rose's granddaughter. You've been holed up in that place too long, I was wondering when you'd find your way here."

I froze for just a second, my smile faltering as a knot twisted tight in my stomach. *What did she mean by that? How much more did she know?*

"Sooner or later, don't we all end up here?" I replied, keeping my voice even, but there was a slight edge to it now on the suspicious side. "We all need to get lost in another world once in a while."

Smooth, Callie. Way to drop hints. What are you doing right now?

"Indeed," Mrs. Lancaster said with a knowing smile that didn't quite reach her eyes. "One of my favorite places to be." She paused for a beat, as if savoring the moment before continuing, "Your grandmother often frequented this store as well. But I'm sure you knew that."

I didn't. And the fact that she seemed to know so much about Grandma Rose made my insides twist with something darker than curiosity—resentment. How could she have been so close to Grandma Rose, while my own mother and I were on the outside looking in? It didn't make sense. How had Grandma found camaraderie with everyone *except* her own flesh and blood?

She said she did it to protect us, but did she? Or was she just making emotional decisions in the heat of the moment, the same way I was now—dodging responsibility, giving in to the impulse to avoid the hard truths, even if only for a little while?

I wasn't blind. My family history was a tangled mess. But now, hearing Mrs. Lancaster speak so easily about my grandmother's visits here, it was another piece of the puzzle I didn't want to acknowledge had just been shoved into my face.

Stop it, Callie, I chided myself, forcing my mind back on track. *You're letting your emotions take over*. This was just *another* strange connection, another reminder that I was being pulled into something far bigger than I'd ever intended.

I glanced at the shelves, fingers tracing a spine idly, but all I could think of was Yk—the Frost King. What he had said. What he *hadn't* said. The way his presence seemed to infiltrate everything I thought I knew about my family.

He confirmed it, I thought, but it didn't help. Not really. The more I tried to suppress the questions, the louder they screamed. What else had my grandmother omitted from her final letter?

I blinked, not sure how to respond. Mrs. Lancaster's cryptic nature was almost more unnerving than her words. She spoke in riddles, but not *just* riddles. There was a strange, underlying truth to everything she said, as though she were dancing around some revelation that I wasn't ready for—or perhaps didn't even want to be ready for.

"I... I'm not sure what you mean," I said carefully, trying to keep the edge of suspicion from my voice.

She studied me for a moment, her expression unreadable, before she nodded to herself. "Oh, I think you do. But it's not the time yet. You'll find your answers. Just be careful where you go looking for them." Her eyes flicked briefly to the shelves of books around us. "Books can be a dangerous thing, you know."

Before I could respond, she turned and wandered off, as silently as she had appeared. I stood there for a moment, trying to shake off the unease that had settled in my chest.

"Is everything alright?"

I looked up and found myself face to face with the owner of the bookstore—James Hendrick, a man in his early forties with an easy smile and a laid-back charm.

Something brushed against my leg, making me jump. I spun around, only to see a black cat weaving around my feet before casually trotting off.

"Yeah, everything's fine," I said, forcing a smile. "Just... Mrs. Lancaster being herself, I guess."

James chuckled softly, but there was a flicker in his eyes —a brief shadow—that I couldn't quite place. "Ah, Mrs. Lancaster. She's got a way of... unsettling people, doesn't she? Hung around Rose too long and picked up her cryptic ways."

I raised an eyebrow, still processing what he'd said. "Seems like it."

He smiled, though it didn't quite reach his eyes, and then leaned against the counter, folding his arms with casual ease. "So, what brings you in today? Looking for anything in particular?"

I hesitated for a moment. What *was* I looking for? I wasn't sure what I was expecting to find, but I knew my curiosity had led me here. "I'm... curious about books on the fae," I said, testing the words as they left my mouth. It sounded ridiculous, even to me. But it was the truth.

His expression flickered again, this time more noticeably —as if he wasn't sure whether to take me seriously or not. After a pause, he finally spoke, his tone light, though his gaze seemed sharper now. "The fae, huh? They've become a pretty hot topic these days amongst romance readers. Sorry to say, I don't carry too many romances, but I do carry books on the myth."

I felt a sudden wave of relief wash over me as I realized James wasn't pushing for some deep, personal explanation.

"Yeah, just looking to entertain myself," I chuckled, my voice light.

He didn't press, just gave a short nod before sliding the book back toward me.

"Well, the fae are definitely different," he said, his voice lower, almost as if testing the air. "I'd say they're a bit... complicated."

I forced a nonchalant smile, the knot in my stomach tightening again. "Yeah, I'm sure."

But my mind wasn't on fae mythology anymore. It was on something else—the Frost King. The way he moved through my dreams, his presence so vivid, so... commanding. His words, his power, his gaze. As much as I tried to shake him off, to erase him from my thoughts, he was stuck to me like gum on a shoe, a silver tether pulling me back to him. *Great,* I thought. *Just what I needed. A centuries-old, ice-cold king haunting my dreams similar to some romantic hero out of a bad fantasy novel.*

Was this part of the guardian's abilities? Had I awakened something with my pitiful little attempts at spellwork? Maybe the universe decided to laugh at me and sent me a frosty nightmare king to spice up my already complicated life. I sighed inwardly. *Oh, yeah. This is exactly what I needed.* I tried to chalk it up to falling more into my "purpose"—as if that somehow made it less ridiculous. Shouldn't a guardian know when the veil was being messed with? I could just picture Grandma Rose, shaking her head at me from beyond the grave. *You're not ready*, she would say, which only made me want to prove her wrong more. Typical.

But oddly, as I thought about it, I stopped feeling as down about my failed attempts at spellcasting. Maybe this wasn't some fluke after all. Maybe this was part of the bigger picture, whatever that was. I'd been so focused on rushing things, trying to make the magic happen now, that I hadn't even considered that maybe I was trying to force something that needed more time to come into focus. *Or maybe I'm just trying to talk myself out of feeling like a total failure. Either way, it's not helping me right now.*

I shook my head, trying to clear it. There was no denying the pull of his presence, though. As much as I hated to admit it, the connection was real. And that, more than anything else, scared me.

CHAPTER 15

CALLIE

As I stood there, lost in the tangle of my thoughts, I didn't notice James watching me for a beat too long. When I finally snapped back to the present, I realized his gaze had softened just slightly.

He cleared his throat. "Everything alright? You seem... somewhere else."

I blinked, then forced a smile that didn't quite reach my eyes. *Right, play it cool, Callie. You've got this.*

"Yeah, of course," I said with a little too much enthusiasm, then added with a half-laugh, "Just, you know, contemplating the meaning of life and whether or not I can survive another week of work." I gestured vaguely at the book in my hand, hoping he wouldn't pry. "Thought I'd do some light reading to help me relax before the next work week starts."

I should start binge-watching shows again. I was sure it

would help take my mind off the nightmares. But of course, the spotty reception at my house turned every episode into a glitchy mess. It's as if the universe was conspiring to make sure I couldn't even escape into fictional disorder for five minutes without a technical hiccup.

James didn't look convinced. His brow arched, but he said nothing, just nodded slowly as if he knew I wasn't being entirely honest. Still, he didn't press.

"Right," he said, offering a small smile, though there was something in his eyes that suggested he wasn't entirely buying it. "Well, I hope the rest of your day goes well."

I bit back a chuckle. "That's the plan," I said, shaking the book in my hand before ringing it up.

I glanced around to see where the bookstore cat had gotten off to while James handed me my change, but I couldn't spot it anywhere. Maybe I'd imagined it—just my mind playing tricks on me, like it had a habit of doing these days. With a mental shrug, I turned to leave.

I stepped out into the cool afternoon air, the door chiming softly behind me as I made my way down the street. The walk to the hardware store wasn't far, just a few blocks, and I could use the walk to clear my head. I needed a new tire for my bike, another excuse to distract me. The Frost King's image still lingered at the edges of my thoughts like an unwelcome shadow. The hardware store's atmosphere was calm, not a lot of people browsing. As I walked toward the bicycle aisle, I spotted a familiar face in my periphery. Tim. Of course, out of uniform.

I sighed quietly, annoyed by his sudden appearance *again*. When did it become less of a coincidence and more of a calculation? He leaned against a shelf in the far aisle, looking impossibly at ease as he flipped through a small tool catalog. His posture was relaxed, but the moment I stepped closer, his eyes flicked up to meet mine, a smirk pulling at the corners of his lips.

"Well, well," he said, his voice smooth and casual. His gaze dropped to the bag in my hand, and he gave a small tilt of his head, as if it was all just too obvious. "I see you made a stop by the bookstore."

I couldn't help but roll my eyes. The last thing I needed today was another weird flirt session with him, but here we were.

"Yeah..." I walked past him to check out the bike tires, quickly making my selection.

"Do you need a hand with your bicycle?" he offered innocently, following close behind me.

"Not here to flirt," I said, keeping my tone light but firm, trying to keep my mind focused on tires and not whatever game he was playing. Lord knows I had enough on my mind these days.

"Flirt?" He raised an eyebrow, clearly not taking my words seriously. "I'm just making conversation, Callie. Not every guy who talks to you is trying to get in your good graces. Some of us are just genuinely curious."

I didn't buy it for a second. "Uh-huh. Sure."

I kept walking toward the register, ignoring him as best as I could. After my ex, I'd sworn off men for a while—figured I'd better get my life together before adding any more chaos. And now, with Grandma Rose's cryptic nonsense and the whole "Frost King" debacle, I was more than aware that getting my priorities straight was no longer optional.

He took a step closer, dropping his voice slightly, almost like he was sharing a secret. "So, what's the real reason you're in here? Trying to fix up that bike, or is there something else I can help you with?"

He glanced at the tools hanging on the nearby shelf with exaggerated interest, waiting for my reply.

I gave him a look that was more exasperated than anything. "I'm not looking for a mechanic. Just a tire."

His smile didn't falter, but there was a flicker in his eyes, a momentary shift that made me pause.

"I'll leave you to it then," he said, his voice dripping with that flirtatious undertone again, though it seemed just a little more serious now. "But I'll be around if you change your mind."

I forced a tight smile, resisting the urge to snap back with something equally pointed. "You do that."

He watched me for a moment before turning away, but not without that lingering glance that made me feel as if I was involved in a strange game he was playing that I wasn't privy to.

As I paid for the tire and headed out of the store, I couldn't shake the nagging feeling that Tim was hiding something—just like Mrs. Lancaster. Did they know each other? The thought made my stomach tighten. There was something off about both of them, something I couldn't quite put my finger on. And of course, they both had a way of talking as if they knew more than they were letting on. Great. Just what I needed—more cryptic weirdness added to the list.

The ride home in the cab was thankfully uneventful.

Once I fixed the bicycle, I would be saving money on rides to and from town.

Walking through my front door had become a mix of conflicting emotions. On one hand, there was relief—finally, home after work or an errand, a chance to unwind. On the other hand, there was the uneasy question if *he* might be waiting for me. Of course, it didn't really change anything. I still had to live here and be a guardian and all that.

After swapping out the tire and washing my hands in the kitchen, I headed straight for my grandmother's study again, making my way past the mirror in the living room.

I grabbed one of the spell books and flipped it open, scanning the pages with a little more urgency than I cared to admit. "There's got to be something simpler in here. Maybe a Protection Spells for Dummies or Protection Spells 101," I muttered to myself.

Or maybe there was a spell in here to help reduce the unwanted nightmares. Honestly, if I could stop dreaming about ice demons and shadowy kings long enough to get some decent sleep, I'd consider myself a winner. Maybe something to calm my nerves. Or better yet, a "How to Get Rid of Menacing Otherworldly Beings in Your Dreams for Dummies" guide. I'd buy that in a heartbeat.

I could practically hear Grandma Rose's voice in my head: "There are no shortcuts, Callie. You have to learn to master the craft." Yeah, well, easy for her to say when she had years of experience and didn't have some king of ice popping into her dreams every other night. Seriously, did he come with a subscription service, or was I just special?

According to him, you're special.

My face flamed. *Stop it.*

A spell for peaceful sleep sounded way more appealing than attempting permanent banishment. After all, if my ancestor couldn't pull it off, who was I to think I'd have better luck? She'd had years of experience with the craft, and *still* couldn't get rid of whatever the hell Ykazar was when he showed up. *No pressure, Callie. And stop thinking about his name.*

Right. Right.

I flipped the sage bundle I'd been drying over the candle, watching the smoke curl up in slow, delicate spirals. Was it ridiculous to feel guilty about wasting money on this? I could've used it for something practical—for instance, in soup. Or a new pair of shoes.

"I banish the thoughts that plague me," I said, trying to sound confident, though I was pretty sure I looked ridiculous. "I close the door on that which should not be... Like *him*."

I waved a hand dismissively toward the corner of the room, as if shooing away a bothersome fly.

As if on cue, the temperature dropped. My breath came out in a small puff of visible air, and I knew—*knew*—he was constantly watching me like the creep he was.

The candle flickered violently as the frigid air wrapped itself around me. I didn't even have to turn around to know who it was. I rolled my eyes without bothering to look.

"Of course," I muttered, turning slowly. Did I accidentally perform a summoning spell or something?

Frosty stood in the doorway, his tall, imposing figure outlined by the faint light from the windows. I was going to have to invest in some space heaters. His presence, as always, commanded the space, a storm on the verge of breaking. The frost didn't just cling to him—it radiated off him, settling into the air, coiling around me thickly.

He chuckled softly, the sound low and mocking, as though the very idea of a spell to banish him was laughable. "Do you truly think something so... simple would work on me? You should know by now, mortals like you cannot hope to control forces beyond your understanding."

He stepped closer, his gaze pressing down on me, his presence almost suffocating. "If you truly wish to do something that matters, look for a spell that addresses what you *really* want."

His lips curled into a smirk, and I felt my annoyance spike, quickly followed by a prickling sense of incompetence. Great. Just what I needed—another reminder that I had no idea what I was doing.

"You cannot sever the tie that binds us—the ties your ancestral bloodline put into play. But by all means, continue. It won't make any difference."

I threw my hands up in frustration, trying my best to look unaffected. "I was just trying to clear my head, alright? Not that you'd care."

I tried to sound nonchalant, pretending I didn't care that he was haunting my every thought. It was easier to act like I didn't than let him see how much he was getting under my skin. I had to play the clueless card now and then, just to keep him guessing. It was the best way to throw him off the trail without giving anything away.

His lips curled into an arrogant, knowing smile, one that made me want to smack it off his face. "A pitiful endeavor, truly," he intoned. "You would do better to seek the means to shatter the curse that binds me, little mortal. Not this... distraction."

"Yeah, well, I'm sure you want to be the most important thing in my life right now," I shot back, my sarcasm on full blast. Honestly, I was beyond pretending I wasn't slightly freaked out. "You know, if you're determined to become some sort of permanent fixture around here, I'm going to have to start charging you rent. Or at least a fee for all this extra, unnecessary annoyance. You could at least chill my drinks or something while you're hanging around, making a scene."

His eyes flickered with something dangerously close to amusement, but there was still that underlying ice—something sharp and lethal. "Such insolence," he snarled, voice dropping to a guttural growl. "I've annihilated entire legions for less."

Always with the empty threats.

I raised an eyebrow, crossing my arms, not entirely sure whether to be terrified or intrigued. "Uh-huh. And here I was, thinking you were just some overdramatic, ice-obsessed landlord. Maybe you should stick to melting snowbanks, Your Frostiness, instead of threatening me. I'm just trying to get some peace around here."

His gaze locked onto mine, cold yet oddly... *penetrating.* "You're not the one in control here, mortal," he said, voice low and full of dark amusement. "You never have been."

I mentally added "rude" to his ever-growing list of qualities—just in case I needed the reminder after the next nightmare. Because honestly, what was a little more annoyance when it came to the Frost King?

"Right. Got it. Thanks for the reminder," I said, turning away. "But seriously, maybe you should consider a hobby. You know, like knitting. Or, I don't know—existing without making my life ten times more complicated than it needs to be?"

I could practically hear the icy sneer in his voice as he replied, "Perhaps eternal imprisonment in your own madness would do you well, mortal. A lifetime spent clawing at your own thoughts, trapped in a world where reality fades to nothing—where every whisper you hear is your own fear, and every shadow is a reflection of your own madness. You might want to reconsider your attitude before you say something you can't take back."

I felt a chill creep up my spine as his words settled into the air, thick and heavy, a weight I couldn't ignore. It was always like this with him—he had this way of turning every conversation into something far darker and more unsettling than I was prepared for. And every time, I couldn't help but feel I was sinking into some sort of abyss I had no control over.

Things were getting way too intense for a Tuesday night.

I forced myself to break the silence with a sarcastic cough. "Well, that sounds *charming*," I said, my voice dripping with fake sweetness. "I'll be sure to keep my attitude in check. Wouldn't want to accidentally end up as a guest in your personal hell, right?"

His eyes flashed, the frost flickering in them. But I wasn't about to let him get the last word on this one.

"Anyway," I added, trying to steer the conversation somewhere I might be able to control, "I mean, with all this time in eternal limbo and all, I'm sure there's something you could take up. Knitting? Stamp collecting? I hear knitting is a great stress reliever."

I half-expected him to snap at me again, but instead, there was a beat of silence. His expression shifted—just slightly, but enough for me to catch the flicker of something... almost human? Maybe? But I wasn't holding my breath. He could've just been plotting my demise in his head.

Still, I wasn't going to let this turn into another one of his ominous rants. No way.

"So, what about it, Ice King?" I continued, crossing my arms like I was negotiating with a toddler. "What's it gonna be? You want to keep threatening me, or do you want to talk about your hobbies? Maybe give me some book recommendations? You know, aside from 'How to Destroy an Entire Family Line 101'?"

His eyes narrowed again, but the edge was gone. For a second, just a second, I could almost believe that maybe I wasn't totally losing it here. But knowing him, that'd probably just make the next time we talked even weirder.

I shot him a pointed look. "Oh, I'm sure *you* can take it back, no problem, right? Because, you know, you're all-powerful and stuff." I threw in some air quotes for extra effect, half-expecting him to lose his composure.

You're on a roll, Callie, best be careful. He might really back up his threats after all and you haven't been able to perform a spell successfully.

To my surprise, he didn't flinch. Instead, he took a slow, deliberate step closer, his presence heavy in the air, making my heart stutter in my chest. "This is not about power," he said, his voice low and unyielding, "but inevitability."

He let the words hang there, an ominous promise, and I had to force myself not to take a step back. Not that it would've done any good. I couldn't outrun a being who could bend reality itself. But still... it felt as if he was inching closer to crossing some unspoken line, and it made me *uncomfortably* aware of how very out of my depth I was.

"Yeah, well," I shot back, trying to mask my growing unease, "I'm sure you're all about fate and destiny and whatever, and yet, here I am, standing—*mostly*—unfrozen in your presence. I think you're losing your touch, Ice King. You're all talk and no... *chill.*"

His gaze darkened, and something flickered in his eyes —a storm building, barely contained. He took another slow step forward, closing the distance between us, his cold presence somehow bending the space to his will.

"You have no idea what your ancestors unleashed," he said, his voice now a deep rumble. "The realms were never meant to be governed by those who cower behind veils and half-measures. I was *born* to rule, not to be locked away like some forgotten relic." His eyes narrowed, lips curling into a smirk. "But your bloodline... they thought they could contain me. They couldn't *comprehend* what they were doing when they trapped me."

He took another step, closing the gap between us until I could feel the chill radiating off him. How was this even possible? He still wasn't fully corporeal, not in the way a living being should be. But there it was, that unmistakable presence—his coldness pressing against me, as though he were standing right beside me in the flesh. Was it the guardian role, I wondered, that heightened my awareness of him? Was it my role—whatever that meant—that made me more attuned to his existence, even if he wasn't fully here?

I tried to push the thought away, but it lingered. How much of this was real, and how much was... *something else?*

"But you," he continued, his voice dropping low, almost coaxing, "you'll understand eventually. The pull... it's already there, isn't it? That connection between us. You can deny it all you want, but I know you feel it."

He reached out a hand, just inches from mine, his fingers twitching, daring me to make the first move. "It's not a matter of *if*, it's a matter of *when*. You will come to understand why it's meant to be this way. And when you do..."

I couldn't help but watch his fingers hovering so close to mine, inviting me to do something stupid. My heart kicked up a notch, but I wasn't about to let him see me squirm.

His words, though... *when*? Oh, great, now he was talking similar to some mystical therapist from hell. This guy would give psychologists a run for their money—more like *psychosomatic terror*, maybe. You know, that perfect mix of "I'm going to ruin your life" and "Trust me, you'll come around to my way of thinking."

Honestly, I wasn't sure which was worse—being afraid of him or his insane amount of confidence that I'd eventually buy whatever nonsense he was selling.

And, somehow, I could feel it—that tight, invisible pull he spoke of, the one I didn't know how to break free from, even if I wanted to.

I pushed the thought aside, keeping my eyes on his outstretched hand. If he thought I was going to play into whatever manipulation he had cooked up, he was sorely mistaken.

His voice trailed off, but the weight of his words was unmistakable. He was arrogantly *certain*—certain that somehow, some way, I would be drawn into his orbit.

CHAPTER 16

YKAZAR

The world outside had changed immeasurably since my entombment. The vibrant hues of life that I once knew had dulled to an oppressive gray, filled with the scent of decay and whispers of forgotten dreams. Yet, here I lingered, a specter in the shadows, watching the living move about their trivial lives. And among them was her—the one who bore the sins of her bloodline, the descendant of the woman who had condemned me to this fate.

Callie. The name felt foreign, yet it rolled off my tongue with a bitter familiarity. She was unaware of the weight she carried, the legacy that bound her to my anguish. As I watched her, the tangled web of my vengeance tightened around my heart, threading its way into every thought.

In the dim light of her gothic home, I observed her every movement—how she rubbed her temples, wearied by the remnants of the day. Her brow furrowed in concentration as she pored over the relics of her grandmother's life, searching for answers in the dusty tomes. Such a futile pursuit, I mused. She had no idea the depths of the darkness she was entangled in.

A blackness that continued to haunt me, pulling my mind back into the madness that kept me company for centuries.

Yet, one barrier remained: the one who held me beneath the thumb of a Summer court bloodline, the ancestral curse that still clung to my soul like a shadow. Now, I was one with the shadows, watching Callie as she moved through her day, a lingering presence bound to the very lineage that had imprisoned me.

She would soon learn the price of her ancestors' sins, and I would ensure that her family line felt the consequences of their actions. The echoes of my vengeance thrummed in my veins, a promise of reckoning that would soon unfold.

I felt the stirrings of anger rise within me, a tempest raging against the wrongs of her forebears. They had sealed my fate in a prison of stone and shadows, and now their lineage danced unawares in the sunlight. They lived, while I rotted in the dark. But vengeance would not be mine if I could not convince her to free me first.

As she brushed the dust off a weathered tome, I noted the flicker of determination in her eyes, a spark that reminded me of *her*. If only she knew that this was merely the beginning of her trials, a warm-up to the reckoning I had planned for her bloodline.

My thoughts twisted with the images of the past, memories of betrayal and fury, yet I forced myself to remain focused. She needed to be guided. Convincing her was imperative. I needed her to understand that the weight of those before her was not merely a burden but an *opportunity* —a means to release me from this eternal prison.

And that required careful manipulation.

I had humored her enough. The time for these verbal games was over.

It was then that the doorbell rang, shattering my dark reverie. Callie, startled from her contemplation, straightened, set down the tome, and headed toward the door. A flicker of annoyance struck me. Who dared intrude upon this moment? My ire grew as I felt the presence of another, a living being I did not wish to witness.

The door creaked open to reveal an elderly woman, her arms laden with what appeared to be some sort of edible concoction and various baked goods—a welcome home gift, I surmised. A gesture of kindness that felt wholly unnecessary and infuriating in its triviality.

"Hello, dear!" the old woman exclaimed, her voice bright and cheery. "I brought you some food! Thought you might need a little something to tide you over from the last grocery shop you did."

I scowled. She didn't need to remind me of Callie and her freedom beyond these walls while I remained trapped among the cobwebs she so eagerly tried to sweep away.

Callie smiled politely, yet I could sense her internal struggle, the yearning to refuse the intrusion weighed against the ingrained politeness of society. I wanted to shout at her, to remind her of the urgency of her situation. Yet here she was, entertaining a distraction, wasting precious moments while I lingered in torment.

"Thank you, that's so kind of you," Callie replied, her voice steady yet tinged with an undercurrent of hesitation. I could see her mind wrestling between the importance of her mission and the allure of companionship—a struggle I found utterly amusing.

As the gray-haired woman stepped inside, I observed how she flitted around the room, her presence filling the space with warmth and noise, a stark contrast to my cold, silent existence. She gestured to the rooms around her with familiarity, chatting away about the neighborhood and how she hoped Callie would settle in well. Each word, each laugh, was a knife in my side, a reminder of the existence I had been stripped of.

"Why waste time with this?" I grumbled inwardly, clenching my fists as I paced the dark corner of the room, unseen yet burning with a desire to intervene, to shake Callie of her nonsense.

She should be searching for a way to break the curse, not engaging in trivial banter. My thoughts spiraled into frustration. The phantom sensation of my torn flesh itched, a constant reminder of all I had endured and the suffering that lingered in my memories. I could almost feel the weight of the generations urging me to act, to influence her, to ignite the fire of vengeance I so desperately craved.

Yet, as I watched, a flicker of something unexpected tugged at the edges of my rage—curiosity. I found myself drawn to Callie in a way I had not anticipated. It was not just the desire for revenge that compelled me to watch her; there was a thread of fascination woven through my ire.

I could easily blame it on her attempted spells, but the thought was laughable—she hadn't even come close to mastering any of them. She was too easily distracted by outside sources.

What was it about her that made me linger, to observe? She was a reflection of the past and yet she seemed so painfully unaware of the role she was destined to play.

As the old woman continued to chatter, Callie smiled and nodded, but I could see the flicker of impatience in her eyes. The warmth of the moment felt alien to me, a reminder of everything I had lost. Amidst my fury, I couldn't shake the strange sensation that enveloped me. It was a revolting feeling, really.

But this was no time for reflection or sentimentality. I had to remain focused. The longer she entertained this distraction, the further she drifted from the path I needed her to take.

The old woman settled into a chair, clearly intent on staying for a while. I felt the heat of my anger flare once more.

"Get to the point, woman! Leave her be!" I seethed internally, my frustration mounting with each passing moment.

"Do you have any plans for dinner tonight?" the woman asked brightly, and my patience snapped. Callie's eyes drifted toward the study, and I could practically hear the thoughts turning in her mind, a battle between hospitality and the weight of her ancestral duty.

"I—I'm not sure yet," Callie replied hesitantly, her voice betraying her inner conflict. "I have some things to—"

"Why don't you come over for dinner instead?" the woman interrupted, blissfully unaware of the storm brewing around us. "It's just a simple meal, but it would be lovely to have you. I make the best chicken pot pie."

The suggestion loomed, tightening around my chest. "No!" I wanted to scream. "You have more important matters to attend to!"

But Callie's expression softened, and I could see the battle in her eyes. She was torn between her desire for solitude and the warmth of community that the old woman offered.

"That sounds... nice," she finally said, and I felt the tide of my acrimony rise.

"Why are you doing this?" I wondered, shaking my head as if I could physically dislodge the absurdity of the moment. "You should be unraveling the mystery of your lineage and your abilities, not engaging in petty social niceties!"

As they continued to chat, I fell deeper into the shadows, wrestling with a tempest of emotions that twisted like vines around my mind. Anger surged through me, a violent tide crashing against the walls of my confinement, but beneath it lurked something darker—a maddening sense of possessiveness that clawed at my insides.

How dare she waste her time on trivialities? Each laugh from her lips a dagger in my flesh. I could almost taste the bitterness of my envy. My thoughts spiraled, wild and chaotic, a cacophony of "She should be focused on me!" that echoed relentlessly in the recesses of my mind. I wanted to lunge forward, to shake her from her ignorance, to make her see the gravity of what was at stake.

Yet there I was, a shadow bound by chains, seething as the woman continued to invite her in, oblivious to the madness unfurling in the dark. The absurdity of it all twisted like a blade; here I was, a tortured soul craving vengeance, and all I could do was watch as she entertained the idea of a cozy dinner.

The plan began to form in my mind—a way to twist her curiosity into an opportunity. I needed her focused on me, on the curse that bound me. Perhaps I could use this moment to plant the seeds of doubt, to instill a sense of urgency in her.

"Callie," I murmured behind her ear, my voice barely a breath against the air as I continued to hide in the shadows, "you must seek the truth. You cannot ignore your destiny."

The old woman paused mid-sentence, glancing around the room as if she had heard something. My heart raced. Had I manifested too soon?

"Did you hear that?" she asked, her brows furrowing with concern.

Callie glanced at her, then shook her head, a puzzled expression crossing her face. "No, I didn't hear anything." But something in the old woman's eyes—a flicker of recognition, perhaps?—made my suspicion itch like a festered wound.

What was she hiding? I couldn't shake the feeling that this woman was more than just a friendly neighbor. Her overly sweet demeanor, and her insistence on bringing food, all felt calculated. My instincts screamed that she knew more than she let on, that there was a hidden agenda lurking beneath the surface of her kind facade. What if she was part of the very curse that bound me?

"Just my old bones creaking, I suppose," the woman laughed awkwardly, but I sensed the tension in the air.

As they resumed their mundane chatter, I felt the darkness within me stir, a mixture of fury and unease. I couldn't let my guard down—not now. If Callie was to uncover her truth, she needed to be wary of those who cloaked their motives in kindness.

I took a breath, steadying myself as I made my way to her side. Inhaling her scent into memory, I whispered, "Now is the moment, Callie. You must feel it—the weight of your ancestors pressing upon you."

And for a brief moment, her expression shifted, a shadow crossing her features as if she had felt the chill of my words. I pressed on, desperate to keep her attention.

"Don't let distractions hold you back. You are the key to breaking the curse. You can free me."

Yet even as I spoke, I felt the irritation simmering in my chest. This woman, this sweet old lady, had become an obstacle to my vengeance. How dare she intrude upon what should have been an awakening of purpose!

With every moment that passed, the old woman continued to prattle on, oblivious to the tension brewing in the room. Callie nodded along, but her gaze drifted toward the direction of her grandmother's study and the remnants of her forgotten past.

A fire ignited within me, a resolve to make my presence felt, to stoke the flames of her curiosity and dread. I would not let her waste this opportunity.

"Callie," I whispered, the words curling like smoke in the air, "do not forget your heritage. You carry the weight of generations. They have wronged me, and you must make it right."

The old woman fidgeted in her seat, her gaze skimming the room until it caught on my lurking presence. In that instant, my lividity ignited, surging through me, impossible to restrain.

Enough of this nonsense!

The doors flew open with a thunderous crash, sending a gust of cold air and snow swirling into the room. I watched with twisted satisfaction as the old woman yelped, and ran out of the house, stumbling in fear.

I had waited for centuries, tangled in a web of rage and regret, the threads of my existence coiling tighter around me with each passing year. The world had changed, as had its people, but the curse—*my* curse—remained. The agony of it gnawed at my insides, ever-present, until Callie. She was the one who could break it. She was the one I had been waiting for.

And yet, there she stood, trembling before me, her wide eyes filled with confusion and fear. I could feel her pulse quicken, hear her shallow breaths, as if she could outrun what was happening.

She couldn't. None of them ever could.

I made my move, letting my presence manifest further, but it wasn't enough. I'd expected fear, but not this. She stood there with her hand hovering over her chest. I could feel her heart racing. She was on the verge of losing herself to the abyss I had been leading her toward.

But there was no turning back. Not anymore.

"Stop wasting time, Callie." My voice was cold, hard, and I watched with twisted satisfaction as she jumped.

She whipped around, eyes wide, her breath catching as she tried to make sense of what was happening. *I* had been in her peripheral vision, a whispering shadow, a presence lurking in the dark, but now—now, I was all there was. She couldn't avoid me anymore.

I hungered for her fear.

Her fingers twitched as though trying to reach for something, anything, to ground herself. "What—"

"Enough." My patience was thin, stretched far too thin. "You do not have time to ask questions you already know the answers to."

The words cut through the air, sharp and unforgiving. She recoiled slightly, but it didn't stop the tremors in her hands or the unease that spread across her features.

But in a split second, it was like her fears had vanished—but I knew better. It was one of her quirks. She masked her fear with anger and jokes, her metaphorical shield she hides behind.

"Are you going to stand there all day making ominous speeches, or are you gonna tell me what is going on here?" she snapped, trying to regain some semblance of control.

If I thought her fear would satisfy my hunger, I was mistaken. It was nothing compared to the hidden fire burning beneath the surface.

I circled her, eyes locked on the subtle way her body tensed with each step I took. "You should be afraid," I murmured.

The air between us was thick, suffocating, but she refused to back down. It was an admirable trait, one that ran through her bloodline—*a trait* that had cost me everything.

She rolled her eyes, and I couldn't help the grin that spread across my face. "Afraid?" she shot back, her voice thick with sarcasm. "Buddy, I'm one bad joke away from completely losing it." She crossed her arms. "Look, I've got enough weirdness in my life already. I don't need you showing up uninvited *again* and making my social calendar even more nonexistent than it already is. These random visits are becoming annoying, to say the least."

I laughed, dark and bitter. "You still think you have the luxury of denying it? Your bloodline is soaked in it, Callie. The truth, the power, the curse—*all of it* is yours. Stop running from it."

She snorted. "Please. I'm *great* at outrunning things. I've been dodging responsibility for years. No offense, but your little 'destiny' doesn't exactly seem like the kind of thing I want to catch."

I took a step closer, the air around us growing colder. "You mock me now," I said, my voice low, "but you'll learn. Some things are so entwined that not even fate itself can tear them apart."

Her eyes widened, and she took another step back, a movement that stirred the predator inside me. Did she have any idea that every step she took away from me only drew me closer? She knew more than what she was letting up. She was playing a game of her own and it thrilled the predator inside of me.

"You don't know what you're talking about," Her face flushed, eyes snapping with a mixture of defiance and desperation.

"Your ancestors made you see it," I growled, stepping closer, my presence pressing down on her. "You are not the first to carry this burden, Callie. But you are the only one left who can end it."

I watched as her delicate throat bobbed, her gaze briefly flicking to my lips before quickly darting away.

"Look, I've got a candle to light and a whole bunch of other more important things to do, so if you'll excuse me—"

The room grew colder, and for a brief moment, the lights flickered. I cornered her against another wall, leaning in so close that my ear brushed against her skin. Her breath, soft and shaky, ghosted across my neck. "You cannot run from me forever."

Her eyes locked onto mine, and for a brief moment, I saw it—the hesitation, the doubt, the slow, dawning realization that maybe the truth was standing right in front of her. But then, just as quickly, the defiance flared back to life. She pressed herself harder against the wall, chin lifted in that stubborn, infuriating way that was starting to drive me mad.

"I don't care who you think you are, or what you want from me, but you are *not* going to order me around like some—"

"Like some *what*?" My words were icy, laced with venom, the kind of venom that had festered for centuries. "A servant? A slave? A tool? Is that what you think I want from you? You think I'll use you and throw you away?"

I raised my hand, letting my knuckle hover just above her skin, barely brushing the air as I traced the line of her jaw without ever making contact.

"Maybe I don't care," she retorted, but I could see the spark of curiosity flickering in her eyes. It made my blood boil, but in a way I hadn't expected and it irritated me to my very core.

I chuckled darkly. "You will get it, Callie. And you will break it—whether you want to or not."

Her breath hitched again, and I felt myself falter. Was

this some kind of spell? The very idea that she could have any control over me, however slight, sent a jolt of unease through my veins.

She darted away from the wall, feigning to pick up something off the floor, all while putting as much distance between us as she could.

I watched her with amusement, the distance between us growing thicker with each breath. She thought she could outrun this, could push me away with the way she wielded her words, but I could feel it—*she couldn't escape.* Not anymore.

CHAPTER 17

CALLIE

The next day, I stared at the journal in my hands, my mind still reeling from the last encounter with Sir Frost-a-lot. The leather-bound book, once supple, was frozen shut somehow as I tried to pry it open.

"Come on, you darn paperweight," I muttered, banging the book against the desk to try and knock off some of the frost. "Spill your secrets already!"

"Such disrespect for knowledge," a chilling voice said from behind me. "Perhaps I overestimated your worth, *mortal.*"

I whirled around, nearly dropping the journal I had been clutching. There he was again, the Frost King, looking as annoyingly majestic and terrifying as before. Even the scowl on his face was irritatingly enamoring.

And he was back to calling me mortal instead of my

name. I was glad for it. I didn't know if I could handle the intensity with which my name rolled off his tongue.

His silhouette continued to flicker in and out of the shadows, a nightmare refusing to be fully formed. The air around him shimmered with an otherworldly cold that sent shivers racing down my spine, leaving me acutely aware of my flannel pajamas—far from suitable armor against his frosty demeanor.

"Oh, it's you again," I said, aiming for nonchalance but probably hitting somewhere closer to 'mildly panicked'. "Didn't anyone ever teach you to knock? Or, you know, stay imprisoned in whatever magical ice cube you came from?"

His eyes narrowed, frost spreading across the floor from where he stood. "You dare continue to speak to me with such insolence?"

I raised an eyebrow, trying to hide the growing fear of the way he made me feel. "Uh, yes?"

For a moment, he looked so genuinely offended that I almost felt bad.

Almost.

"I have brought empires to their knees, frozen oceans with a mere thought. I am—"

"Yeah, I get it," I interrupted, waving a hand dismissively.

I would be lying if I said annoying him didn't tickle some part of me. Was it wrong of me to be attracted to his scowls and irritation? I was always in a state of confusion when he was around and that made me uneasy.

"You're a big deal in the ice cube tray."

I was acutely aware of a few things at that moment.

His face contorted with vexation, and the temperature

dropped so low I could see my breath. During our verbal sparring, I made a conscious effort to ignore the madness lurking behind his eyes, determined not to let him see that it was getting to me. It was possible that one day, my words could lead to my death by hypothermia.

"Insolent female!" he snapped, finally dropping the mask he'd been wearing. His voice was sharp, icy with barely contained fury, and the title made my skin prickle, though I forced myself to pretend I didn't care. "The world will once again know the true meaning of winter's wrath."

As his words echoed through the icy air. Something happened the other day during Mrs. Lancaster's visit, something I couldn't understand quite yet. Speaking of which, I needed to apologize to her for how things went down. Eventually. When I had the chance.

The intensity of his rage was palpable, a storm brewing just beneath the surface. What did it mean for someone like him to hold such power? I felt a surge of doubt creeping in. Did I really possess the ability to hold such a force at bay?

But true to who I was, in weird situations such as this, I couldn't help what happened next.

I laughed.

"Okay, Ice Queen, deep breaths. No need to be so dramatic."

He hesitated and I began to wonder if my deflection tactics would allow me to live to see another day after all.

He stepped closer, towering over me with a confidence that was becoming unsettlingly familiar. His presence seemed to freeze the air between us, a cold that wasn't just temperature but something deeper, heavier. When he spoke again, his voice dropped an octave, the tone sending a shiver through me that had nothing to do with the temperature.

"Search your blood, your memories. The knowledge is there, buried deep. Speak it, Callie. Speak my name and set me free."

This ice demon was giving me emotional whiplash worse than a car crash. One minute, he was an arrogant, condescending jerk, and the next, he was practically begging me for... what? To say his name? Was he trying to guilt-trip me into freeing him? Oh, and let's not forget the whole "my bloodline bound me, now I want revenge" spiel.

What a mess.

Who needed to binge TV shows when my life was practically a season of drama on its own?

I took a step back, bumping into the desk, my nerves a bit shaken. It was something that was happening more often than it should. "Yeah, no. That sounds like a terrible idea. How about we stick with something simple? I'll call you... Bob. You look like a Bob."

"Bob?" he sputtered as he shook with indignation. "You dare reduce me to such a common moniker?"

Who says this kind of stuff?

It was his fault I was feeling this way. Didn't he realize that his seriousness and dramatic comebacks just fueled my inner snark?

I shrugged and crossed my arms, hoping I came off confident rather than trying to protect myself. "Would you prefer Icicle? Frostbite? Ooh, how about Icey-shiver-me-timbers? That last one might be a bit of a mouthful."

His hand shot out, grabbing my wrist as he pulled me

closer to his face. The cold of his touch burned, and I gasped, catching me off guard.

"I grow tired of these games, little mortal."

I tried to pull away, but his grip was like iron. Coolness radiated from his skin. This close, he smelled lightly of freshly fallen snow.

"Why?" I demanded. "Why me? Why now?"

We were going in circles and I knew it.

For a brief moment, his fierce expression wavered, giving way to something almost vulnerable. The hard lines of his face softened, and I caught a glimpse of uncertainty in his eyes, a flicker that contrasted sharply with his earlier rage. It was as if the armor he wore so proudly had cracked, revealing a glimpse of the man beneath. But just as quickly as it appeared, the moment vanished, replaced again by the storm brewing in his gaze. I was left wondering if I had imagined it all.

What happened to you?

Stop it, Callie. Who cares what happened to him? He's all but admitted what he's going to do once he's free.

"The blood of the one who bound me flows through your veins," he said, his voice thick with ancient bitterness. "You haunt this place, dangling freedom just out of reach. Just like your ancestors, you torment me—but with you, it's far worse. It's why only *you* can undo what was done."

I blinked, processing this. The shift in his expression had caught me off guard, leaving me momentarily disoriented. The certainty of what he was saying weighed heavily on me, though I tried not to show it. This push and pull was a dangerous game, and I wasn't sure if I was ready to play.

After our last tense encounter, I finally had a moment to

regain my bearings. He intimidated me more than any person I had ever encountered. I wasn't going to admit that I had needed at least a day to recover from the whirlwind of emotions he put me through.

"So, what you're saying is," I began slowly, "my family kicked your icy behind, and now you need me to undo their hard work? Sorry, but I'm not in the habit of undoing my ancestors' achievements. Especially when those achievements involve keeping scary frost pops locked up."

He released my wrist, turning away with a growl of frustration. His reactions to my quirks shouldn't have drawn me the way they did, but here we were at a strange impasse.

"You do not understand the forces at play here. The balance of power, the fate of realms beyond your comprehension."

And in the blink of an eye, he was back to his usual condescending tone. I resisted the urge to roll my eyes, but something about the way he spoke, all dripping with bitterness and ancient resentment, made me wonder if maybe— just maybe—he wasn't the only one with some weird coping mechanisms. It created this bizarre, uncomfortable camaraderie between us that I really didn't want to unpack.

"You're right, I don't understand," I admitted. "All I know is that you show up, uninvited, start making demands and threats, and expect me to just go along with your 'free the ancient evil' plan. From where I'm standing, that makes you the bad guy in this story."

He whirled back to face me, his eyes blazing with an ethereal blue light, captivating me. "I *am* the 'bad guy' in this tale, foolish girl. I am a force of nature, as essential to the balance of the world as the sun or the sea."

Despite the hammering of my heart, I couldn't decide whether to be scared or just mildly entertained by his theatrics.

"A force of nature, huh?" I needled him further, not fully understanding my own reaction to him. "So, what, you're like global warming, but in reverse?"

His jaw clenched, and I swear I could hear ice cracking somewhere in the distance, making me straighten. "Your ignorance is matched only by your insolence. I have led armies that would make your mightiest warriors tremble. I have shaped the very face of the world with my power."

I crossed my arms once again, trying to look unimpressed while ignoring the way my teeth were chattering. "Uh-huh. And yet here you are, begging for help from a 'foolish girl'. Not very mighty of you, is it? I mean, if you're so powerful, why can't you free yourself?"

The air around us crackled with unsettling cold energy, and frost patterns swirled across the walls—intricate, icy tattoos, a chilling reminder of the power he wielded. My heart raced, caught between fear and a strange thrill, as I braced myself for the worst.

But then, surprisingly, he seemed to deflate slightly, as if the storm brewing inside him had suddenly lost its strength. The blazing intensity in his eyes flickered, dimming to something less volatile. It was a stark contrast to the icy atmosphere, and I felt a strange mix of relief and confusion wash over me.

What was happening? Had I imagined the shift in his demeanor, or had I accidentally struck a nerve? I couldn't help but wonder what was hiding beneath that icy exterior —what had shaped him into this. The warrior from my nightmares, the one who seemed unstoppable, had been reduced to this... a prisoner of his own madness.

"The magic that binds me is... complex," he admitted, his voice low and filled with a bitterness that seemed ancient. "It uses my own power against me. The stronger I become, the more securely I am trapped."

Despite myself, I felt a twinge of sympathy. Being trapped by your own strength? That sounded awful. But then I remembered the way he'd threatened me, the casual cruelty in his eyes, and I hardened my heart.

"That sounds truly tragic," I said, my voice dripping with faux sympathy. "Have you tried yoga? I hear it's great for working out the kinks."

Once the words left my mouth, my face flushed at the accidental double entendre.

He stared at me, bewilderment replacing anger for a moment. "You mock me still? Even knowing what I am capable of?"

I shrugged, trying to project a confidence I didn't feel. "What can I say? You haven't done anything to me yet, apart from giving me a seriously bad case of goosebumps."

A slow, cold smile spread across his face and I blinked a few times to stop myself from getting distracted.

"I simply need you to speak my name," he purred, his voice slipping into something darker, almost hypnotic. "To acknowledge me, to give me life once more. Just a word from your lips, and I will be free from this suffocating silence. You, Callie, have the power to undo the chains that bind me —don't you see? It's all within your grasp. One word. One whisper... and everything changes."

His gaze sharpened, cold and calculating, as if he could

already taste the fear curling in my chest. "What are you so afraid of, Callie?" he murmured, his voice low and velvety with menace. "You carry the bloodline of those before you. By freeing me, I would owe you—be bound to you. Under your control."

He took a step closer, and despite myself, I felt a shiver crawl down my spine. "Doesn't that tempt you? To hold my fate in your hands, to bend me to your will? To finally wield the power your ancestors only dreamed of?"

He shouldn't be as seductive as he was. How could a person strike both fear and intrigue at the same time?

The words slithered into my thoughts, dark and enticing, wrapping themselves around the edges of my mind. I wanted to scoff, to dismiss him outright, but something about the way he spoke made my heart beat a little too fast.

"Control you?" I forced the words out, my voice a little sharper than I intended, though I wasn't sure if it was out of defiance or fear. "I don't even have control of my own life right now, let alone whatever *this* is."

I gestured vaguely at the air between us, trying to make my point, but it felt weak, like I was grasping at straws. His eyes glittered, an ancient gleam of amusement flickering in the depths of his cold stare.

I couldn't shake the feeling that he was somehow reading my thoughts, unraveling my doubts just by looking at me. My reactions around him irritated me and I think he knew it.

He turned to me and began to circle around the journals, speaking in a much calmer tone than when we started. "It is your duty to break the curse. Your destiny. I would be free to reclaim my rightful place in the world. To bring back the glory of the eternal winter, to reshape this soft, weak world into something stronger," he paused, his eyes flicking to mine for a moment, "more beautiful."

I raised an eyebrow, skepticism bubbling to the surface despite the way his choice of words made me feel.

"Stronger and more beautiful?" I echoed, unable to hide the bite in my tone.

His vision of an eternal winter sounded more of a bleak, frozen wasteland than a masterpiece of strength and beauty. Who was he to decide what made the world beautiful? Did he truly think a landscape of ice and desolation could rival the warmth of life and growth?

His fervor was almost contagious, and part of me was intrigued by his passion. But I couldn't ignore the chilling implications of his words. He envisioned a world where beauty thrived in frost and shadows, one where the sun's light was banished, leaving only an endless winter.

I sighed. "Uh-huh. And where do I fit into this winter wonderland of yours? Because I've got to tell you, I'm more of a beach vacation kind of girl."

He reached out, and I had to resist the urge to flinch, bracing myself for him to grab my wrist again. But this time, his movements slowed, and his cold fingers brushed against my cheek. A shiver ran through me, and I mentally berated myself.

"You would have a place of honor, of course. The one who freed me, who saw my true worth when others sought to keep me chained. You could rule by my side, Callie Winters," he whispered, tilting his head. "Imagine it— endless power, eternal youth, the world reshaped to your desires."

My lips slightly parted, caught off guard by the intensity of his words. For a moment—just a moment—I was tempted. The image he painted was undeniably seductive, a vision of power and beauty that tugged at something deep within me. I could almost physically see it: a world cloaked in shimmering frost, every surface glistening, a landscape both haunting and breathtaking.

It was as if I was watching it in high definition.

But then reality crashed back in, pulling me from that enticing reverie. I thought of the world I knew—a world of warmth and change, where life blossomed in vibrant colors and the sun coaxed flowers from the earth. It was a place filled with laughter, with the gentle hum of nature thriving in all its messy glory. The thought of that world flickered like a beacon in my mind, reminding me of the beauty found in diversity and growth.

How could I trade that for his cold vision? I shook my head slightly, trying to dispel the allure of his words. It was an alluring fantasy, but it came with a price I wasn't willing to pay.

I stepped back, breaking contact with his icy touch. "Thanks, but no thanks. I'm not really the 'ruling the world' type. I can barely balance my budget, let alone lead an eternal winter kingdom. Besides, who would make the coffee? Can't exactly grow beans in a perpetual blizzard, can you?"

His face darkened, the temperature plummeting. "You refuse me? After all I've offered you?"

I squared my shoulders, steeling myself as I met his gaze. His words hung in the air, heavy with the weight of his expectations, and I could feel the intensity of his disappointment cutting through the cold. It was as if the very atmosphere was responding to his anger, pushing against me, daring me to back down.

"Yep. Consider this my official 'thanks but no thanks' to your frosty hostile takeover. I'm keeping your name under wraps, Sir Shiver. You'll get no magic words from me."

His eyes flickered, a brief moment of something darker flashing across them as if the strain of holding back his madness was beginning to show. For a second, I saw something raw in him—an edge of desperation.

Then, just as quickly, it was gone, replaced by that familiar cold, calculated control. But the shift didn't escape me. His lips pulled back into a tight, humorless smile, and I could feel the tension in the air snap as his voice dropped a shade colder.

"You think this is a game?" His voice was sharp, almost breaking through the icy calm he'd been trying to maintain. "You truly believe that denying me, denying *yourself*, will save you from what's coming?"

The silence between us stretched, and for a moment, I almost regretted provoking him. The air thickened, freezing around me, but I stood my ground, refusing to show weakness.

He leaned in, just inches from my face now, his cold breath brushing my skin. "You are more amusing than I anticipated, little mortal," he said, his voice a mix of admiration and venom. "But humor won't change your fate."

I forced myself to hold his gaze, my pulse hammering in my ears. "You keep saying that, but you know, it kind of sounds like a broken record."

A flicker of something dark and dangerous flashed in his

eyes, but he only smiled, and this time, the smile wasn't amused. It was something far colder.

The silence hung heavy between us, thick with tension. I could see the muscles in his jaw tightening, a flicker of something chaotic dancing behind his eyes. It was as if a storm was brewing just beneath the surface.

For a long moment, we stood there, locked in a battle of wills. I could feel the cold trying to seep into my bones, to wear down my resolve. But I held firm, wrapping myself in the warmth of my conviction.

Finally, he stepped back, and as he did, his form began to dissolve into the air. The once formidable figure was now a wisp of shadow and frost, swirling like a fading echo of winter's breath. Ethereal tendrils of ice curled around him, glistening in the dim light, as if the very essence of cold was reluctant to let him go.

The world around us shimmered, the colors blurring and shifting, as though the fabric of reality itself was bending under the weight of his departure.

As he disappeared, the remainder of his final statement echoed through the room: "The winter always returns, little flame."

Then he was gone, leaving me alone in a room that suddenly felt far too large and empty. I slumped against the desk, my legs shaking and my head in my hands.

CHAPTER 18

CALLIE

What had possessed me to grab my bike after a long shift, I'll never know.

The bike ride was quickly proving to be an exercise in self-punishment. The old thing creaked and groaned, one bad turn away from giving up entirely, and I wasn't sure if I was dealing with a bike or some kind of angry mechanical pet that didn't want to be ridden. The rusty chain caught on every other rotation, making me grunt in frustration. I was working harder than I had anticipated—mostly because the bike wasn't doing much of the work.

By the time I reached the park, I was sweating profusely as if I ran a marathon. And not a fun, light jog kind of marathon. No, this was the kind where you start out thinking, "Hey, I'll get in a nice workout," and then five minutes later you're cursing your poor life choices and wondering how you're going to survive the next twenty miles.

The park, as it turns out, was *packed* by Odom's standards. Because, of course it was. I couldn't just have a peaceful bike ride to clear my head. No, I had to share the space with every jogger, dog walker, stroller-pusher, and someone who was clearly trying to break the world record for most children in one vicinity.

I skidded to a stop, yanked the bike onto a patch of grass, and kicked the tires in irritation. Why did I think riding through a park full of families and happy people was going to be a good idea?

"Well, this is just fantastic," I muttered, watching a kid zoom by on a scooter, doing wheelies. "I came out here to escape everything, and now I'm stuck surrounded by a thousand happy faces and a bike that feels more like medieval torture equipment than a mode of transportation."

I plopped myself onto the nearest bench, rubbing my sore palms. This was supposed to be my moment of peace, but instead, I'd been thrown into the middle of a sitcom where the universe was the punchline. I stared at the peaceful pond in front of me, trying to calm my racing thoughts, but every time I closed my eyes, all I could hear was the icy voice of the Frost King echoing in my mind.

I sighed dramatically, as if the universe was listening, and finally let my irritation bubble over.

"It shouldn't be this hard. I mean, he was already trapped, right? All I had to do was ignore him and he would stay in the same place," I grumbled.

I kicked at the grass, and my mind wandered back to icey. I was tired of thinking about him. Seriously, why couldn't I just have one day where he wasn't hovering in the back of my mind, freezing my thoughts into sharp, uncomfortable shapes? I needed to get away from him, even if it meant literally getting away from my own house.

I grabbed the bike, determined to get a few more moments in. Maybe if I could sweat out some of the frustration, I'd feel better. It wasn't a good plan. I didn't even have a good bike. But it was all I had.

The ride back home was even worse than the ride out. The chain slipped more than usual, making weird grinding noises that sounded like the bike was trying to file for divorce. Every time I tried to change gears, the bike would protest, forcing me to pedal harder than I should have had to. My legs were burning, my arms were sore, and I was so done with this day, I could've dropped the bike in the middle of the street and walked the rest of the way home.

As I finally pulled into my driveway, completely out of breath, I took a moment to stare at the bike with disgust.

"You're dead to me," I muttered at it, too exhausted to even be angry. "We're done. You don't get to be my transportation ever again."

I dropped it on the ground with the same amount of grace I'd seen in a toddler trying to walk for the first time and trudged toward the house. I stumbled through the door, kicking off my shoes and dragging myself to my bedroom before collapsing face-first onto my bed. The scent of the quilt enveloped me, and I rubbed my sore muscles, willing the tension to dissolve.

"Maybe I'll grow a six-pack while I'm here," I grumbled, cursing the bike.

The weight of disappointment continued to press against me as well as the thought of trying another spell. I could feel my eyelids growing heavier at the thought.

I decided to take a hot bath, hoping the warmth would soothe my aching body. As I sank into the old claw tub, the steam enveloped me like a comforting hug, but my mind refused to settle. The images from the text swirled in my thoughts, taunting me even in this moment of supposed relaxation.

Eventually, drowsiness overcame me, and I slipped into a light sleep. I jerked awake, water splashing over the side of the tub as I groaned. I was too tired to clean, and the longer I stayed in the water, the more likely it seemed that I'd create an even bigger mess. Unplugging the tub, I watched the water drain before exiting and wrapping a towel around me.

Getting back into my pajamas, a yawn escaped as I crawled into the bed, cocooning the sheets around me. But what awaited me in my slumber was anything but peaceful. I was thrust into a world of shadows and whispers, ancient realms bathed in twilight. I wandered through vivid images of crumbling ruins, the echoes of laughter mingling with the soft rustle of leaves.

Then, I saw her—my grandmother's portrait hanging in a grand hall, her eyes moving through the darkness, as if she were alive and watching me.

"Find the truth, Callie," she seemed to say, her voice a blend of wisdom and warning. But before I could answer, the scene shifted, and I was face to face with the King of Frost, a figure cloaked in ice and shadow. His oceanic gaze was chilling, sending shivers straight to my soul.

"You've come to me," his voice echoed, cold and haunting. The wind howled through a desolate, frozen forest. I felt trapped, my heart racing as the world around me dissolved into frost and darkness, the portrait of my grandmother fading from view.

The cold bit deep, a chill that sank into my very bones, but it wasn't just the temperature that made me shudder. It was the creeping *presence* of something ancient, something malevolent, that hung in the air, as thick as the fog that swallowed the room. A silence stretched too long as if the world itself was holding its breath.

And then, from the corners of my vision, they appeared.

First, the wraiths—a dozen or more, their pale, translucent forms drifting silently through the gloom. They didn't make a sound, but I could feel their eyes on me, unblinking, watching. Their faces were empty, hollow, eyes like black voids that seemed to suck in the light around them. I froze, my heart pounding in my chest. They weren't just shadows —they were aware. Alive. And they were waiting for something.

Before I could gather my wits, the floor trembled beneath me. Low, rumbling growls echoed through the air, and the wraiths seemed to move aside, parting as if to let something through.

The wolves came next—massive, gaunt creatures, their white fur matted and slick, eyes glowing with an unnatural hunger. They prowled, circling, their lips pulled back to reveal sharp, jagged teeth stained dark with blood that wasn't their own. The air around me grew thick, suffocating, as if they were closing in, waiting for the right moment to pounce. I could hear their breathing now, rasping and wet, and my pulse quickened.

I tried to step back, but my feet were frozen to the floor,

my body gripped by an invisible force that kept me rooted to the spot. I was prey. They could smell my fear.

And then, the ground shook harder. My vision blurred, and before I could even process what was happening, they were here—the giants. Massive beings. Their footsteps made the floor crack beneath them as they moved, the air thick with the smell of dirt and death. They were cloaked in shadows, their forms huge and indistinct, looming like ancient titans from some forgotten legend. Their eyes glowed faintly as they bent low, watching me with cold, unblinking stares.

I could feel their gaze, heavy and oppressive, suffocating. They towered over me, each movement making the air ripple, and I realized with a sickening certainty—they were not here for me to fight.

I was nothing to them—not really. Their reactions to me were just echoes of something deeper, something I couldn't grasp yet.

And then, the roar. It was so loud, so ferocious, that I felt the vibrations in my chest before I even saw it. I looked up, and there it was—dragons made from ice.

A frozen, monstrous shape against the dark sky. Its scales gleamed similar to shards of broken glass, reflecting the dim light in a thousand directions. It let out another earth-shattering roar, its breath frigid as it unfurled its wings, blocking out everything above me. The ground seemed to shake beneath the weight of it, and my entire body went rigid as it circled, its eyes locked onto mine with a predatory hunger.

The dragon's gaze bored into me, the air crackling with its power. And I felt a chill in my soul—this was no myth.

This was no dream. This creature had existed long before humanity, and it was *real*.

But what did it want with me?

The creatures closed in, the wraiths weaving through the fog like smoke, the wolves circling with their hunger palpable in the air, the giants looming as if the world itself was bending under their weight. I couldn't move. I couldn't breathe. I was drowning in the pressure, in the dark power surrounding me.

A voice echoed through the chaos—low, familiar, but so *other* that it sent a tremor through me.

"Callie." It was as if the earth itself was speaking, the voice vibrating through my bones, chilling me from the inside out. It was ancient, *familiar*—yet wrong. And in its wake, the world seemed to slow, every second stretching into eternity.

I tried to answer, but the words wouldn't come. My mouth went dry. My heart pounded in my chest so loud, it drowned out everything else.

And then I felt it—a presence behind me. The temperature dropped further until the air was thick with the stench of rot and decay.

I tried to turn, my body refusing to obey for a second as if wading through deep waters but there it was—a figure cloaked in shadow. I couldn't make out its face, but the weight of it pressed down on me, the feeling of being watched by something that had seen the beginning and the end of time. I couldn't look away, and I couldn't breathe.

The creature spoke, its voice like gravel scraping against stone. "She is not yours to claim."

Was it speaking to me, or someone else? I glanced

around, my pulse quickening, but the space where I stood was empty—just me, alone in the silence.

Before I could react, everything shifted. The creatures, the shadows, the cold—they all vanished, as if they'd never been there at all. The darkness retreated, leaving me standing alone, gasping for air. My skin was clammy, my heart hammering in my chest as I struggled to regain my bearings.

"Callie."

I jolted awake, heart pounding, drenched in sweat. The room was dim, the moonlight spilling through my window, casting eerie shadows on the walls. The nightmares clung to me like cobwebs, and I couldn't shake the feeling that I was being pulled into a web of secrets I wasn't ready to face.

I sat up, rubbed my eyes, and took a deep breath, steeling myself for the inevitable—staying awake for the rest of the night.

"Great, just great," I muttered, pushing myself out of bed. *Thanks a lot, Frost King. This is all your fault, I'm sure of it.*

I trudged toward my grandmother's study, every step feeling heavier under the weight of everything my mind witnessed. Was this a warning of things to come? I need to get a better grasp on my abilities. I need to practice more.

Entering the study, I flicked on the light, dimly illuminating the shelves lined with ancient tomes as well as all the journals scattered on the floor where I left them.

"Ugh, look at this mess," I groaned, eyeing the volumes as if they were sentient beings conspiring against me. "Why couldn't you have left me an instruction manual, Grandma? Something along the lines of 'Here's how to navigate your ability without losing your mind.'"

I grabbed the first book off the floor—a heavy leather-bound volume that weighed a ton. "Let's see if you're any better than the last one," I grumbled, opening it with a flourish. I could feel my frustration bubbling over from the lack of sleep.

I flipped through the pages, each one more convoluted than the last. "Why can't you just label this or create a table of contents or something?"

As I continued to rummage through the texts, my stomach growled. "Oh great, just what I need—my body staging a rebellion against my quest for knowledge. Thanks for the reminder."

I debated calling one of the food brochures left in the kitchen drawers but decided to hold out a bit longer, grabbing another book.

I leaned back in the chair, rubbing my temples in frustration.

Focus, Callie. Dragons. Maybe the dream was pointing to something about dragons. That could make sense. Dragons had power, they had myths, they were... well, not Frost Kings, but close enough.

I reached for another book, ready to dive into something that would keep my mind off the mess that was *him*. But then I heard it—a faint sound, barely there, a whisper in the night. A soft, almost imperceptible meow. It came from outside the window.

I froze, my hand suspended in midair, the book forgotten in my grip. I blinked a few times, trying to shake off the odd sensation creeping up my spine. How long had I been in this house? A month? The strangest thought slipped into my mind, uninvited.

Maybe I was overthinking it, but ever since I'd arrived in Odom, the cat population had gone from zero to a handful. It wasn't exactly an infestation, but enough to raise an eyebrow. Some weird, cosmic feline conspiracy was in play, just biding its time until I cracked.

I hesitated, still unsure if I was just jumping to conclusions. But that niggling feeling at the back of my mind? It wasn't going away.

I stood up, my feet moving before I could talk myself out of it. Time to check it out.

I stepped cautiously toward the window and peeked through the curtains. At first, nothing. The yard was quiet, shadows stretching across the forestry, the soft glow of the moon giving everything an eerie, almost dreamlike quality.

Then I saw it.

A pair of glowing eyes, staring back at me from the shadows near the cusps of trees.

A cat, I assumed. A black one, probably the same one that had been haunting the bookstore, though I couldn't be sure. But it didn't *move* like a regular cat. It just stared, those eyes gleaming as if they knew something I didn't.

I blinked. When I looked again, it was gone.

I stared out into the night, my heart thudding in my chest. I needed to get some sleep.

Shaking my head at myself, I shuffled back to my grandmother's study and flipped through her journals, hoping the words would distract me. But it wasn't long before my eyelids grew heavy and the darkness crept in, pulling me under like a tide I couldn't fight.

CHAPTER 19

CALLIE

I stumbled into the kitchen, bleary-eyed and caffeine-deprived. The clock hanging over the ancient stove showed 3:17 AM, mocking my terrible life choices. My head throbbed from hours of poring over cryptic texts about seasonal courts, and my eyes felt as if they'd been rubbed with sandpaper.

"Coffee," I mumbled, fumbling with the coffee maker. "Sweet nectar, don't fail me now."

As I waited for the life-giving brew to percolate, I glanced out the window. The forest was eerily still, blanketed in a thick layer of white once more.

I blinked a few times. Snow?

"Your mortal beverages are a poor substitute for true power," he said, lounging against the doorframe like he owned the place. Which, given that he'd been here longer than I had, maybe he kind of did.

"Yeah, well, some of us prefer our power in liquid form, thanks," I retorted, grabbing the biggest mug I could find before I got crankier. "Not all of us can subsist on the tears of our enemies or whatever it is you eat."

He raised an eyebrow. "I do not eat, Callie Winters. I simply am."

"Of course, you don't.

I poured my coffee, the rich aroma filling the kitchen and momentarily drowning out the crisp, pine-scent that seemed to follow the Frost King everywhere. I took a sip, sighing in contentment as the warmth traveled down my body.

As if growing a sixth sense, I could feel him move closer, and I fought the urge to step back—a bad habit I was beginning to form around a predator. "Here you are, awake at this hour, poring over ancient texts. Seeking understanding. But you could be so much more, Callie. If only you'd embrace your destiny, speak my name—"

"Not happening, Ice Cube," I interrupted, scowling at the purr in his tone. "Talk about a one-track mind."

He sighed. "You are as stubborn as you are beautiful. Very well."

Beautifu—

Before I could fully absorb his words, he waved his hand. The air shimmered, and suddenly the kitchen table was laden with steaming plates of food. The scent of freshly baked bread, savory meats, and sweet pastries filled the air, making my mouth water involuntarily.

"What—how—" I stammered, staring at the lavish spread before me, my eyes wide in disbelief. There was no way. He was toying with me. This had to be some sort of sick joke. Wasn't this the first spell I failed? I shot him a glare, trying to hide the mix of confusion and... yeah, a little jealousy. How was he so good at this when he still wasn't at full power?

"You need sustenance," he said simply. "Your mortal form weakens with each passing hour. Eat, Callie Winters. Regain your strength."

I narrowed my eyes. "Is this some kind of trick? Like, if I eat the food of the Fae, I'll be trapped here forever or something? Do you know how many guys have slipped something into a woman's magical meal? It's the oldest trick in the book."

He laughed, a low, knowing sound. I couldn't help but notice he didn't deny my mention of the fae—nor did he ask what I might have learned about them.

"This is no fairy tale, little flame. The food is real, conjured from the kitchens of the finest chefs in the mortal realm. Eat without fear."

My stomach, the traitor, growled loudly, betraying me in front of him. I shot him another glare. His smile only widened, clearly amused. My stomach, apparently determined to make its own decisions, growled again—this time louder, as if to say, *Okay, fine, I'll eat.* I sat down, eyeing the spread warily, wondering just how much of it I'd regret later.

"If I turn into a popsicle or start speaking in riddles, I'm blaming you."

I blamed my lack of sleep for what was clearly a descent into partial insanity. I took a tentative bite of what looked to be the most perfectly roasted chicken I'd ever seen. Flavor exploded across my tongue, and I couldn't hold back a moan of appreciation.

"Oh my," I mumbled around a mouthful. "This is amazing."

Bob watched me eat, and for a moment, I could have sworn there was an expression of... fondness? It flickered across his face, softening the sharp angles that usually defined his demeanor. But that thought sent a wave of disbelief crashing over me. No, that was ridiculous. Evil ice guys didn't do fond.

I stole a quick glance at him, trying to decipher the glimmer of something in his icy blue eyes. Maybe it was just the dim light playing tricks on me, or perhaps I was imagining things entirely. His usual stoic intensity was still there, lurking beneath the surface, but there was an unfamiliar warmth that made my stomach flutter uncomfortably.

As I devoured the meal, I felt strength returning to my limbs, the fog of exhaustion lifting from my mind. I hadn't realized how hungry I'd been, how much I'd been neglecting my own needs in my frantic research.

"Thank you," I said grudgingly as I finished, wiping my mouth with a napkin that felt softer than any fabric I'd ever touched. "That was... unexpectedly decent of you. Glad to see you're finally contributing something around here, considering you're going to be haunting my life indefinitely."

He lifted his chin, a gesture that might have been gracious if it weren't for the glint in his eyes. "You are of no use to me weakened and addled by hunger, Callie Winters. Consider it enlightened self-interest."

"Right. Because everything you do is for your own bene-fit. No chance you might actually care about my well-being or anything."

His lips twitched, and for a fleeting moment, I caught a glimpse of something unguarded, a flicker of laughter in his eyes. But just as quickly, the mask slipped back into place, the chill returning. It reminded me that beneath any semblance of warmth, he was still the embodiment of ice and danger.

"Caring is a mortal weakness," he said, his voice colder than usual. "One I shed centuries ago."

I shook my head internally, scolding myself for even entertaining the idea that he could be anything other than an adversary. Evil ice guys didn't do fondness, and I needed to remember that.

I stood up, suddenly feeling the need to move. "Yeah, well, maybe that's your problem. All ice, no heart. Must get lonely, being so cold all the time."

He moved with an unnatural speed, appearing suddenly right in front of me. His hand seized my chin, and I gasped at the unexpected contact. His touch was cold, yes, but not painfully so. It felt more like the first breath of winter air—crisp, invigorating, and oddly refreshing.

"You know nothing of loneliness, little flame," he murmured, his voice low and intense, each word laced with a haunting weight. "Centuries trapped between worlds, neither here nor there. Unable to touch, to torture," he whis-pered, running the pad of his thumb across my lower lip, sending an electric jolt through me, "to truly exist. You cannot fathom the depths of solitude I have endured."

I swallowed hard, my heart pounding as his words

coldly wrapped around me. The intensity in his gaze felt almost suffocating, as if he were peeling back layers of my own defenses, forcing me to confront the strangely raw, but morbid, vulnerability in his confession. I could see the flicker of pain behind his icy facade, a glimpse into a world I had never known.

"That sounds awful," I managed to say with a bit of sarcasm to his torture remark, my voice trembling slightly as I fought to maintain my composure. The air between us felt charged, heavy with unspoken emotions

He smiled, but it was a sad thing, fragile as new-fallen snow. "Your pity is unnecessary. But your understanding... that, I would value."

I reluctantly stepped away from him, the heat of his touch lingering on my skin. It tingled with an unfamiliar intensity, and I found myself rubbing the spot absently, as if trying to erase the memory of his electric contact.

"Understanding doesn't mean I'm going to free you, you know. I still think you're dangerous."

He laughed, the sound surprisingly warm. "Oh, I am dangerous, Callie Winters. More than you can possibly imagine. But perhaps... perhaps not in the way you think."

With a wave of his hand, the remnants of the feast disappeared, leaving the kitchen as spotless as if it had never happened.

"Come," he said, moving toward the study. "You seek answers. Let me show you where to look."

Against my better judgment, I found myself following him. Was this why they warn you not to feed stray animals? What in the world was I doing?

The study was as I'd left it, books and papers strewn about in organized disarray. But now, in the pale light of pre-dawn filtering through the windows, it seemed different. More alive somehow, as if the very air was charged with potential.

Bob moved to a bookshelf I'd overlooked before, running his fingers along the spines of ancient novels.

"Your ancestor was a formidable woman," he said, his voice tinged with what might have been respect. "She understood the true nature of power, the balance required to wield it."

He selected a book bound in midnight blue leather, its cover unmarked save for a single silver star.

"This," he said, holding it out to me, his expression serious, "contains the answers you seek. But be warned, Callie Winters. Knowledge, once gained, cannot be unlearned. Are you prepared for the truth it holds?"

I hesitated, my hand hovering over the book, torn between curiosity and trepidation.

His eyes met mine, and for once, I saw no guile in them —no playful malice or hidden agendas, just an earnest intensity that made my pulse quicken.

I swallowed hard, feeling the weight of his gaze like a physical force. "What if I'm not ready for what it reveals?" I asked, my voice barely above a whisper, the uncertainty spilling out.

"Surely, you jest," he chuckled, his voice dripping with both amusement and something darker. "After centuries of solitude, I find your company... surprisingly refreshing. A rarity."

The moment our fingers brushed against the cover of the book, a jolt of energy coursed through me, a promise of revelations yet to come. And in that heartbeat, I realized that I was stepping into a realm far beyond my comprehension, where the truth could very well change everything I thought I knew.

"And if what I learn helps me keep you locked up for good?"

He smiled villainously. "Then you will have proven yourself worthy of the power you possess. But I do not think that will be the case, little flame. I think you will find that the truth is far more complex than you imagine."

As he began to fade, I called out, "Wait! I... thank you. For the food, and for this."

As much as I enjoyed poking holes in his arrogance and knocking him down a peg or two, I *could* be nice as well, when I wanted to.

He paused.

For a moment, I saw something in his eyes. "Do not mistake kindness for weakness, Callie Winters. I am still what I am. But perhaps... perhaps you are becoming more than you were."

With that, he vanished.

Taking a deep breath, I sank into the armchair, the book clutched tightly to my chest as if it were a shield against the swirling ambivalence in my mind. My thoughts were a chaotic storm, struggling to reconcile the terrifying ice guy I had first encountered with this new, more complex figure before me.

He was still dangerous, still manipulative, and that icy

veneer was ever-present, but there was something else—a flicker of unexpected gentleness that caught me off guard.

"What am I doing?" I muttered to myself. "He's the bad guy, remember? The one you're supposed to be keeping locked up?"

Maybe, just maybe, there was more to this story—and to Bob the Frost King—than I'd realized.

I glanced down at the book in my hands, feeling its weight as a tangible reminder of the knowledge it contained. What had once seemed a simple quest for answers had transformed into a tangled web of emotions and revelations. Could I trust him? Could I trust myself to navigate this dangerous territory without getting burned?

I started reading, quickly losing myself in tales of ancient magic, forgotten realms, and seasons that had waged battles for centuries. The stories blurred the lines between good and evil, where heroes and villains were defined not by their actions but by the shifting allegiances of courtly beliefs and ancient values. One tale spoke of a queen who was revered as a savior, yet in another's eyes, she was a tyrant who sacrificed countless lives to uphold an ideal that was as fragile as it was misguided. In one kingdom, the warriors fought for freedom, only to realize they had become oppressors themselves, blinded by their own righteousness. Another spoke of a fallen god, once considered a destroyer, now praised for his attempts to bring balance to a world of unyielding chaos.

Each story seemed to twist and turn, drawing me deeper into its web, until I wasn't sure if I was reading about the past or the present—or even the future. Was the line between right and wrong so easily drawn, or did it simply depend on which side of the coin you were standing on? The further I read, the more I realized: in these tales, no one was truly innocent, and no one was truly guilty. Everyone had their reasons. Everyone had their truths.

I closed the book with a sigh, a sense of unease settling in my chest. Was this what I was getting into? Would I, too, be forced to navigate these shifting truths, these tangled webs of power, loyalty, and betrayal? Was this where my bloodline had been leading me all along—toward a fate where my actions, too, would be painted as either heroic or damning depending on the whims of the world around me?

As the first rays of dawn crept over the horizon, casting the snow-covered forest in shades of pink and gold, I couldn't help but wonder: maybe the real prison wasn't the one that held the Frost King. Maybe it was the one I had been slowly drawn into—built from the very bloodline I'd inherited.

The thought clung to me like ice, suffocating and cold. Was the real prison not the one that held the Frost King captive, but the one my bloodline had woven for me long ago? A prison made of ancient bonds, blood-soaked promises, and the weight of something I couldn't yet understand.

As the first rays of dawn peeked through the curtains, painting the remnants of snow outside in soft hues of pink and gold, the room seemed to close in around me. My pulse quickened, and I couldn't shake the feeling that everything was spiraling out of control. The Frost King's words—the promise of fate, of destiny—drifted through my mind again, similar to a song I couldn't unhear.

You will understand. You will come to me.

I squeezed my eyes shut, trying to shake it off, but my heart thudded in my chest, louder with every passing second. Was it all part of the plan?

But just as I was about to turn the page, a sudden noise broke through the silence—the faintest creak from somewhere in the house. My heart skipped.

I wasn't alone.

CHAPTER 20

CALLIE

The air in the study suddenly shifted. The hairs on the back of my neck stood up, and I got that creeping sensation of being watched.

"Bob, if you don't stop this creeper behavior, I swear I'm going to invest in a warehouse-sized space heater," I called out, not bothering to look up from the information I was reading.

"My, my," came a voice that was decidedly *not* Bob's icy baritone. "What an interesting little mortal you are."

I whirled around, nearly toppling off my chair in the process. Floating in the middle of the room was a being that made my brain hurt just to look at it.

She—at least, I thought it was a she—seemed to shift and change with every blink, like a montage given form. One moment she was breathtakingly beautiful, the next terrifyingly alien.

"Uh," I said eloquently, backing away slowly. "I don't suppose you're here to tell me how I can save on my car insurance?"

The being laughed, a sound similar to shattering glass. "Oh, you are delightful. I can see why he's so fascinated by you."

I frowned, my curiosity momentarily overriding my fear. "He who? Bob? Wait, are you like... his ex or something? Because I gotta tell you, I am not getting in the middle of some centuries-old lover's spat."

As the words left my mouth, I instantly regretted them. *Great, Callie. Smooth.* But the fact that it made me feel uneasy—unsettled in a way I couldn't quite pinpoint—had nothing to do with the awkwardness of the situation.

I didn't understand why, but the idea that there could be *someone else* in his life, that he might have some ancient, long-lost lover—or, god forbid, a *current* one—did something to me. A cold knot had formed in my stomach. I wasn't sure if it was jealousy, or just some dumb reflex that made me defensive, but the feeling was uncomfortable, like trying to wear shoes that were a size too small.

I focused on my breathing, trying to push the irrational discomfort away. But still, I couldn't shake the weird little flutter of something deep in my chest.

Whatever. Not my problem.

The being's form solidified slightly, taking on the appearance of a woman with skin like polished ebony and hair that seemed to be made of living flame around ears a little too pointy.

"You speak of the Frost King with such familiarity," she said, her voice now a low, melodious purr. "How intriguing."

I should've brushed it off, but I felt a knot tighten in my stomach. How *intriguing*? What did she mean by that?

I shrugged. It was a force of habit. "Yeah, well, when someone keeps popping up uninvited in your home, you tend to get familiar. Look, not that this isn't a lovely chat, but who exactly are you and what are you doing in my grandmother's house?"

The being smiled, revealing teeth that were just a bit too sharp to be human. "I am Zainah, emissary of the Summer Court. And I am here, little mortal, because we have sensed a disturbance in the balance. A stirring of ancient power that should have remained dormant."

I wanted to say something sharp, to vent my frustration about the constant, unwelcome visits and the flood of new, unsettling information with a snarky remark. But the words wouldn't come. Instead, all I could manage was a pregnant silence, thick with the weight of everything I didn't want to deal with.

Finally, I groaned, slumping back into my chair, careful not to drop the book in my hand. *Seriously? Now you're telling me you sensed something?*

"You've sensed?" I muttered sarcastically, barely holding back my eye-roll. "Just now? Not when Bob first appeared or anything?"

I shook my head as if that would somehow banish the creeping suspicion settling in my gut.

I'm going to need a lot more coffee. I swear, if I don't get a break from all this weirdness soon, I'm going to lose it.

I cast a sideways glance at the corner of the room, half-expecting Bob to be lurking there, watching me with an amused smirk. But to my disappointment, he wasn't.

Zainah's eyes narrowed, the flames of her hair burning brighter. "You speak of him so casually. Do you not understand the danger he poses? The destruction he would bring if freed?"

I felt my throat tighten, a wave of unease crashing over me. *Was anyone trustworthy?* I wasn't about to spill any more information to her.

There was something off about Zainah. Something in the way she asked questions—she was fishing for answers, waiting for me to slip up. I wasn't about to make that mistake.

Pressing my lips into a thin line, I clenched my hands at my sides. If she wanted to know about Bob, she could figure it out on her own.

It was time to deflect.

I tucked the book under my arm and held up my hands. "Hey, preaching to the choir here. I'm the one trying to figure out how to keep him locked up. Though a little help wouldn't go amiss, if you're offering. These books are about as clear as mud, and twice as messy."

Zainah glided closer, her form shifting again until she looked almost human, save for the glow in her eyes. "You seek to maintain his prison? Curious. We had heard whispers that the last of the guardian's line had come to free him."

I guffawed like no one ever guffawed before. First of all, who was whispering about me? Secondly, why would they whisper it to her? "Yeah, no. Hard pass on unleashing eternal winter, thanks. I enjoy my seasons changing and my world unfrozen."

She studied me intently, looking straight through me.

"You are... not what we expected," she said finally, her voice quiet but heavy with meaning. "Perhaps there is hope yet."

I blinked, my mind scrambling to keep up with the words. *We?* Who was this "we" she kept mentioning? Was she referring to the entire Summer Court? The same Court that had rejected my ancestor because of their illegitimacy but was now more than happy to use them when it suited their purposes?

Anger simmered just beneath the surface, hot and bitter, crawling up my chest, trying to claw its way out. The hypocrisy was so thick I could almost choke on it. Generations of my bloodline were used, discarded, and then yanked back into the mess—pawns in a game too twisted to even comprehend.

Despite the insomnia and the nightmares that clung to me, I could feel the pieces of the puzzle slowly starting to click into place. Every sleepless night, every cryptic message, every bizarre encounter was starting to form a clearer picture. And I kept it all to myself, because honestly? I wasn't sure if I was just losing it or if my assumptions were right.

But the more I observed—especially with Zainah's sudden reappearance and her smug, Frost King-like air—the more my theories started to take shape. It was almost as if the universe was handing me breadcrumbs, and I was trying to convince myself I wasn't crazy for following them.

My ancestor had been rejected for the simplest of reasons—something as trivial as a bloodline imperfection. And somehow, my grandmother had followed suit, repeating the same mistake by rejecting my mother and me.

Here I was, born into the middle of something *much* bigger and far more dangerous.

What kind of twisted game was this?

"Gee, thanks," I muttered. "Always nice to exceed rock-bottom expectations. Look, not that this isn't fascinating and all, but I'm kind of in the middle of something here. So unless you've got some magical cliff notes on 'How to Keep Your Ice Apocalypse Locked Up Starter Version', I should probably get back to it."

Zainah's lips curved into a smile, a mix of amusement and something deeper that I couldn't quite place. "Oh, young one. You have no idea of the forces you're dealing with, do you? The Frost King is but one player in a game that has spanned millennia. And now, it seems, you have become a piece on the board."

I felt a cold shiver trail down my spine, but I fought to keep my expression neutral. *I knew it.* The idea of being swept up into some ancient cosmic chess match didn't exactly sit well with me, but I wasn't about to let her know that. No way. Let her think I had no idea what she was talking about.

"Right," I said, crossing my arms in a way that was probably a little too defensive. "The Frost King. Millennia of 'game playing.' All sounds *super* intriguing. I mean, you really should get out more, Zainah. You're starting to sound like a character from one of those cheesy fantasy novels. You know, the ones with all the prophecies and destiny stuff?"

Zainah's smile didn't falter, but I caught a flash of some-thing—amusement or maybe just pity—behind her eyes. I was not in the mood to be pitied, especially not by someone who could make fire flare up just by running her hand through her hair.

"Do you truly think I jest, Callie?" she asked, her tone gentle, but the underlying seriousness made my stomach twist.

I bit back a sigh, forcing my mind to focus. How does everyone keep knowing my name? There wasn't enough coffee for this.

"I don't *care* to be part of any game. As if one magical stalker wasn't enough, now I've got an entire supernatural chess club after me. Can't a girl catch a break? I don't even play chess!"

Zainah raised an eyebrow, clearly not buying my act. She leaned in slightly, her voice dropping low. "I know you understand more than you're letting on. You feel it, don't you? The pull. The connection. The way the pieces are slowly falling into place. All that power lying dormant inside you."

I felt my stomach lurch, a prickling sensation creeping up my spine. I had to respond carefully. Part of me wanted to snap at her, tell her to cut the crap, but the rest of me... *the rest of me was listening.*

The truth was, *I did feel it.* There were things happening in my life lately that I couldn't explain—things I didn't want to think about, let alone confront. The weird way the house seemed to hum at night, the way the air changed when I touched certain objects, and the strange dreams that had started clawing at my mind, persistent and uninvited.

Suddenly, the temperature in the room plummeted. Frost began to creep across the windows, and my breath came out in visible puffs.

"Oh boy," I grumbled, trying to push down the rising anxiety in my chest. *Of course* he chose now to appear.

The hairs on the back of my neck stood up as I watched a swirling vortex of frost and shadow begin to materialize before me. A shape formed in the ice, tall and looming.

Speak of the devil...

His presence filled the room like an icy storm, his eyes blazing with fury as they locked onto Zainah. There was no mistaking the overwhelming power radiating from him—as the air itself trembled at his very being.

"You dare intrude here?" he snarled, his voice as cold and sharp as the edges of a blade. Ice crystals formed in the air around him, miniature snowstorms that seemed to freeze everything in their path. The intensity of his voice made my heart race. It wasn't just the sound—it was the *weight* of it. The kind of power that came with centuries of animosity and authority.

Zainah didn't flinch. If anything, the corners of her lips curled into something that almost looked like amusement and anticipation. But there was no mistaking the tension that filled the space between them, thick and electric.

"I was not invited," Zainah replied, her voice steady and calm, in stark contrast to the storm of frost and wrath building in front of us. "But neither were you."

The Frost King's gaze narrowed, and the temperature in the room plummeted another few degrees. I could see my breath clouding in front of me, my hands beginning to numb from the chill. *Why did everything around here have to be so... dramatic?*

"You are far too bold for someone who hasn't earned such liberties," he growled.

Zainah remained unfazed, her posture relaxed. "I am exactly where I need to be, Frost King. You have no claim over me."

His lips curled into a twisted smile—if you could even call it that. It was a cruel, cold expression, one that promised nothing good. It shouldn't be so attractive at the moment, but I digressed.

Zainah stood her ground, her form flickering between fire and shadow. "We have every right to be here, Frost King. The balance is threatened. The Summer Court will not stand idly by while you plot your escape."

I looked between them, as if watching a tennis match between two nuclear warheads.

"Callie," he said, his voice gentler than I'd ever heard it. "Are you unharmed?"

I blinked, thrown by his apparent concern. The dichotomy of his nature—both predator and protector—wove a complicated thread between us, and I wasn't sure how I felt about it. "Uh, yeah. We were just having a lovely chat about how I'm apparently the worst chess piece ever. You know, typical Tuesday night stuff."

Zainah's eyes narrowed as she looked between us.

"Fascinating," Zainah murmured, her voice low and contemplative, as if she were studying a rare artifact or a particularly complicated puzzle. Kind of rude when I was standing right here. "The bond between you... it's not what we anticipated at all."

I blinked, unsure whether I'd heard her right. A *bond*? Between me and who? Before I could ask, her eyes shifted from me to the Frost King, and instinctively went on the defense.

"Whoa, hold up," I said, holding up my hands like I was trying to stop an oncoming train. "There's no 'bond' here. Just a reluctant roommate situation and a whole lot of property damage." I paused, trying to wrap my head around her words, my pulse quickening.

I really should've read more before coffee. How did I miss this? Sure, I was getting used to his presence, but it was more being slowly smothered by a growing fungus than any kind of... bond. She had to be talking crazy.

I could feel my face heat up, but it wasn't embarrassment. No, this was pure disbelief, as if I'd just been told I was related to Bigfoot or something.

A smirk flickered at the corners of Bob's mouth, and I scowled. His reaction was only making my rising panic worse. Irritatingly, he chuckled, as if he found my distress amusing. For the first time, I wanted to punch him.

"The thirst for knowledge suits you," he said, his voice almost approving. "You're proving yourself more useful than I anticipated."

I rolled my eyes. "Yeah, well, forgive me for not being thrilled about being caught between the supernatural equivalent of the Bloods and the Crips."

Zainah tilted her head, confusion flickering across her ever-changing features. "I do not understand this reference."

"Nor I," the Frost King muttered.

I couldn't help it. I laughed. The absurdity of the situation—me, standing between two ancient, powerful beings, making cultural references they didn't understand—was just too much.

"Okay, real talk," I said, crossing my arms and leaning

back, trying my best to sound casual despite the swirl of anxiety building in my chest. "Why exactly are you here? You can see with your own two eyes that he's still stuck, right?"

Zainah, however, didn't even acknowledge my question. She just launched into her explanation as if I hadn't spoken at all. "The balance between Summer and Winter has long been maintained through a delicate truce. But now, with the possibility of the Frost King's release..."

Something inside me snapped. I was already tired of being referred to as "mortal"—as if that alone made me less than them—but it was the way she spoke to me that got under my skin. As if I was some pet she could boss around at will. It didn't matter how the whole guardian bloodline thing had started—this was modern society in the human world, where women didn't have to put up with being dismissed or belittled.

At least Bob always made sure to remind me that I mattered in some twisted way. He may have been an arrogant, icy pain in the butt, but at least he *saw* me. This one, though? She seemed determined to remind me of my utter insignificance. And that? That was something I wasn't about to let slide.

I crossed my arms, shooting her a look that I hoped conveyed just how fed up I was. "Oh, I get it now. So, the 'great balance' of Summer and Winter is all about treating me like a dog on a leash. Well, I'm sorry, I didn't realize that the *mighty* Summer Court had such low standards for who gets to feel important."

Zainah's eyes narrowed, her expression shifting from calculated to downright venomous. She took a step closer, her voice cool but tight with anger. "You think this is a game, *mortal?*"

I wasn't backing down. "Yeah, I do. You've been playing it this whole time. I'm just over here trying not to lose my mind while you prance around with your air of superiority and tell me what *my* bloodline's capable of. You want respect? Start by showing it."

The silence between us crackled with tension. Zainah's nostrils flared as she fought to keep her composure, but I saw the way her hands clenched into fists at her sides. I couldn't help but feel a tiny bit smug. Let her stew in that.

The air crackled with supernatural tension as Bob and Zainah squared off. The temperature fluctuated wildly—one moment freezing, the next scorching—as their powers clashed.

"The balance must be maintained," Zainah said, her fiery hair blazing brighter.

I was tired and I was *fed up*.

I turned on my heel, storming off into the living room with my book, leaving them both to their devices. A few moments later, I felt a sharp, electric tingle in the air. The hairs on the back of my neck stood up. Zainah's voice, laced with fury, sliced through the tension between us.

"Don't you dare turn your back on me, mortal!"

CHAPTER 21

CALLIE

I barely had time to react before a bolt of radiant, blinding light shot through the air, whizzing past my ear. The searing brightness blinked out almost instantly, morphing into shards of ice and then water, splashing against the floor at my feet.

Did she just—?

Before I could process the bizarre attack, Bob stepped forward, his cold presence radiating off him in waves. The temperature in the room dropped by several degrees, and I swear the air itself seemed to stiffen with the weight of it. Ice spread in slow, deliberate patterns across the floor with every step he took, the chill crawling up my legs, sinking into my bones.

I wanted to step back, but something about his gaze pinned me in place. Those glacial eyes locked onto mine, unblinking and intense, like I was the only thing in his world. It made my skin prickle, as though his stare alone could freeze me from the inside out.

"She is under my protection," he said, his voice a deep, low rumble—a distant thunder gathering in the mountains. The words carried with them a weight of unspoken authority, as if this simple statement could bend reality itself. But there was something darker in the way he said it, something... possessive, maybe even territorial, that had me holding my breath.

I blinked. "I'm what now?"

"The mortal requires no protection from us," Zainah said, her voice smooth but with an edge that sent another chill through the room. Her figure flickered, her human form shimmering and distorting similar to heat waves on a summer day, but then something else—something far more otherworldly—began to push through. The air around her seemed to vibrate with a pulse of heat, making my eyes water and my chest tighten as if the very room had grown too small. "It is from *you* she needs safeguarding."

The scent of burning pine overtook the room as their powers continued to clash, a bizarre juxtaposition that underscored the ferocity of the moment. It was a heady mixture that sent my senses spiraling, amplifying the chaos unfolding around me.

My teeth chattered uncontrollably from the rapid temperature shifts, each icy gust cutting through me only to be followed by a wave of warmth that felt almost oppressive. I could feel my heart racing, adrenaline pumping through my veins as I struggled to maintain my footing amidst the swirling energies. Static electricity crackled in the air, making my hair stand on end, and I brushed a hand through it in a futile attempt to tame the wild strands that danced around my head.

This is getting out of hand in a hurry.

"Look," I said, trying to sound reasonable despite my mounting panic, "how about we all just take a nice deep breath and—"

The windows exploded inward.

I dove behind a floral chair as shards of glass and splinters of wood rained down. The smell made me want to gag.

Through the broken windows poured a dozen figures that seemed to be made of living light, their edges blurring and shifting. The temperature dropped even further, and my breath frosted in front of my face.

"This day," I muttered, peering over the edge of the desk, "just keeps getting better and better."

The figures moved with unnatural grace, but as my vision adjusted to the strange light, I realized they weren't rays at all. They were actual beings of pure light, their forms rippling like sunbeams through water. The smell of meadows and fresh rain made my nose tingle.

"The Summer Court," Bob snarled, ice crystals forming in his hair. "Come to ensure your prison holds, have you?"

My heart lurched.

These weren't enemies—they were the good guys, right?

"The boundary weakens," one of the light beings said, its voice a soft, ethereal melody. The sound sent a shiver through me, not from cold, but from the strange, unearthly presence of it. The being's glow pulsed softly, almost imperceptible, as if the very air around it was alive with power. "We cannot allow him to break free."

I pressed myself against the wall, a silent observer of the

impending trainwreck, the book still clutched in my hands. I wasn't about to let it get burned. I'd never find another copy.

I mean, they were right. He shouldn't be allowed free. Bob was a monster, he'd said so himself. He wanted to freeze the world, and kill countless innocent people. I should help them reinforce his prison. That thought flickered through my mind like an unsettling flash of light, but I couldn't hold onto it.

Bob *had* made it clear—he wasn't some misunderstood antihero. He was dangerous. He *was* the threat. He wanted to unmake the world, and, to be honest, that wasn't something someone should be let out to do. I couldn't ignore the weight of that. The world was at risk.

I ran a hand through my hair, trying to sift through the mess of thoughts spiraling through my brain. I groaned inwardly. *Why is everything so complicated?*

"The girl comes with us," another light being declared, its voice high and chime-like, resonating with an unnatural harmony that sent a chill down my spine. "She's too dangerous to leave here. Her blood could undo everything."

Wait, what? How did this get turned on me?

My heart skipped a beat. *My blood?* I looked around at their shimmering forms, their ethereal glow blurring the edges of reality. My pulse quickened, my throat tightening with panic.

"I'm not going anywhere," I said, my voice wavering despite my best efforts to sound firm. My stomach churned, but I forced the words out. "I just got this house."

"You don't understand, child," the first being said. "Your

very presence weakens his bonds. We must remove you—permanently to solidify his imprisonment."

Wait...

What!

Before I could formulate a response, the temperature plummeted sharply, the air growing heavy with an ominous chill. I shivered involuntarily as Bob moved to stand between me and the two beings, his presence a formidable barrier against the encroaching threat. It was a stance that spoke volumes.

"Touch her, and I will destroy you all," he said menacingly.

I knew I should be afraid of him. He was the villain in this unfolding drama, the Frost King wrapped in layers of danger and darkness. Yet, as the summer beings advanced with their harsh, blinding light, a strange sense of safety enveloped me in his presence.

"She is mine," he growled.

As the summer beings drew closer, their light was sharp and suffocating, illuminating the space with a blinding intensity that made me squint. I felt their energy crackling in the air, hot and overwhelming, as if standing too close to a roaring fire.

Zainah's laughter cut through the tension sharply, echoing off the walls with a cruel, mocking tone. It sent a chill down my spine, and I couldn't stop the sudden spike of annoyance anytime she opened her mouth. It wasn't just the condescension in her voice—it was the fact that she was so sure of herself, so sure of *everything*.

The light beings around her flared, their brilliance so

intense it made the air shimmer. As if standing too close to a bonfire—their very presence was trying to burn me alive.

Zainah took a slow, deliberate step toward me, eyes narrowed. "That's exactly the problem," she said, her voice dripping with amusement. "Her power calls to yours. You *are* a threat, Callie. Your bloodline's curse, the one you've been so blissfully ignorant of, pulls you toward him. And it's only a matter of time before he gets free—and when that happens, it won't just be your precious little world that's destroyed."

Oh.

My.

Goodness.

These "good guys" of summer wanted to kill me just because I might be a threat to his release. No one told me my death would be the answer. They were supposed to be beings of light, but they were willing to murder an innocent person just to keep their prisoner secure.

Just how dark can you get?

I could see the flicker of power in Bob's eyes, a storm brewing behind that icy facade, and it stirred something deep within me—a flicker of trust, perhaps, or a strange, compelling urge to stand my ground.

"No," I said, my voice stronger now. "You don't get to decide anything about my life."

"It's for the greater good," one of the light beings insisted, its voice laced with a chilling sense of righteousness. It circled us slowly, its luminous form casting strange shadows against the walls of the room. "One life against the millions he would destroy."

Bob's ice met their light in explosive bursts, sending

shockwaves through the air. Each collision erupted into a dazzling display of color and sound, shards of frost, and beams of radiant energy scattering like fireworks. The room erupted into pandemonium, the very fabric of reality warping under the intensity of their clash.

I ducked and weaved through the mayhem, adrenaline surging through my veins as my mind raced to process what was happening. The air crackled with energy, a whirlwind of sensations that left me disoriented. I could hear the sharp cracks of ice splintering and the searing hiss of heat meeting cold. It was a symphony of destruction that filled my ears, drowning out my thoughts as I fought to stay focused.

Yes, Bob was evil.

Yes, he wanted to freeze the world.

But right now, he was the only thing standing between me and beings who wanted to kill me "for the greater good."

I had to make a choice.

When forced to choose between certain death and an evil ice king... well, sometimes you pick the evil ice king.

Bob roared in lividity, the sound shaking the house's foundations. A wave of arctic cold burst from him, freezing three light beings enough to slow them, but not stop them as the ice immediately began to thaw and melt around them.

I held onto my grandmother's spell book, clutching it to my chest. The leather was warm under my fingers.

"If anyone's got some helpful spells," I whispered to it, the fear for my life constricting my chest, "now would be a great time to share."

The pendant around my neck suddenly flared to life, the metal searing against my skin. I let out a sharp hiss, jerking back instinctively as the heat became unbearable. I leaned forward, twisting the chain to dangle it away from my skin, the warmth spreading like a fire, burning through the fabric of my shirt. My fingers fumbled in a frantic attempt to put distance between it and me, but the warmth was relentless.

In my haste, I dropped the book I had been holding, watching as it tumbled to the floor. The pages fluttered open of their own accord, stopping on a section titled "Warding Against the Void." The words seemed to glow, rearranging themselves into modern English before my eyes.

"Oh, now you're helpful," I muttered, fingers trembling as I flipped through the pages. Bob's ice shields were already starting to crack under the assault of summer magic.

"Give us the girl," the light beings demanded, their voices harmonizing into something terrible and beautiful. "Her death will ensure his eternal imprisonment."

Bob snarled, but I could see his power weakening. The once powerful icy aura surrounding him, which had been so sure and strong, was starting to flicker. A calm before a storm. These beings—whoever they were—had clearly helped imprison him before. They knew how to weaken him. How to break him.

And I couldn't let that happen. No, I wasn't playing their games.

"Callie," he called, his voice strained. "Speak my name. End this."

"Not happening, Bob," I muttered, finally finding the page I needed.

A spell for amplifying power. Not breaking his prison—I wasn't that stupid—but maybe giving him enough strength to drive them back.

The light beings struck again, their magic burning through Bob's defenses. He stumbled—actually stumbled—and my heart dropped. If they got through him, I was dead.

"Sorry, Grandma," I whispered, pressing my hand to the spell page. "But I don't think these are the good guys."

Power surged through me, cold and ancient, flooding my veins with an energy I could barely comprehend. The pendant at my neck pulsed, its warmth now replaced by an overwhelming chill, like I was tethered to something far greater than I ever imagined.

I could feel it connecting with Bob's magic, intertwining with his frozen power in a way that made the air crackle. His icy shield—already formidable—began to shift, turning from brittle crystals to something far stronger, similar to steel or diamond, pulsing with a quiet, terrifying hum. The force was growing. It was *working*.

At that moment, something inside me clicked. I *understood* Bob—more than I ever had before. Controlling that kind of power, that raw, ancient force, was intoxicating. It was like standing on the edge of a cliff, feeling the pull of the wind, knowing you could either fly or fall.

And just as I thought I might have a chance to push back, a sharp voice sliced through the rising tide of power.

"Enough!"

Zainah's command cut through the space, shattering the moment. The spell I had begun to weave faltered and twisted in mid-air, the energy recoiling violently as she raised her hand, halting my magic with a snap of her fingers.

Instinct kicked in before I could think. My hand shot out, grabbing the first thing within reach—the cinnamon candle that had fallen to the floor—and I threw it. The glass container whizzed through the air.

But the projectile went wide. The candle ricocheted off the edge of the mirror on the opposite wall, sending it tipping sideways. For a moment, everything slowed. My heart stopped. The mirror shifted just enough to catch the spell I had been channeling.

Time seemed to stretch as I watched in horror, knowing what was about to happen.

The mirror became a conduit, reflecting the raw magic I had been desperately trying to control. The spell ricocheted off the glass, like an unholy shard of ice, and shot straight toward Bob.

His eyes flickered, wide with surprise as the mirror's reflection of my spell slammed into him with a force I hadn't expected. The shield of ice he'd woven around himself shattered, and the icy energy cascaded over him, spiraling around his form.

For a split second, I thought I saw his figure waver—the magic had cracked through something deep inside—but before I could process what was happening, the air went *Artic*.

Bob stood, motionless, eyes glowing with a new intensity, the ice now swirling around him like a violent storm. And in that moment, I realized—what had been set in motion couldn't be undone.

I backed away, my breath catching in my throat. "Uh... whoops?"

"What have you done?" one of the light beings cried. "You fool! He'll destroy everything!"

What have *I* done? Apparently, Zainah could do no wrong.

"Maybe," I admitted, watching frost spread across the walls in intricate patterns. There was no turning back now. "But at least he's honest about wanting to kill me. You pretend to be righteous while planning my murder."

Bob cackled. "Oh, little flame. You continue to surprise."

His power, amplified by my spell, surged forth in a breathtaking display of strength, bursting outward like a shockwave. The air around us shimmered with raw energy, and I felt the very ground tremble beneath my feet. The light beings shrieked in shock, their cries echoing through the chaos as tendrils of ice shot forth, wrapping around them with a relentless grip.

The temperature in the room plummeted as Bob's magic surged, forcing the very air around us to freeze. I could feel the weight of his power bearing down, wrapping around us in an impenetrable cocoon of cold. His ice spread quickly, coating the floor and walls in an intricate lattice of frost, a barrier of crystalline armor that encased the Summer beings.

Zainah shrieked in fury. "This is *nothing!*" She tried to push through the freezing walls, her radiant form flickering like a dying flame, but the cold wrapped tighter, binding her movement, forcing her to retreat. Her eyes were wild with anger as she summoned more light, trying to burn through the ice, but the glow sputtered in the face of Bob's overpowering chill. The frost expanded, curling around her arms and legs, trapping her.

"You think you can stop me with this?" Zainah spat, her voice a venomous hiss. Her fingers stretched outward, sending bolts of blazing light at Bob, but he was unfazed, stepping forward with the unshakable authority of someone who had long ruled the cold.

Bob's eyes were frozen storms, an unspoken command running through them. "You've forgotten who holds the true power of winter," he growled, his voice a deep, rolling rumble. With a flick of his hand, the ice intensified, closing in around Zainah and her companions. The heat from their bodies began to evaporate, the steam rising in thick clouds.

I watched, frozen in place, as the Summer beings struggled, their forms warping in the cold, flickering like fading candles. They tried to fight back, but the force of Bob's magic kept pushing them further away. The ice was not just a barrier; it was an oppressor, crushing them with the weight of centuries of winter's rule.

CHAPTER 22

CALLIE

As I stood there, clutching the pendant around my neck, my pulse hammering, I could feel the raw, undeniable power of winter coursing through me. The pendant grew warm in my palm, but it wasn't a comforting warmth. It was an acknowledgment, a bond, something deeper than what I understood. At that moment, I wasn't just a mortal caught in the middle—I was part of this.

Zainah's fury grew as she tried to break free, her light twisting in angry spirals around her. Her radiant form flickered and dimmed with each passing second as the ice continued to encircle her. She screamed in frustration, her voice rising to a deafening pitch. "You think you've won? You've only sealed your doom, girl."

But Bob was relentless. His ice spread further, the walls groaning under the pressure of the light against the cold. A battle of wills, fire against frost. I could feel the tension crackling in the air. Bob's grip was unwavering.

"You should have never come here," he said, his tone laced with contempt. "Everything succumbs to winter —*even* your precious light."

In one powerful motion, he slammed his hand against the ground, sending a shockwave of ice sweeping across the room. It hit Zainah with the force of a thousand winters, sending her sprawling back, her light dimming further as the frost seized her.

Her ire reached a boiling point, and with a furious roar, she sent a blast of energy directly at me—an explosive ray of pure sunlight. I barely had time to react as the beam surged toward me, hot and blinding.

"Callie!" Bob shouted, his voice full of warning.

In a blur, his hand shot out, a wall of ice rising between me and Zainah's attack. The light collided with the ice, bursting into a cascade of steam and sparks. Bob didn't flinch. The wall held strong, the impact of the blast leaving a faint echo of warmth against the unyielding cold.

Zainah staggered back, her power draining with each failed attempt to break free. "You can't hold us forever, Frost King," she snarled, her voice dripping with venom. "The Summer Court will rise, and you will fall."

Bob stepped closer to me, his presence a force of nature. "You will see," he replied, his voice steady and final. "Winter always comes."

As the air between us thickened with the weight of his words, I couldn't help but feel the weight of the battle shifting. Bob was not just fighting for survival— he was fighting for something much older, much deeper. And I was right in the middle of it, caught between the fire of Summer and the ice of Winter. A pawn, perhaps, but one whose power had yet to be fully realized.

And somewhere, deep down, I couldn't shake the feeling that this was only the beginning.

With a final pulse of blinding light, ice shattered.

"This isn't over," they warned as they retreated. "We'll return. And next time, we won't be so merciful."

Then they were gone, leaving behind only the lingering scent of summer meadows and the bitter taste of betrayal in my mouth.

I slumped against the wall, exhausted. Bob stood tall beside me, his expression fierce and unyielding, the embodiment of winter's resolve.

"Just so we're clear," I told Bob, who was watching me with those intense frozen eyes, "this doesn't change anything. You're still the bad guy."

"Am I?" he mused, moving closer. Frost followed in his wake. "I'm not the one who tried to murder an innocent girl today."

"No, you just want to murder everyone by freezing the world," I shot back. "Don't pretend you're any better. I helped you because they wanted to kill me, not because I believe in your cause."

He smiled. "And yet you did help me. Tell me, Callie, how does it feel to side with the villain?"

I closed my eyes, trying to ignore how close he was, how his cold presence made my skin tingle. "It feels necessary. That's all. Sometimes you have to work with monsters to survive."

"A monster, am I?" His voice was soft, dangerous. "Then why do you trust me more than them?"

"I don't trust you at all," I lied. "I just... I know what you are. You've never pretended to be anything else. They hide their darkness behind light and righteousness, but they're willing to sacrifice an innocent life for their cause. At least you're honest about your evil."

He laughed again, and this time it sent shivers across my skin. "Oh, little flame. You have no idea how honest I can be."

I opened my eyes to find him inches away, his glacial gaze boring into mine.

"I will freeze this world," he said softly. "I will plunge it into eternal winter and reshape it as I see fit. But you, Callie Winters..." his cold fingers traced my cheek, "you, I would spare. Rule beside me. Be my queen of winter."

What is with this guy taking liberties in touching me this way? My mind screamed in protest, a whirlwind of confusion and denial. This was the Frost King, the villain of my story, and yet here he was, offering me power and a place by his side. My heart raced, not from fear, but from the intoxicating allure of his words and the undeniable chemistry that crackled between us.

But I couldn't allow myself to get swept away by his charm.

I jerked away from his touch. "And there's the sales pitch again. Not interested in being your evil ice queen, Bob. I helped you fight them off because I want to live. That's all."

His smile was knowing, predatory, a flash of white teeth that sent a shiver down my spine. It was the kind of smile that hinted at secrets, at the depths of his intentions that lay just beneath the surface. The way his lips curved suggested he was fully aware of the effect he had on me, a hunter reveling in the thrill of the chase.

As he leaned in slightly, getting down on one knee, the air between us thickened with tension, charged with an unspoken challenge. There was a glint in his icy blue eyes, a flicker of amusement that made it clear he was savoring this moment. It was as if he found delight in my uncertainty, a game that he was determined to win.

I felt exposed beneath his gaze, as though he could see right through the carefully constructed walls I had built around my heart. The nature of his smile suggested that he saw me not just as a potential ally, but as something to be claimed, a prize to be won in the grand scheme of his eternal winter.

A part of me wanted to flee, to escape the magnetic pull of his presence, while another part was drawn in, captivated by the darkness and danger that surrounded him. I was standing at the edge of a precipice, teetering between desire and self-preservation.

"For now, perhaps," he spoke softly. "But you've taken your first step into darkness today, little flame. And darkness, once tasted, is not easily forgotten. The truth is far more complex than you realize."

I wanted to argue, to deny it. But I could still feel the echo of his power mingled with mine, cold and seductive. I had chosen to help him, knowing what he was, and what he wanted to do.

What did that make me?

"Get out," I whispered. "I need to clean up this mess and

figure things out. Because next time they come, I might not be so willing to help you fight them off."

He stared at me arrogantly. My pulse quickened, and I could feel a mixture of defiance and intrigue rising within me. I refused to be a mere pawn in his game, but I couldn't deny the flicker of curiosity he ignited.

"As you wish," he stated flatly, getting to his feet. "But remember this moment, Callie. Remember how it felt to embrace the cold, to let your power merge with mine. Remember that they would kill you without hesitation, while I offer you a crown."

Then he was gone, leaving me alone with my thoughts and the lingering chill in the air.

I looked around at my devastated study, at the frost patterns still decorating the walls. I had helped an evil ice king fight off beings of light and summer. Beings who were trying to protect the world from him.

"What have I done?" I whispered to the empty room.

But I knew the answer. I had chosen to survive, no matter the cost. And something told me that cost was only going to get higher.

I just hoped I'd be able to live with myself when this was all over.

If I survived at all.

I took a deep breath, trying to steady my shaking hands. I had already made enough of a mess today, and I wasn't about to let the house fall apart completely. Flipping through the book again, something inside me *clicked,* as if the power surge had unlocked a part of my mind that had been dormant. The words on the pages shifted, rearranging themselves in a way that made perfect sense now—things I hadn't understood before suddenly fell into place.

The incantation buzzed in my mind, the words both foreign and oddly familiar at the same time. I could feel the magic stirring in my chest, thrumming like a heartbeat.

This was it. Time to fix my stupid mistakes.

I recited the spell again, louder this time, the words trembling slightly on my tongue. I could feel the magic pushing back against me, testing my resolve, but I wasn't going to back down. I *needed* this to work.

At first, nothing happened. The frost on the walls just glistened mockingly, as if the house itself was laughing at my attempt. But then, slowly, the temperature in the room shifted.

A faint, electric tingle ran up my arms, the kind of sensation you get when you're standing too close to a charged power line. I felt it before I saw it—the ice that had once consumed the walls started to recede, cracking and crumbling away in delicate, almost graceful fragments.

It wasn't just dissolving—it was *rebuilding*.

The floorboards that had splintered from the sudden freezing began to lift back into place, the jagged edges smoothing out as if they'd never been damaged. The shattered windows slowly repaired themselves, the shattered glass reassembling like a jigsaw puzzle, turning from jagged shards to clean, clear panes that reflected the soft glow of the candlelight in the room.

The walls, once covered in a thick web of ice, now hummed with a strange warmth as the frost melted away, revealing their original structure beneath. It was as if the house was breathing again—the spell wasn't just fixing the damage, but reviving the very heart of the place.

My pulse quickened. It was working. *It was really working.*

The air felt warmer, the oppressive chill lifting as the icy patterns on the walls slowly disappeared, leaving behind only faint, swirling designs that looked almost as if they belonged there.

The whole room seemed to sigh in relief. A low hum vibrated through the walls, the magic settling like a quiet storm after the bedlam. The only thing it didn't fix were some of the broken chairs.

I couldn't help but smile, a little in awe of what I had just done. For a moment, I almost forgot who I'd been helping, who had caused all of this in the first place. This wasn't just about survival anymore—it was about control. About proving that I could still hold power over my own fate, no matter how much it seemed as if the world around me was conspiring to strip that away.

The book I had dropped earlier lay quietly on the floor, its pages still perfectly intact. I bent down to pick it up, my fingers brushing the smooth surface of the cover, and for a fleeting moment, I felt a sense of accomplishment.

But just as I straightened up, my eyes caught the glimmer of light reflecting off the newly repaired window. It was still dark outside, the shadows long and thick against the glass, but something in the air had changed.

A sense of... anticipation.

I froze.

The warm glow of the candlelight flickered, casting

strange, long shadows across the walls. I thought I heard a faint whisper—soft, almost imperceptible.

My heart skipped a beat, and I instinctively reached for the pendant around my neck, which was now humming with a strange warmth. A warning, or maybe a reminder. My gaze darted to the door, half-expecting to see him standing there, watching me with those cold, unblinking eyes.

But there was nothing.

The house was quiet again, peaceful, as if it had never been shattered by the power of the Frost King or the Summer beings. And yet, that strange sense of unease wouldn't leave me.

I had done it. I had fixed the house.

But something told me that the real battle—the real storm—was only just beginning.

And this time, I wouldn't be able to rebuild *everything* so easily.

CHAPTER 23

CALLIE

The sound of the truck pulling into the driveway echoed through the still morning air. I glanced up from the half-finished cup of coffee in my hand and sighed. This was it. The replacement chairs had finally arrived.

After surviving the impromptu war in this house and some rest after my "fix-it-all" spell as I liked to call it, I'd finally given in and ordered a few things from the local furniture shop.

I grabbed my jacket, tossed the last of my coffee into the sink, and headed out the door just as the delivery truck idled in the driveway. The back doors swung open, and I saw two guys getting out, both wearing uniforms with the name of the delivery company emblazoned on the front.

And, of course, one of them was Tim. Because with a town this small, why wouldn't he be here?

Tim flashed his usual easy grin as he spotted me. "Well,

well, if it isn't the woman of the hour. Tired of being surrounded by all that vintage floral chaos, huh?"

I bristled, the all-too-familiar discomfort curling in my stomach. His advances were just as unwelcome as they'd ever been.

"Hey...Tim?" I still wasn't sure what his name was.

"It's Trent, actually," he replied while putting on a pair of leather gloves.

I blinked, feeling the familiar awkwardness creep up on me. "Right. Trent. Sorry." I gave a small, tight smile and rubbed the back of my neck.

Tim—no, Trent—was still grinning, clearly enjoying my discomfort. His eyes had that glint of amusement, as if he knew exactly what he was doing. "No problem," he said, moving toward the truck, casually glancing me up and down. "So, what're you getting delivered this time? Something more...*you*?"

I stiffened, my guard going up instinctively. The last thing I needed was to get wrapped up in whatever game he was playing.

"Just some new chairs," I said, tucking a loose strand of hair behind my ear, trying to sound casual. "Nothing too exciting, really."

I just needed him and his partner to drop the stuff off and leave. Was that too much to ask?

"Ah, new chairs, huh?" Trent chuckled, his eyes twinkling. "I guess that means you're getting rid of the old and bringing in the new. Starting with the furniture?" He flashed another smile, taking a step closer, and I could smell the faint hint of woodsy cologne. "You sure you're not just looking for a change in... *company*?"

I fought the urge to roll my eyes, but only just. My inner snark was practically begging for release, but I had to keep it together. I needed them gone.

I raised an eyebrow, crossing my arms. "Well, I figure if I'm going to have a bunch of furniture staring at me all day, it might as well be something that doesn't make me feel like I'm living inside a floral nightmare."

Trent chuckled again, taking another step closer, and I couldn't help but notice the subtle shift in his posture. He was trying to see if he could get under my skin.

The air around me grew... colder, almost imperceptibly at first. A faint gust of wind swept through the open door, and I could feel a prickling chill crawl down my spine. My skin goosebumped, but I wasn't about to let it show.

"Fair enough. So, new chairs and a new vibe, huh? Sounds like you're trying to make some... changes."

Another icy breeze cut through the door, this one colder than the last, making my teeth clench as if the wind itself were trying to remind me that I wasn't alone in the room. I exhaled sharply, trying to shake off the uncomfortable sensation.

"Right," I said, forcing a tight smile. "And some changes don't involve, you know, company who can't take a hint."

I winced internally. That was a little too sharp, even for me, but it was out there now. I glanced at the other guy, who was carefully setting down a box by the door, clearly pretending he wasn't witnessing this little exchange. Good, let him stay in his oblivious bubble. Trent, however, didn't seem to take the hint.

He grinned, completely unbothered. "Well, I'm good at taking hints. Just not the ones that aren't said out loud."

He took a few steps up the front porch and leaned a little closer, his eyes practically gleaming.

"You sure you're not just avoiding the *right* kind of company, Callie?"

The air dropped another degree. A sharp gust of wind sliced through the door frame, hitting me directly in the back. I fought the urge to shiver, but I could feel the faintest trace of frost creep across the windowsill.

I needed to end whatever this was, and quickly.

"I'm just trying to avoid people who can't seem to understand the concept of personal space," I said, stepping back just a fraction, crossing my arms tighter.

Another gust of frigid air howled past the door, slamming it slightly ajar, making the temperature drop even more. Okay, now I was getting the impression that I wasn't the only one who was a little bit irritated.

Trent's smirk only widened, as if I'd just handed him a challenge he was more than eager to accept. "Guess I'll have to work on that then."

"Yeah," I said, finally feeling my patience start to crack, but I forced out a sweet smile. "Maybe when you're done with the delivery, you can work on the whole 'getting out of my way' thing."

I wasn't sure if that was a threat or a suggestion, but it sounded like I was losing the battle of wits with him—and that just wasn't gonna happen.

"And what exactly is in your way? I can help you move it while I'm here," he offered pseudo-innocently.

A bone-chilling gust of wind slammed through the house, rattling the windows and setting off a low creak in the rafters. The temperature plummeted, and a quick, frosty breath of air brushed possessively against the back of my neck, cold as ice.

Trent glanced up over the door, then back at me, his grin widening. "Seems you might be needing a handyman for some of these drafty windows. The cold will keep you up at night."

I could almost feel the Frost King's gaze burning at the back of my head. Look, it wasn't as if I was enjoying this conversation either.

"What I need is for you guys to finish the delivery and head back to work. Thanks for your time." I couldn't help myself. My lips twitched despite my better judgment. But at that moment, the air grew so cold that I had to rub my arms to stop from shivering. My breath puffed out in a cloud of white.

For a split second, I thought I saw something flicker in Trent's eyes—something sharper than the usual playful gleam—but it was gone in an instant. He just chuckled, leaning back a bit, unbothered by the cold. "Anytime, Callie. Glad to be of service."

I pivoted on my heel and strode inside, making it clear with every step that I had zero interest in continuing this little exchange.

Mission accomplished? Maybe not. Because as I crossed the threshold, I felt it—the sharp, biting chill that lingered in the air, a reminder that the Frost King was still very much present, whether I liked it or not.

THAT NIGHT, THE NIGHTMARES CAME AGAIN.

The same dark, suffocating space. The cold, as if being trapped inside a frozen cavern, pressing down on me from all sides. A vast stretch of snow, endless and consuming, with no sign of escape. Above me, a sky full of swirling, frozen clouds, as though the world itself was made of ice. Every breath was akin to inhaling shards of glass. I could feel something—*someone*—lurking just beyond my reach, watching, waiting.

The ominous weight of its gaze pressing against me, a shadow that never quite moved into the light. I tried to scream, but my mouth wouldn't move. I couldn't even twitch my fingers, frozen in place by something cold and ancient.

And then, from the snow, a dark figure emerged. A dragon? A man? It didn't matter. The shape grew closer, its presence freezing everything in its wake, and as it reached for me, I couldn't move, couldn't breathe, couldn't fight back. The claws... the wings... the eyes, glowing with an unnatural light.

The scene shifted, and suddenly, I was no longer in the snow. I was there—in the darkness, in the cold. Shackled to the floor of an endless, yawning cavern. The walls were made of nothing, an infinite void that pressed in on me from all sides. There was no escape. No way out. Just the oppressive weight of the blackness, thick with suffocating silence.

The stench hit me first. Iron. Copper. The unmistakable, cloying scent of blood mixed with something worse—something darker, more ancient. It clogged my lungs, choking me with its heaviness. The metallic tang burned my throat with every breath.

I gasped, my body trembling, but it didn't help. I

couldn't breathe. I couldn't see. Only the suffocating air and something phantom digging into my skin.

I tugged at the restraints, but they were unforgiving. Invisible chains cut into my wrists, my ankles, holding me tightly to the jagged floor. The coldness seeped into my bones, making the binds feel like ice against my flesh. I pulled harder, desperation clawing at me, but it didn't budge. Whatever magic this was bound me in this place.

My mind raced, but it couldn't focus. The air was thick, pressing down on me with an unseen force. My heart pounded in my chest, each beat louder than the last, a countdown to something I couldn't even comprehend. I was trapped. This wasn't a dream, it couldn't be—it felt too *real*.

I desperately struggled against the restraints again, my breaths shallow, quick. Panic was rising in me now, crawling up my spine. What were the implications? *Where was everyone? Where was I?*

The thought of being alone in this place, of being forgotten, of being held here in silence forever, made my mind want to fracture.

My body shifted and scuffled in the stillness, a noise that felt far too loud in the vast emptiness.

No. No, no. This can't be happening.

I pulled harder, straining, my body screaming for freedom, for air. And then, the air shifted.

I felt a cold, unnatural draft rush past me, sending a wave of frost creeping over my skin. My breath hitched, heart thudding in my chest.

A sound broke the silence, low and rumbling, like distant thunder. A voice, deep and agonized, filled the space.

"No... no!" The voice roared, raw and broken. The words

came with such force, such anguish, that the ground seemed to tremble beneath me.

"You'll all pay for this!"

I winced at the sound of it. His voice, filled with pain, with fury. It shook me to the core.

I could feel the air around me growing colder, the frost creeping up my limbs, my throat closing with a chill that froze me from the inside out.

"No..." The voice, guttural and desperate, echoed through the cavernous dark. It wasn't just a voice anymore. It was a sound of pure anguish, an endless cry, the roar of a beast in torment, locked in a prison of its own making. It was a sound that reverberated through the very fabric of my soul.

A final, desperate roar echoed through the void, resonating with a deep, primal power—familiar and terrifying in its intensity.

And in that instant, my throat tightened, suffocating. Familiar hands gripped me, and an icy blade pressed against my neck, cold and unyielding.

I jerked awake with a gasp, my heart pounding in my chest. My body was drenched in sweat, the remnants of the nightmare lingering like a weight on my shoulders. I sat up, eyes darting around in the chilling darkness, trying to shake off the feeling of something lurking just out of sight. The room was quiet, the house still. Nothing out of the ordinary.

Except... there was something on my chest.

My eyes widened with sudden panic. Something shifted against me. I held my breath, straining to make sense of it.

It was warm. Purring.

A cat?

I blinked rapidly, my mind foggy with the remnants of sleep. Slowly, I turned my head to look down at my chest. Sure enough, there was a jet-black cat curled up on top of me, its body rising and falling gently with every breath I took. It was average-sized, with glossy fur that seemed to shimmer faintly in the moonlight streaming through the curtains. Its golden eyes gleamed like two little lanterns, reflecting the light in a way that made it seem... almost magical.

It had to be the same cat from the bookstore, and the one I caught in my backyard the other night.

I stared at it, confused. How had it gotten in? I was sure I'd closed the window. There was no way it could've just appeared on my bed, was there?

The cat blinked up at me slowly, as if it were assessing my confusion. It gave a small, almost content purr and stretched its paws out, digging them gently into the soft fabric of my pajama top, making itself more comfortable.

I rubbed my eyes, still unsure whether I was dreaming or not. But the cat was real. I could feel the warmth of its body against mine, the softness of its fur brushing against my hand as it nuzzled closer.

Okay, well. It could be worse. It could be that raccoon deciding to make another midnight appearance.

Sighing, I gently shifted my new feline companion off my chest. It didn't protest—just blinked at me lazily, as if it had all the time in the world. I swung my legs over the side of the bed, and the moment my feet hit the floor, it was back on me, rubbing against my calves in that annoyingly affectionate way that cats do.

"Hey, little fella. Did you follow me? What am I going to

do with you?" I muttered under my breath, feeling a wave of annoyance mixed with the phantom memories of the cavern. "Of all the things I could have dealt with tonight, you show up."

The cat mewed softly and gave me a look. I could have sworn it was judging me.

"Yeah, yeah, I know," I said. "I'm sure you have some sort of tragic backstory involving an ancient curse or maybe you're the reincarnation of some long-dead royal pet. Who am I to judge? I mean, I'm dealing with the nightmare of living in a haunted house with a creepy king of winter. So yeah, a mysterious black cat that follows me around is nothing."

I winced. Okay, maybe I was getting a little too sarcastic for my own good, but when your life suddenly decides to take a turn into the weird and unexplainable, you have to find a way to cope. And for me, that meant snark. Lots of snark.

The cat gave me another slow blink as if to say, "Really? This is your solution to a strange, magical apparition in your home?"

"The raccoon put you up to this, didn't he? I don't even know if it was a he or a she." I sighed. "You know, I kind of felt bad about spraying that weird stuff outside. It doesn't matter now, I guess."

I straightened up, feeling slightly ridiculous for having a one-sided conversation with a cat. "Fine. I'll feed you, and you can be on your way. You're lucky I'm a sucker for house animals. Though cats have been on my bad side since the incident with my ex."

It meowed as if in protest.

"Yes, I know it has nothing to do with you."

The cat followed me without hesitation as I padded toward the kitchen, tail flicking lazily behind it. It was almost cute, in a *you're-keeping-me-up-at-three-in-the-morning-for-no-reason* kind of way.

As I opened the fridge, I thought about how much weirder this night could have been. The spring or fall court could have shown up. Yeah, I'd take a simple cat any day.

I blame all of this chaos on Bob. His appearance in my life has led to nothing but a slow descent into losing my mind and making further questionable decisions.

"Frost King, indeed," I muttered, grabbing a can of tuna from the pantry instead. "The guy who wants to freeze the whole world and thinks *I* can help him. But sure, here I am, feeding a random stray cat tuna at 3 AM, as if this is normal."

Maybe I was destined to become this town's eccentric cat lady after all. The irony of it all didn't leave me.

I shook my head, popping the can open and scooping the tuna onto a plate. The cat was watching me, its golden eyes fixed on the food like I was about to hand it a diamond. I set the plate down on the floor in front of it, still ranting under my breath.

"Honestly, what happened to my life? Hindsight, one could even say I used to have it together. I had a job, a normal apartment, a good routine, and now... now I'm hosting an impromptu feline dinner party while dealing with cryptic, ice-themed royalty and the possibility that I might be the one that's cursed."

The cat began eating, its tail flicking back and forth in a

satisfied rhythm. I stared at it, half in disbelief and half in resignation.

"Well, at least you're not trying to kill me," I muttered, half sarcastic, half relieved. "Not yet, anyway."

As it licked its paws and cleaned its face like it had all the time in the world, I leaned back against the counter. "Great. Tomorrow, I'll wake up, deal with whatever is happening with Bob, and wonder how much stranger my life can possibly get before it just turns into a full-blown circus. And you, mister, will probably still be here—probably shedding all over my sheets. I'll just have to make room for you on the list of things that have gone utterly insane in my life."

The cat paused in its eating, glanced up at me again, and blinked slowly. I could almost hear the thought process in those glowing golden eyes.

"Okay, okay," I relented, raising my hands in mock surrender. "Maybe you're not so bad. You just picked the *worst* possible time to show up."

Or maybe—just maybe—the universe knew I needed something to vent to before I completely lost my mind. Maybe my grandmother sent the cat. She always did have a way of sending just the right things at the right time.

This house, and the pendant for instance.

I shook my head, half-laughing at myself. *A cat as a guardian angel? Really, Callie?*

It finished the tuna, then sat back, licking its paws with a dignity I found deeply irritating at the moment.

"Well, I'm glad you're enjoying it. Now, if you'll excuse me, I have a whole list of other things to worry about—like sleeping, for example. Which I'm pretty sure you're not helping with."

The cat yawned in response, stretching out its front paws and giving me an utterly unbothered look, as though to say, *I'm not the one who can't sleep.*

I grunted, turning toward the hallway. "Right. I'm the one who can't sleep. You didn't have to be so rude about it."

I sighed again, rubbing my eyes. The bed was calling me. I just hoped I didn't have another nightmare, especially now that I had yet another uninvited guest who seemed perfectly content to make itself at home.

As I walked back toward my room, the cat followed closely behind, tail swishing back and forth like a metronome, steady and unhurried.

"Fine," I muttered. "Just don't expect me to pet you all night long. I'm not that easily charmed."

The cat meowed, as if to say, *You already are.*

CHAPTER 24

YKAZAR

For the first time since Callie had channeled her power into me, I stepped beyond the confines of the prison walls—freedom, if only for a fleeting moment.

Her abilities—*my power*—coursed through me, raw and heady, and I reveled in it, tasting the air around me with a clarity I hadn't felt in centuries. This world, this realm, was mine to take, as it had always been, had it not been for the shackles that had bound me so long. But no longer. I was free, and nothing would keep me from what I was owed.

I felt the tug of her presence even now as if she were the anchor that held me to this reality, the tether to the physical world. She didn't understand it yet, but she would. She *had* to. She was mine. I could feel it deep inside me, in the power we shared, in the connection that neither of us had fully grasped—bound together by a drop of winter's blood.

As I moved through the unfamiliar streets of this mortal realm, a shadow among shadows, I found myself tracking Mrs. Lancaster. A mortal, yes, but one with secrets I plan to reveal. That day in Callie's home ignited something in me—an unrelenting spark of both curiosity and irritation with her presence. She was the one who had been so close to Callie's grandmother, the one who thought she could manipulate and control what belonged to me.

And I had allowed it, for a time.

I followed her down the street, my steps silent, unseen. Her ignorance of my presence was the greatest mistake of all. She thought she could weave her schemes, maneuver her pieces around the board, all while pretending to be in control. But she—and the rest of them—had no idea what they were truly dealing with.

They thought they could play their clever little game, thinking they could pull the strings and use Callie as a pawn, just as they had done with her grandmother.

They were wrong. They were all wrong.

I was in control now.

The old woman looked left and right before disappearing into the candle shop. Of course. It had always been a place of secrets, of whispered words, of quiet deals.

They thought they could control her bloodline. They thought they could use her as a tool to preserve their fragile alliances between courts. They underestimated her—and they underestimated me. Callie might have been unaware of the depths of her power, but she would soon understand her role in this dance, whether she liked it or not. I would make sure of it. And if I had to break her trust, destroy everything she held dear to show her how small their control was? Then so be it.

I watched as the shopkeeper emerged from the shadows, her steps deliberate, her face calm but hard. There was nothing innocent about her, not even in her mortal shell. She was just another piece in a game that had gone on far too long.

I listened in, unseen, as Mrs. Lancaster joined her. Their conversation was hushed, too soft for even my ears to catch fully, but I could hear enough to confirm my suspicions of their intentions.

"They don't know yet," the shopkeeper murmured, her voice tight with anticipation. "But when she does..."

"When she does, it will be too late," Mrs. Lancaster cut in, her tone dripping with a venom I hadn't expected. "She's *ours* now. The Spring Court will not stand by while the Summer Court makes their moves. And when the guardian learns the truth, when she understands her role, she'll do as we've planned."

I bristled at the mention of what *belonged* to me, my fingers curling into fists at my sides, nails biting into the skin. The audacity of these mortals, to think they could use her for their gain, to manipulate the power that ran so deeply in her blood—my blood.

A low, almost imperceptible hum thrummed through my chest, like the beginnings of a storm. The frost within me stirred, as if it, too, recognized whom she belonged to. I could feel the cold creeping up my spine, the chill swirling through my veins, a reminder of the power that had been buried for so long.

"She'll be easier to handle than her grandmother," the

shopkeeper said, almost fondly. "Rose was too proud. Too stubborn. She was clever to send her daughter away but with the reemergence of her granddaughter—Callie doesn't know yet what she can do. Once she awakens..."

Mrs. Lancaster's lips twisted into a cruel smile, one that sent a sharp prick of cold through me. "She'll be our weapon. The Spring Court will rise again, restored to its rightful reign."

The words pierced through me, igniting a deep, primal hunger for blood and vengeance. The Spring Court thought they could simply claim what was never theirs. I chuckled darkly, the sound twisted and hollow.

My mind splintered, fragments of madness creeping in at the edges, curling around my thoughts. Visions of desolation flooded my senses—my throne reclaimed, my enemies crushed beneath the weight of my wrath. The world reduced to ice and ruin, just as it should be. I would make them pay for daring to think they could control what was mine.

And Callie would be the perfect instrument of that destruction. The thought made my skin crawl with a maddening mixture of desire and possessiveness.

"And when she realizes her true power?" the shopkeeper asked, as if speaking the words to herself.

Mrs. Lancaster smiled, cold and calculating. "She'll do what must be done. If it wasn't for us, her Grandmother would have never called her back here. She'll destroy the Summer Court and take down the Winter Court while he's still imprisoned. From what I can tell, she had no intentions of freeing that monster. The Spring Court has the backing of Woodland Trolls."

My nostrils flared at this information. Oh, how the weaker races band together with a false sense of hope. It seems the Spring Court has been quietly making their political moves and alliances over the centuries.

The shopkeeper nodded. "I miss home. I hate being stuck here in this realm."

"As have I. But all in due time, my friend." I watched with disdain as Mrs. Lancaster patted the shopkeeper's hand. "It's why this mission is so important. Once it's done, we'll finally return home for good."

"I know you're right. But some days, the wait is excruciating."

With a subtle nod, Mrs. Lancaster slipped out of the shop, her footsteps muffled by the thick silence of the darkened streets.

Centuries locked away in a living tomb had gifted me a patience that stretched beyond mortal comprehension. Gliding through the shadows, I followed her every step, watching as she slipped into a small, unassuming house on the outskirts of town. She settled in effortlessly, completely unaware of the storm that was about to descend upon her. As she washed her face in the dimly lit bathroom, her breath began to fog. I watched with wicked satisfaction as the mirror spidered with frost—thin, delicate cracks spreading like veins of ice. The cold crept through the room, thickening in the air as my presence swelled, suffocating the warmth around her.

She paused, her hands stilling on the edge of the sink, and for the briefest moment, her eyes widening with doubt.

Then, the madness came—slow and deliberate. I let it consume me, a dark hunger unraveling in my chest. The frost on the glass thickened until it resembled the cold stare of death itself.

The temperature dropped sharply, a biting chill that turned the air heavy, suffocating. She trembled, her breath ragged, each exhale more desperate than the last as the frost spread. Her wide eyes flickered in panic, searching the empty bathroom for some refuge, some escape from the creeping cold that seemed to close in from all directions.

The frost on the mirror writhed, an unnatural, malevolent force, crawling along the edges of the glass. It pressed in on her, colder than anything she had ever felt, its icy tendrils reaching toward her with predatory slowness, closing in like a web around a helpless insect.

She gasped, her chest heaving as the cold licked at her skin. Her hands shook as she gripped the sink, but it was no use. The frost encased her arms, her fingers frozen in place, her legs stiffening as though the very marrow in her bones had turned to ice. Her body quaked, but the sound of her fear—the frantic beating of her heart, the shallow gasps— was muffled by the cold, by the eerie silence that had fallen over the room.

She opened her mouth to scream, but no sound came. The air had thickened, and her breath froze in her throat, choking her. The frost continued to creep up, curling around her neck, over her shoulders, as though the very room was consuming her.

They had trifled with the wrong king. The hunger for retribution, for the restoration of my power, spread through me like an unrelenting chill, freezing everything in its path until nothing remained but cold, bitter satisfaction.

And then it came to my wicked delight—the realization.

Her eyes locked onto the mirror, now a reflection of nothing but ice. It was too late. She could feel it, the suffocating chill, as the frost wrapped itself tighter, tighter, around her chest, her throat. My hand, though unseen, controlled the ice, a living extension of my will.

The contrast of her warm blood seeping down to the ground made me shudder with relish. It reminded me of the way Callie felt with every touch—how her warmth fought against the cold of my presence, resisting the pull I had on her, yet unable to escape it.

Desire and rage collided within me, the chilling need for vengeance against those who had wronged me clashing with a new, unexpected hunger—one I hadn't foreseen. Since her arrival and my awakening, I had planned to manipulate her, to use Callie to gain my freedom. But now... now I couldn't shake the unsettling suspicion that it was *she* who had been manipulating *me*.

Every moment I spent in her presence, I felt something shifting, something beneath the surface I hadn't anticipated —something I might not be able to control. The idea gnawed at me, the creeping chill of winter biting at my heels. Was I the predator, or was she the true force driving this game?

The room seemed to grow darker, colder, until the very walls of the bathroom appeared to buckle under the weight of the frozen nightmare I had brought. With a mental flick of my wrist, blood splattered against the walls, running down until they too froze in place. What remained of her body went still, the last shuddering breath leaving her lips in a final, futile gasp.

I let the silence hang heavy in the air for a moment

before dropping her frozen body, shattering it into a million pieces.

My thirst for revenge was far from satisfied by this measly sacrifice. It only deepened, a cold, insatiable hunger that could never be fully slaked.

And with a final cruel twist of my power, the frost retreated, as though it had never been. The warmth of the room returned, but only to show the empty, lifeless fragments of flesh that had once been her. She was gone—nothing more than a frostbitten memory.

The very punishment they had sought to inflict upon me.

And with the sacrifice of this martyr, my power swelled. Her life essence from the other realm absorbed into me, feeding the hunger that had gnawed at my core for centuries. My strength, now stronger than before, pulsed through me like a living thing, thrumming with a new, intoxicating force.

I could feel the balance tipping, my freedom drawing near.

I turned away from her shattered remains, leaving behind the remnants of her life. With each step, the shadows around me deepened, the cold swirling tighter, as if eager to follow. There was still one final piece to claim—the last tether to the life I had once known, to the one who had unknowingly become the key to unlocking my prison.

Callie.

Her name lingered in the air, sharp and sweet. The last thread of my freedom rested on her tongue. She had no idea how little control she had, how deeply her blood called to mine. It would only take the slightest nudge, the smallest thread of manipulation. I would guide her, push her, until she was in my grasp.

With a cruel, satisfied smile, I stepped into the shadows, the world outside a blur as I made my way back to the one place where my destiny awaited.

My little blood of winter.

CHAPTER 25

CALLIE

I woke to the sound of cracking ice.

The noise echoed through the house like gunshots, followed by a bone-chilling roar that made my teeth rattle. The temperature plummeted so fast my breath froze midgasp.

"Oh no," I muttered, scrambling out of bed. "No no no..."

The floorboards creaked under my feet as I ran to the study, nearly slipping on patches of black ice that hadn't been there when I'd gone to sleep. The smell of ancient magic, sharp and bitter like frozen metal, filled my nostrils.

I skidded to a stop in the doorway, my heart lodging somewhere in my throat.

Bob stood in the center of the room, but he wasn't his usual eerily composed self. Ice exploded from him in violent bursts, spreading across walls and ceiling in jagged patterns.

His form flickered between solid and shadow, a glitch in reality.

"What did you do?" I demanded, wrapping my arms around myself as the cold bit through my flannel pajamas.

His head snapped toward me, and I stumbled back. His eyes blazed with an unholy blue light, and frost crystals formed in the air around him.

"The barriers between realms grow thin," he said, his voice resonating with power. And your blood, little flame..." His smile was terrible to behold. "Your blood calls to mine."

"That's..." I swallowed hard. "That's not creepy at all. Look, maybe you should—"

Another explosion of ice cut me off. Cracks spread across the magical barriers that held him. I could see them now, glowing lines of power that were starting to splinter.

"Stop!" I grabbed the nearest grimoire. "Whatever you're doing—"

"I'm not doing anything, precious girl." His laugh sent icicles crashing from the ceiling. "This is all you. Your power, your heritage, calling to mine. The prison weakens."

Horror gripped me as I realized he was right.

I could feel it.

A pull in my blood, a resonance with his magic that grew stronger with each passing second. The spell that had held him for centuries was breaking down, and somehow, I was the cause.

"No," I said, backing away. "I won't free you."

"You already are." He moved toward me, more solid now than I'd ever seen him. His feet touched the ground, leaving frozen footprints on my grandmother's rugs. "Can't you feel it, Callie? The bond between us grows stronger."

"There is no bond!" But even as I said it, I felt the lie.

Helping him fight off the Summer Court, caused something to change. The connection between us had deepened, whether I wanted it to or not.

He reached for me, and for the first time, there was a newfound strength behind his grip. His fingers were still cold as death, as he held onto my arm.

I screamed.

Not from pain—though his touch burned like frostbite—but from the surge of power that rushed through me at the contact. Ice and ancient magic flooded my veins, and suddenly I could see... everything.

The layers of spells that made up his prison, the threads of power that bound him, and the weakening points where my magic had begun to erode the barriers.

"Beautiful," he breathed, pulling me closer. The scent of winter storms overwhelmed me. "Do you see now? Do you understand what we could be together?"

I struggled as his eyes glazed over as if enjoying my reaction. After a few moments I was able to jerk away, my skin tingling where he'd touched me. "We are not together. This isn't beautiful—it's wrong. You're evil!"

"Evil?" He flashed a wicked smile. "I am a force of nature, little flame. Neither good nor evil. I simply am."

"Yeah? Tell that to all the people you want to freeze to death."

He shrugged, the gesture somehow elegant despite its casualness. "The weak will perish, yes. But the strong will survive, adapt. Evolution through ice and snow. And you..."

His eyes raked over me possessively. "You are already proving your strength."

Another crack appeared in his prison, this one accompanied by a sound of breaking glaciers. The temperature dropped further, and frost began to creep up my legs.

"Stop it!" I tried to move, but the ice held me in place.

"I'm not doing this, remember?" He circled me slowly, each movement imbued with a predatory grace. "Your power calls to mine. The prison weakens because you want it to."

"I don't! I would never—"

"Not consciously, perhaps."

He leaned close, his breath against my ear. "But deep down, in the darkest corners of your soul, you yearn for what I offer. Power. Freedom. A throne beside mine."

"I'd rather die," I gritted out, struggling to break free from the hold he had on my legs.

"No." His voice hardened. "You will live, Callie Winters. You will live and rule at my side as my queen."

The casual possessiveness in his words wrapped around me like a vice, sending chills down my spine that had nothing to do with the biting cold of his presence. There was a commanding authority in his proclamation, a certainty that left little room for debate. My heart raced, caught in a tumultuous blend of fear and something dangerously akin to excitement.

"I don't recall being consulted about this career change," I snapped, trying to hide my fear behind sarcasm. "Besides, I'm more of a summer person. Better beach weather."

The ice around my feet crept higher, reaching my knees. "You jest to hide your fear. It's adorable, but unnecessary. I would never harm what's mine."

"I'm not yours!"

But even as I said it, the prison cracked again. This time, something fundamental shifted. I felt it in my bones, in the very air around us.

"Say it," he whispered, his voice silk over ice. "You know my name, Callie. I can see it in your eyes. Feel it trembling on your lips."

I shook my head, struggling to comprehend the weight of his declaration. It was as if he had woven a spell with his words. "I don't... I won't..."

"You do know it." His fingers traced patterns of frost on my arm, a gesture both intimate and alarming. "It's there, in your blood, in your bones. Say it, little flame. Give me my name."

My throat went dry as the word built up inside me, dangerous and forbidden.

"Y-" I caught myself, biting my lip hard enough to draw blood. "No."

"So close," he purred, pulling me against him. The scent of midnight frost made my head spin. "I can feel it, little flame. The way your power calls to mine. The way my name burns in your throat, begging to be spoken."

"Please," I whispered, not sure if I was begging him to stop or to come closer. "I can't..."

"You can. You will." His lips brushed my ear before trailing the tip of his nose along my jaw. "Say it, Callie. Free us both."

The first letter formed on my tongue again, and I swallowed it back with a gasp.

"Your name is Bob," I said desperately, trying to break the spell he was weaving, fighting against whatever was happening to me. "Just Bob. Nothing else. You're just an evil ice cube with delusions of grandeur."

Bob threw his head back and laughed, the sound echoing with triumph. Ice and snow swirled around him like a storm, and when it cleared...

He stood before me, fully corporeal. No longer trapped between worlds, but present in a way he hadn't been before. Power rolled off him in waves, making the air crystallize and the windows frost over.

"I'm not yours," I said again in a weak whisper.

"Not yet," he agreed, reaching out to trace my cheek with a cold thumb. "But you will be."

I tried to jerk away, but the ice still held me fast. "This doesn't change anything. You're still trapped in the house. The prison may be weakened, but—"

"Oh, my little flame." His smile was terrible in its beauty. I stiffened as he leaned in, his movement swift and unsettling, and licked the bead of blood off my lower lip with an intimacy that made my skin prickle with awareness. He sighed deeply, as if savoring the moment. "The structure was never the prison. It was merely the anchor. And now..."

His words trailed off, thick with meaning I didn't want to understand.

He gestured, and a swirling vortex of snow and darkness appeared beside us. Through it, I caught glimpses of an alien landscape—jagged ice peaks, endless winter, and a palace that seemed built from frozen starlight.

"Now, I have just enough freedom to show you your future kingdom."

His demeanor was unwavering, an unyielding force that left me feeling both vulnerable and trapped. It was clear he was not merely making a suggestion; he was laying down a challenge, asserting his will in a way that left little room for resistance.

The notion that my fate was already decided sent waves of defiance bubbling to the surface. "No. No way. I am not going anywhere with you!"

"You don't have a choice. The old lady was an easy sacrifice, one I would lay down at your feet again if given the chance," The ice encasing my legs spread higher, numbing my skin. "Winter ends in this realm, little flame. And I will not leave you here for the Summer Court to find."

What? How could he just drop that bomb so casually? My mind struggled to process it, each thought slipping through my fingers. What had he done to her? The question echoed, but the answer felt just out of reach, tangled in a web of confusion and disbelief.

And why was the Summer Court after me? Shouldn't they be after him?

"They're the good guys!" I struggled against the ice again, my muscles burning with the effort, but it was useless. The cold wrapped around me like chains, its grip tightening with every movement. "They're trying to protect the world from you!"

The words felt hollow, slipping off my tongue, a lie I was trying to convince myself to believe. But who was the good guy here? Was it the Frost King, with his icy promises and cryptic words? Or was it them—the ones who kept insisting they were saving the world, while every choice they made seemed to drive us further into chaos?

I didn't know anymore. I used to have a clear sense of what was right, who was on the side of light, and who was on the side of darkness. But now? Everything was a blur of gray. Every move felt it could tip me into something worse, something I couldn't control. I was tangled up in this fight, but I didn't know which side would even protect me—or if there was a side left to protect me at all.

So I screamed the words anyway, hoping they would stick. Hoping I would believe them.

"They tried to kill you," he reminded me, his voice darkening with a possessive edge, a shadow wrapping around his words. "They would sacrifice you without hesitation. I, on the other hand, would destroy the world for you."

A cold chill ran through me, sinking deep into my bones. His words were too smooth, too assured, as if he had already made the decision for me. Like my life had never been my own, not in his eyes. My heart pounded, an unsettling mixture of fear and something I refused to name, rising in my chest. This was madness.

I recoiled, shaking my head, forcing my voice through the tremors. "You're a monster!" I spat, the words bitter on my tongue. How could he think I would want to be a part of that twisted logic? The very idea of destroying everything— just to claim me—made me sick.

But his eyes? His eyes never wavered. They were locked onto mine with an intensity that made it feel he could tear the world apart just to see if I'd break along with it.

"Yes." He pulled me closer, and this time when he touched my face, his hand was warm.

Impossibly, terrifyingly warm.

"I am a monster. I am the darkness that makes the light seem brighter, the cold that makes warmth precious. I am winter incarnate, and I will remake this world in ice and snow."

The ice reached my waist now, spreading up my torso. I couldn't feel my legs anymore.

"But you, Callie Winters..." he continued, his voice softening to that of a lover's caress. "You, I would keep. My queen, my anchor, my living flame in an endless winter."

"Please," I whispered, hating the tremor in my voice. "Don't do this."

For a moment, his pupils contracted. "The Summer Court comes. I feel them approaching, burning through my defenses. They will kill you, little flame. And that, I cannot allow."

The ice reached my chest, crystallizing around my arms, trapping me in his embrace. The portal beside us grew larger, and through it came the smell of clean snow and ancient magic.

"When you know me better," he said, pulling me closer still as the ice completely encased me, "you'll understand. Everything I do, I do for you."

He was spewing nonsense. It was never about me and always about him!

"That's what makes you a monster," I managed through chattering teeth. "You actually believe that."

He grinned, sharp and cold and possessive. "Perhaps. But I'm the monster who will keep you safe."

His fingers traced my jaw, so light at first that it barely registered. But then, it was as though a spark ignited deep within me, a current of something older, darker, coiling through my veins. Suddenly, knowledge flooded my mind— ancient, terrible knowledge that bubbled up from somewhere deep in my blood. It was as though I could feel the weight of centuries pressing down on me, whispering secrets I wasn't meant to know.

A name. A name that tasted comparable to ice and starlight on my tongue—sharp, powerful, impossibly beautiful.

I tried to hold it back, to clamp my mouth shut, to stop it from spilling out.

His smile deepened, a dangerous, seductive curve of lips. His thumb brushed over my lower lip, a slow, deliberate movement, savoring the taste of my surrender. And then, without warning, he leaned in. His breath was ice on my skin, and his kiss? It was as if the world itself froze in that instant—dangerous, possessive, and so deep that it was more than a kiss. It was an invasion.

His lips were cold, but the fire inside of me threatened to consume me alive. I burned with an intensity that sent a shiver straight to my core, unraveling me inch by inch. I couldn't breathe, couldn't think—just felt, just existed under the weight of his kiss. His hands were everywhere now, pulling me closer, pressing me against him with a force that left no room for escape.

The world outside ceased to matter. There was only him.

When he finally pulled back, I was breathless, my skin tingling with a strange, intoxicating heat. His eyes were dark —dangerous, yes—but there was something else in them now. Something deeper.

"You're mine now," he whispered, and I knew at that moment that whatever I thought I had before... was already lost.

"*Ykazar,*" I breathed, and immediately knew I'd made a terrible mistake.

Power exploded around us. The air itself seemed to shatter, and his triumphant laugh shook the foundations of reality. His eyes blazed with unholy joy as the last threads of his prison snapped.

"Finally," he growled against my cheek, his voice low and rough, vibrating through me. "The sound of my name on your lips... it's decadent torment. My freedom, *your* voice."

Horror and something else I refused to name coursed through me as I realized what I'd done. "No... I didn't mean—"

"But you did. Deep in your soul, you did, little flame."

The last thing I saw was his triumphant face as he pulled me through the portal followed by a blur of a black tail. The last thing I felt was his cold lips pressing against my forehead in a mockery of a loving kiss.

The last thing I thought was: I should have bought that space heater.

Then darkness and winter swallowed me whole.

And somewhere in the endless winter of his realm, I heard him laugh.

ECHOES OF FROST AND DECEIT (BOOK 2)

The frost deepens, and the stakes grow higher.

After the chaos of her arrival in the Fae realm, Callie finds herself under the cold, calculating "protection" of Ykazar, the ruthless king of Winter. As Ykazar reclaims his throne with brutal efficiency, Callie struggles to navigate a world where power is everything—and loyalty can be bought. But as political intrigue unfolds and rival fae courts vie for alliances, Callie discovers something that may make her more dangerous than she ever imagined: latent magical abilities that even she doesn't fully understand.

Forced into the role of Ykazar's consort for political gain, Callie fights the growing pull between resistance and an undeniable connection. Her defiance fuels Ykazar's cruelty, but as his enemies close in, she finds herself caught in a web of rebellion and betrayal, unsure of where her true loyalties lie. Secretly aiding the growing dissent against Ykazar's rule,

Callie becomes a pawn in a much bigger game—one that could cost her everything.

When Ykazar uncovers her betrayal, his retribution is swift, punishing everyone except Callie. But in their confrontation, he reveals a prophecy that binds their fates together—whether she wants it or not. As Ykazar's past and present collide, Callie must choose: will she save herself, or will she be forced to confront the twisted connection that has bound her to him from the beginning?

Betrayal. Magic. Prophecy. And the line between love and power is thinner than ever.

WORD FROM THE AUTHOR

Reviews are so important for independent authors because they help readers discover books they like. Please consider leaving a review if you enjoyed this book. Just a line or two is all that's needed and it would really mean a lot.

AUTHOR BIO

Sophea Chan is the creator of cutesy yet dark fantasy romances, where nightmares intertwined with sugar-spun dreams, and the paranormal harbors hearts capable of epic love.

The night not only whispers fear, it sings of love. Who else could stuff her face with food, while crafting enthralling stories of romance and adventure? Readers should plan to discover the most fearsome creatures who have yearnings and vulnerabilities, and that bravery can be found in the gentlest souls.

In Sophea's world...every monster has a story.

https://sopheachan.carrd.co/

Also by Sophea Chan

ENCHANTED ELEMENTAL EMPIRES SERIES

Cursed Bonds

Whispers of the Past

Echoes of the Fallen

ANTHOLOGIES

Romancing the Rogue Vol 1

Romantic Realms Vol 1

Beyond the Depths: A Bite of Winter and a Sip of Trouble

FROSTFIRE SERIES

Bound by Ice and Shadow